THE JAM SANDWICH DETECTIVES

CLARE THOMPSON

For Mum & Dad,
who got me through school without a parent-chat group in sight.

1
———

RACHEL

'Shit!'

The morning had *started* well. Rachel had only snoozed her alarm twice.

The kids were up and dressed. They had eaten a healthy breakfast and drunk some freshly squeezed orange juice. Their school uniform was ironed and spotless. *The only time it would be either of those things all year.* Their shoes were polished and their hair was brushed.

'Shit, shit!'

They stood by the door in their new coats, holding their new school bags containing lunchboxes full of healthy sandwiches made with fresh bread, juicy fruit picked from the local farm and homemade treats.

Rachel smiled. Ready on time. You could tell it was the first day of term... *There is no way this is going to last.* As she picked up her keys she took a quick look in the hallway mirror.

'Shit, shit, shit!'

She had showered, dressed and even put on some make-up, but her hair looked like she'd just rolled out of bed, and if they didn't leave *that exact second* they would be late.

'What does *shit* mean?' asked Charlie.

'Erm, ask your teacher,' said Rachel, grabbing one of Megan's sparkly princess scrunchies from the console table and shoving her hair up into something resembling a bun.

'Mum!' said Megan, rolling her eyes, before turning to her little brother and taking him by the shoulders. 'Do *not* ask your teacher.'

'Let's go,' said Rachel, bundling her two children out of the door. 'We are going to be late.'

'But we need to take a doorstep photo,' said Megan, posing in front of the red front door. 'We take one every year and this will be Charlie's first one in his uniform.'

'Fine,' said Rachel, scrabbling about for her phone. 'Say cheese!'

Megan stood sideways, hand on her hip, flicked her hair to the side and raised two fingers into a sideways peace sign. *When did she get so grown-up?*

Charlie shouted 'Gorgonzola!' at the top of his voice, then stuck his tongue out and let out a puff of air from the other end.

One week in Italy over the summer and now he's a cheese expert.

'Eww,' said Megan, holding her nose and elbowing her brother in the ribs. 'You smell like stinky blue cheese.'

Charlie burst into tears and Megan raised her hands as if to say *I didn't touch him*, just as Rachel tapped her screen to take the photo, whilst also yelling, 'Leave your little brother alone, Megan!' Probably not one for the album, but it was all they had time for.

Megan rolled her eyes.

'Time to go,' said Rachel, wiping Charlie's tears away. 'C'mon, no tears on your first day.'

Rachel took a deep breath as they stepped onto the playground. She held on tight to Charlie's hand, more for her sake than his.

'There's Lottie,' said Megan. 'Can I go and say hi?'

'Of course,' said Rachel, adding, 'have a good day,' as she knew that was it and she wouldn't see her daughter again before the bell went.

'Bye, Mum,' said Megan, without looking back and she skipped off.

Rachel squeezed Charlie's hand.

'I'm scared,' he mumbled.

She crouched down to his height and looked him straight in the eyes. 'There is nothing to be scared about.'

'But my heart is beating.' He put his hand to his chest.

Rachel laughed. 'That's a good thing, Charlie. I'd be worried if it wasn't!' This got her the smallest of smiles in return.

The truth was that her heart was beating too; beating fast. She didn't tell Charlie, but as she looked around the playground and saw the sun-kissed mums, the Lycra-clad mums and the Insta-mums gathering in their cliques, she was transported right back to her own time at school where, if you weren't sporty or popular or beautiful, you didn't fit into any group and you just sort of floated your way through school... until you knew who you were and where you belonged.

Rachel still felt like she was floating now. She had finished school about twenty-five years ago but still she floated through life.

Despite the fact that it would help them prepare for adult life, Rachel prayed that her kids wouldn't have to deal with the inevitable groups of kids that you had to be cool enough or sporty enough or clever enough to be a part of.

She kissed Charlie on the nose.

'You will have the best day,' she said. *And from then on school will only get worse,* she didn't say.

The bell rang and she jumped out of her thoughts.

'Bye, Charlie!' She waved, as he strode off more confidently than she could have imagined or hoped for. More confidently than she herself had ever done.

He didn't even look back.

No tears. No wave. He was gone. And Rachel had a sudden thought. *What do I do now?* For the past eight years she'd had at least one of the kids by her side, almost twenty-four seven, but now, suddenly, she was all alone.

'What a brave little boy,' said a voice over her shoulder, and Rachel jumped again. 'Jane,' she said. 'Nice to see a friendly face. How was your summer?'

'Lovely, thanks. Got time for a quick wine to catch up?'

'Bit early, isn't it?' said Rachel, looking at her watch but with no real intention of turning the invitation down.

'The pub are doing a special first-day-back breakfast,' said Jane. 'They normally open the bar too.' She winked. 'I guess they know we'll need a drink!'

Rachel smiled. 'Oh, well in that case, would be rude not to!'

They found a cosy corner and ordered a couple of glasses of Pinot.

'It's like being back in Italy,' said Rachel, as she took her first sip.

'How was your holiday?' asked Jane.

'Ah, it was bliss,' said Rachel, with a brief smile. 'But it left me with this feeling...'

'That's called sunburn,' said Jane, glancing at Rachel's shoulder as she adjusted her top to cover the red skin.

'Not sunburn.' Rachel rolled her eyes. 'I'm talking about the *is this it?* feeling. I mean it can't be... all those weeks of packing school bags, washing uniform...'

'Ironing uniform...' Jane nods.

'Optional,' laughed Rachel, before continuing. 'Making packed lunches, cooking, cleaning, tidying up, hoovering, food shopping, washing up... the list is endless. And for what? One week in the sun! That can't be it, can it? There must be more.'

Jane took a very long sip of her wine. 'I guess so,' she said eventually.

'I used to be an executive PA,' said Rachel. 'I used to organise important business meetings, meet fascinating people, have dinners with clients in swanky restaurants.'

Jane raised one eyebrow. 'Sorry if I'm not fascinating enough for you!'

'I didn't mean... you know what I meant... I just feel like I used to be important and now I'm just a mum. And not a very good one at that.'

'I know what you meant,' said Jane. 'And if it makes you feel any better, I'm just a mum too.'

'Well, you're a better mum than me, you iron for a start... took me a good twenty minutes to even find my iron this morning!'

Jane laughed, then fell into a pensive silence, which moments later was interrupted by the Insta-mums bursting through the door.

They bustled around the bar before sitting down a couple of tables away, where they immediately started posing for selfies and taking photos of their drinks. Rachel knew that before she could say *Pinot Grigio* those photos would be all over social media covered in hashtags.

#nineoclockwineoclock

#firstdayfizz

#backtoschoolbubbles

'Oh hi, Jane,' came a high-pitched voice as one of them noticed someone outside of their little bubble of bubbles. 'Didn't see you there.'

'Hi, Natasha,' said Jane, raising her wine glass. 'Happy Back-to-School Day!'

Natasha raised her glass back. 'Gosh, I do hope the little darlings are getting on okay? My baby, Freddie, has just started in Reception. It is such a big day for the whole family, now that they are all at school.'

'You know Rachel, don't you, Natasha?' Jane gestured towards her. 'Her Charlie started today too.'

'Oh, did he? Bless,' said Natasha, sounding ever-so-very patronising.

Rachel smiled a fake smile. She knew that Natasha knew full well that Charlie was starting today too. They had lived on the same street since before Charlie and Freddie were born. They'd had a coffee once when they first met, back when Rachel just had Megan and Natasha just had the twins. Natasha had made a comment about not knowing how people can live in such clutter whilst eyeing the toys strewn around Rachel's living room floor.

'Well, unfortunately we don't have a playroom,' Rachel had said at the time.

'How do you cope?' Natasha had asked with faux sympathy, looking at her as if she'd said, *We don't have a toilet.*

Rachel had not invited her over again and she had never been invited to Natasha's house, although from the number of pictures she had seen of it on Instagram she could tell you more about it than she could her own.

'Anyway,' said Natasha. 'Must dash... that Prosecco won't drink itself.'

Rachel waited until she thought she was out of earshot and

said, 'Oh, bless those darlings, having to drink all that Prosecco,' in her best Natasha voice.

Jane stifled a laugh as Natasha shot a look back over at them, and they both dived head first, back into their Pinots.

'She's harmless enough,' said Jane, when she came up for air.

'That's what they used to think about cigarettes,' replied Rachel, looking at her watch. 'Anyway, I'd better get back. I told Phil I would let him know how Charlie got on this morning. He's in the office this afternoon, so I want to catch him before he goes.'

'Of course,' said Jane, downing the rest of the glass. 'Lots to do myself.'

'Don't rush on my account,' said Rachel, smirking. 'Stay, relax, get in on the selfies. After all, you look a lot more Instagrammable than me!'

She meant it as a compliment, but Jane looked slightly offended. The truth was that Rachel was always impressed with how amazing Jane looked. Stylish clothing, neat hair, perfect make-up. Even at eight thirty in the morning she always looked great. Rachel was jealous. She never seemed to find the time to make herself look even half presentable. Of course, she knew where the time went, but she would rather spend an extra half an hour in bed than styling her hair, just to drop the kids at school.

When Rachel got home she made herself a coffee and sat clutching it at the breakfast bar, deciding that in hindsight 9am was far too early for drinking wine.

While she decided what to do with her first day of freedom in six weeks, she aimlessly scrolled through her phone. Now that Charlie had started school she had five days a week to fill. That felt like a big wedge of time. Sure, she had enough housework to keep her occupied but she would surely go insane if that's all she had to do.

She stopped scrolling. There it was.

Crying into my Prosecco this morning but feeling supported by these other amazing mums. *#mumlife #mumnetwork #inittogether #firstdayofschool*

Natasha had 50,000 followers. Rachel wondered why on Earth 50,000 people cared about Natasha crying into her Prosecco. She flicked through the selection of filtered photos that Natasha had posted to accompany the profound statement, and there, in photo five, was Jane, clinking her glass with the Insta-mums.

Rachel laughed. 'She loves it,' she accidentally said out loud.

'Who does?' asked Phil strolling into the kitchen, wearing his pyjama bottoms with a shirt and tie. This was what *hybrid working* did to stylish men. Turned them *into* hybrids. Like a centaur. Professional, working, sexy man on the top half, slob on the bottom. As Rachel caught her own reflection in her phone screen, she realised that she – and her mum-bun – had no right to comment.

'Oh, no one,' said Rachel.

'How did Charlie get on?'

'Well, he walked through the door brilliantly. If they are graded on walking through doors, he'll be top of the class.'

'What time does he finish today?' Phil asked, ignoring Rachel's sarcasm.

'No idea,' said Rachel, partly because she knew it would get a laugh: they had been discussing over dinner last night how needlessly complicated the schedule for the new Reception intake's first week was, and partly because she actually had no idea.

She leafed through the bits of paper piled at the end of the dining table. 'It's in here somewhere. Think it's eleven thirty, or could be eleven forty-five...'

And that's when it happened.

PING!

She picked up her phone and looked at the screen.

'Shit!'

'Everything okay, love?'

> Natasha added you to Reception Mums #inittogether

Christ! thought Rachel. *Even the mum-chat has a hashtag!*

> Natasha (Freddie's mum) is typing...

> Natasha (Freddie's mum): Please welcome Charlie's mum, Rachel, to the group.

> And don't forget pick-up is at 11.45am today.

'Bloody hell!' Rachel looked up at Phil with panic in her eyes. 'I've been added to another flippin' mum-chat.' She paused before adding. 'Charlie's pick-up is eleven forty-five.'

2

JANE

Jane didn't want to interfere, but she knew what Rachel was like. She'd never navigate her way through having two children, in two classes at school, without the help of the Reception mum-chat.

She knew that Rachel had muted the Year Four mum-chat some time ago – back when it was the Year Two chat – but the difference was that when it came to Year Four, she had Jane to keep her in check, remind her of things that she might have missed... *will have missed.* But Jane didn't have a child in Reception, so Rachel was now going it alone, which is why Jane had asked Natasha to add her to the chat over a glass of early morning Prosecco.

Of course, Natasha had been only too happy to.

'I just completely forgot about Rachel,' she had said. 'Silly me!'

Jane smiled. 'Thanks, Natasha.'

Jane had never told Rachel she was already in a mum-chat with Natasha, and a handful of the other mums. She was embarrassed to admit that the group was called *Yummy Mummies* and contained most of the mums that Rachel usually rolled her eyes at. The ones that she referred to as the Insta-mums. The ones who posted their perfect lives on social media.

'They're not that bad,' Jane would say to Rachel. This would be met by the standard eye roll.

She had decided some time ago that she just wouldn't mention to Rachel she was in a group chat with them. The truth was, they really *weren't* that bad; well, most of them weren't. Natasha could be a bit much, but this whole lifestyle and her persona was more of a job for her. She had tens of thousands of followers on Instagram and got paid to promote products and wear certain clothes. The hashtag *#schoolrunfashion* was probably the most used on her Instagram grid, where she posted daily photos and reels of the outfits she wore as she walked the kids to school. For Natasha, the school run seemed to be like stepping out for a night in Soho; mum-style.

Jane always tried to look her best when she left the house, not that her husband ever noticed. Even if it was only to nip the kids to school or pop to the shop for a pint of milk, she made an effort. But having to put together a new outfit every day and style it with the right accessories and hair was a lot for her to think about first thing in the morning. She had, however, been known to check Natasha's Insta feed as soon as she woke up to help her decide what to wear. She assumed it must be easier if you are sent packages and packages of clothes from all the best brands.

Her phone pinged. It was the Yummy Mummies chat.

> Natasha (Twins' mum): Victoria is on one already! Saw her on my way home from the pub…

> Amy (Rosie's mum): Oh no! What's she done now?

> Natasha (Twins' mum): She's asked me to message the reception mums for her and invite them to a Bake Off party at her house, so she can recruit some more bakers for the PTA.

> Amy (Rosie's mum): New blood!

> Beth (Oliver's mum): Ha! Like an audition? Presumably you told her to get lost?

> Natasha (Twins' mum): Actually I didn't. Thought it might be fun... see the newbies squirm for a bit!

Jane started to type: *That's a bit mean...* then thought better of it, but in case anyone had seen that she was typing she wrote something else...

> Jane (Lottie's mum): Oh dear... good luck to them! LOL!

> Amy (Rosie's mum): They're going to need it!

> Beth (Oliver's mum): Happy to be off the baking hook... for a little while at least!

Jane imagined Rachel's face switching from irritated grimace to dawning horror when she saw the invite to a Bake Off party at Victoria's house. The thought made her giggle.

Victoria was chair of the parent teacher association for Castle Upperhill Primary School. Most of the parents moaned about the PTA because well, don't parents already do enough? Why do they need to be constantly guilt-tripped into baking cakes, then buying back said cakes, just so the school can buy laptops and tablets for the kids? They got by without laptops and tablets. But despite their moaning, parents do like eating cake, so a team of willing and talented (*talent optional*) bakers is essential. It is *for the kids* after all, which is a great excuse when you're shoving in a large slice of chocolate gateau on day three of your diet.

Being on the PTA was a thankless task. Jane knew this only too well and had, more recently, tried to avoid it. *Once they get you, that's it!* She had seen other mums crumble and regret it for the rest of their primary-school lives. Her next-door neighbour, Debbie, was one of those mums. She now only seemed to speak in grunts. Whenever Jane said, 'Hello,' she made a strange noise back and shuffled off to carry out the latest mission bestowed upon her by Victoria.

Debbie was vice chair of the PTA. She started with delusions of grandeur, a hope that when Victoria stepped down she would be elected the chair. But Debbie was still waiting, even though Victoria's only child was all grown up, studying photography at university, and hadn't been at the primary school for years.

Jane wondered whether she should warn Rachel about the Bake Off, but decided that she had already interfered enough. Rachel was a big girl, she would be able to say no, just like she had done for the four years their daughters had already been at the school.

Their daughters, Lottie and Megan, had been best friends since pre-school. So, Jane and Rachel had been friends since then too. Jane always thought it was nice to have a fellow mum to confide in, although she had never fully let her guard down. Perhaps it was the worry that they were only friends because of their children. Perhaps it was the worry that if their daughters fell out... so would they. Either way, she always felt the need to impress Rachel, to keep her on side.

Jane thought about what Rachel was saying earlier in the pub. About what it was all for; one week in the sun... Jane hadn't even had a week in the sun. Not for about three years. Ben's shifts kept him very busy and he always did a lot of overtime. He never said outright that he needed the overtime because Jane didn't work, but sometimes she felt like it was implied. She knew that he loved going to work, that he loved his job. Jane would have loved his job too. They met at police training, but when Lottie came along they decided that Ben would work and Jane would become a stay-at-home-mum, a homemaker, a housewife; whatever you choose to call it.

Jane was totally fine with this *of course*, she didn't mind one bit.

She kept her home beautifully. Her daughter Lottie was always well presented, as was she. She was always on top of her daughter's schedule: what she needed to wear, what she needed to take to school, what she had to read or what homework she needed to do. It was a lot to think about and although she found it stressful at times, she never let on. She was like a beautiful swan above the water, with her feet paddling frantically underneath.

She knew that Rachel was the opposite, openly scatty and frantic, and perhaps that's why they got on so well. Jane tried not to be as *over the top* with it all – to use Rachel's phrase – as the Insta-mums were. She was on social media but only posted a few pictures when something special happened, or when her house was especially tidy, or... okay so she did post quite a bit. But she worked hard to keep her home spotless so she deserved to show off a little, didn't she? Not daily updates on her outfit or home like Natasha though. No, that was too much.

She sighed as she looked around her kitchen. The kids' (one actual kid and one man-child) cereal bowls were beside the sink, crumbs all over the worktop where she had prepared their lunchboxes, the dishwasher was still full of last night's dinner plates and both the washing machine and tumble dryer needed emptying too.

She made a cup of tea.

She sat on the sofa and put the telly on. She watched as a woman with perfectly manicured nails and pristine make-up told her what the best cleaning products were. She picked up the remote and switched it off. After one quick slurp of her tea she went back into the kitchen and started cleaning. By the time she had finished her tea was cold, so she put it in the microwave and turned the dial to twenty seconds.

She sighed.

She couldn't stop thinking about Rachel's words earlier. *What is it all for?*

'No,' she said out loud to herself. She wasn't about to start moping. She had it all: the perfect husband, the perfect home, the perfect family. She had nothing to mope about.

She snapped out of her low mood, took her pinny out of the drawer and made two loaves of banana bread, some scones and a chicken pie for dinner.

She let out a satisfied sigh.

She took out her phone and snapped a picture.

Oh, why not? she thought, as she posted the picture to Instagram.

Busy   Afternoon!   #backtoschoolbaking   #mumlife #lovemyfamily

3

RACHEL

PING!

PING!

PING! PING! PING!

'You're popular this morning,' said Phil, as he buttered his toast.

Rachel picked up her phone and rolled her eyes at the Reception Mums #inittogether chat.

Frankie (Billy's mum): Billy came home without his school jumper yesterday. Don't suppose anyone else has it?

Natasha (Freddie's mum): Not here, lovely. I swear there's a black hole at school that they disappear into.

Sarah (Mia's mum): Just checked Mia's bag and can't see it I'm afraid.

Gina (Harry's mum): Harry didn't bring it home, sorry.

Jo (Millie's mum): Hope you find it.

There was a flurry of new PINGS, all the messages saying pretty much the same thing. Some people offered some *excellent* advice on looking in the lost property box and others made wild accusations about whether the garment in question was named.

'For God sake,' said Rachel. 'She doesn't need twenty-eight people telling her they don't have it... If you haven't got the jumper you don't need to reply.'

'Who are you talking to?' asked Charlie, as he sat down at the breakfast bar.

Rachel looked up from her phone screen and realised that Phil had disappeared and Charlie had taken his place.

'You can turn the pinging off, you know?' said Phil, reappearing from the downstairs loo.

'Yes, I know, I just... I am trying to be more *on it* this year. You know, on top of it all. I don't want to miss anything.'

'Yeah,' said Megan, joining them at the breakfast bar. 'You should really get your act together, Mum. The day I went in dressed as Matilda, when it wasn't even World Book Day was the worst day *EVER!*'

'Isn't Matilda just a girl wearing a school uniform?' asked Charlie.

'She is,' agreed Phil. 'And I'm sure no one even noticed.'

'Everyone noticed!' said Megan. 'I had this big red stupid bow in my hair and...'

'Like the one you have in now?' asked Charlie.

Megan's cheeks turned the same colour as her bow and she stuck her tongue out at her brother.

'Mum!' he shouted. 'Megan's being mean to me.'

Rachel ignored them all and scrolled through the list of people on the mum-chat, trying to put faces to names. It was hard to learn dozens of new kids' names as well as new parents, all in one go, but she knew some of them from pre-school or older siblings.

Frankie (Billy's mum) – keeps herself to herself.

Sarah (Mia's mum) – flirts with all the dads.

Gina (Harry's mum) – total newbie – has no idea what's going on.

Jo (Millie's mum) – bright and breezy.

Faye (Paige's mum) – bit of a snowflake.

Natasha (Freddie's mum) – everyone knows who Natasha is.

That is when her message pinged up.

> Natasha (Freddie's mum): Victoria Sandwich wants to invite all the new reception mums to her Bake Off party. Friday night. 7pm. Bring your best bakes. She is expanding her team of bakers for the PTA events (The Big Bake Sale is coming up) so this is your chance to shine!

No one typed anything for at least two minutes.

> Natasha (Freddie's mum): Any questions give me a shout…

Still nothing. Rachel couldn't believe that no one was asking. She started to type but then saw that other people were typing, so she waited with bated breath.

> Jo (Millie's mum): Sounds lovely. Think I'm busy unfortunately.

> Gina (Harry's mum): Is this like an audition? Will we be judged? What are the rules?

Rachel couldn't hold it in any longer.

> Rachel (Charlie's mum): Is… her name really
> Victoria Sandwich?

Victoria had been chair of the PTA for years. How had Rachel never known that was her surname? She chuckled to herself.

'What's so funny?' asked Phil.

'Victoria Sandwich,' laughed Rachel.

'My favourite,' said Phil.

'There is nothing funny about cake,' added Megan, seriously. She loved the *Bake Off* show on the telly. In fact, so did Rachel, although she couldn't bake to save her life.

'Are you making one?' asked Charlie, thinking about his belly as usual.

'No, I'm not,' said Rachel. 'Although I might have to. There's this thing on Friday. They need new bakers for the PTA.'

Phil's brows shot up and his eyes widened as he stared at her. 'Do not get involved,' he said, with fear on his face. 'I've heard about these PTAs. They get you in and then that's it, you will never be free.'

'Give over,' said Rachel, laughing at how serious he looked. 'I've decided to get more involved with school life this year. You know, give something back.'

'What, like food poisoning?' laughed Phil.

'Hey!' Rachel threw a tea towel at him. 'My baking isn't that bad. Although, maybe I should get someone to help me.'

'Well, don't say I didn't warn you.' Phil's stern expression returned.

Natasha (Freddie's mum): @Rachel yes that is her name. She has gone back to her maiden name after getting divorced a couple of years ago.

Rachel (Charlie's mum): What? Her parents actually named her that? Brilliant!

Sarah (Mia's mum): LOL!

Natasha (Freddie's mum): All right ladies, grow up! This is a kind space. @Gina to answer your questions; yes it is, yes it will and I will send over some guidance from Victoria.

Gina (Harry's mum): Oh right. Thanks. Sounds a bit daunting.

Natasha (Freddie's mum): Here you go… Message forwarded: Ladies, this is your big chance. Get involved and do your bit for the kids. All our events involve cake, but we don't want naff cakes. We want the best. Bring a homemade cake along on Friday and I'll choose three bakers to add to our baking pool. They must look perfect, taste perfect and contain NO NUTS! What fun! Thanks V xx

Sarah (Mia's mum): No pressure then.

Rachel (Charlie's mum): What fun!

Gina (Harry's mum): Oh gosh, I'm going to try and make a lemon cake. How exciting!

Is it exciting? wondered Rachel. It sounded terrifying to her but she really wanted to take a cake and experience one of Victoria's famous parties. She'd never been invited to one before and they were always notorious for producing a bit of gossip.

Greg (Masie's dad): I make a mean red velvet but not sure I fall under the 'ladies' category so, looks like I'm not invited.

Faye (Paige's mum): Oh gosh. Hadn't realised there were dads on this chat!

Sarah (Mia's mum): They don't bite @Faye. @Greg I'm sure it's no problem that you're a man, but give the amateurs a chance, don't you own a chain of bakeries?!

Faye (Paige's mum): Does he? Well, that's a bit unfair, isn't it?

Sarah (Mia's mum): It was a joke @Faye!

PS. I'll make an Earl Grey and ginger cake with mirror glaze and gold leaf decorations.

Rachel laughed out loud. She liked Sarah's sense of humour.

Several other people chimed in; a couple with cakes they were going to bake and quite a few in support of Greg and his velvet cake, and one or two more moaners that had clearly never heard of 'Greggs' the Bakers!

The messages were flowing. Rachel was proud of herself for getting involved as she typed.

Rachel (Charlie's mum): I'll make a coffee & walnut.

Then nothing.

Tumbleweed.

Rachel swiped down from the top of her phone screen to refresh her feed.

That's weird, she thought, the messages had been pinging through. Where had everyone gone suddenly? But then her thoughts turned to the fact that she couldn't bake.

'Do you want me to take the kids to school?' asked Phil.

'Shit!' said Rachel, looking at the kitchen clock.

It was 8.35am and they needed to leave in the next five minutes, maximum.

'No, I'll take them,' said Rachel, downing the rest of her lukewarm tea.

'Really?' Phil eyed her.

She looked down at herself as she sat, phone in one hand, mug in the other, still wearing her pyjamas and fluffy slippers.

'Do you mind?' She smiled sweetly, as she typed again in the mum-chat.

> Rachel (Charlie's mum): Is it PE today?

Rachel breathed a sigh of relief after a quick dash round the house locating trainers, white socks, a hair bobble and Charlie's toilet roll castle creation. His teacher was going to love him; second day of school and taking in uninvited homework. Still, it was a pay-it-forward for the mountains of crap that would undoubtedly filter its way home over the next year. Reception was basically the school's recycling programme.

She had shoved some cheese and crackers, a brown banana and a packet of crisps into a lunchbox just in the nick of time. It didn't look in any way appetising, but as she handed it to Megan, Charlie eyed the concoction of food and asked for the 257th time why he couldn't have packed lunches. So, Rachel explained again that *his* school dinners were free, and that she knew he wanted a Super Mario lunchbox but he couldn't have one while the government were willing to pay for his lunch.

'I wish they'd pay for my lunch,' Megan said, taking her lunchbox. 'So I didn't have to eat this.'

Rachel waved them off and quickly shut the door before any

of the other mums saw her mis-matched pyjamas. She decided that she had better go upstairs for a shower before she got an eye roll from Phil on his return. She had time to make another quick cuppa first though, so it was ready for her when she was done.

As she waited for the kettle to boil she thought about baking a cake for Friday. She looked at her phone again and saw Jane's latest post:

#backtoschoolbaking

Oh Jane! She was becoming one of them. Rachel shook her head, but then an idea started to form. She typed out a message to Jane:

> Don't suppose you could knock me up a quick coffee and walnut for Friday? Oh, and pretend I made it? Pleeeaaase! I would be forever grateful.

She hit send and crossed her fingers for a reply. Surely Jane would do her a little favour? She knew Rachel was busy preparing for a job interview. She was sure she had mentioned it. Plus, Rachel couldn't bake to save her life, but hopefully Jane would help her out.

Jane replied straight away:

> You do know that Victoria is allergic to nuts?

'Shit!' Rachel said to the empty room. No wonder her suggestion of a coffee and walnut cake had gone down like a cold Gregg's sausage roll.

4

————

JANE

Jane rolled her eyes and chuckled as she read Rachel's message. Not only was she planning on cheating in the baking contest but she was going to give the chair of the PTA an anaphylactic shock at the same time. Probably not the best way to make a good impression.

How about a Victoria sponge? Jane typed as a suggestion.

Probably safer... replied Rachel. *A Victoria sponge for Victoria Sandwich.*

Jane shook her head and checked her cupboards. She was sure she already had all the ingredients. A quick look confirmed that she did and she messaged Rachel back.

> Jane (Lottie's mum): All set.

> Rachel (Megan's mum): Thank you. You're a star!

Jane wondered if she was a mug, making Rachel's cake for her, but she liked Rachel. She seemed genuine, unlike some of the other mums. Natasha for example was always overly polite but Jane knew she was the type of person who would be making bitchy comments about you the moment your back was turned.

Jane's friendship with Rachel had grown as their daughters, Megan and Lottie, became closer too. Jane was glad that she'd bonded with Rachel. Like her, she didn't seem to have a close circle of friends. She wasn't unpopular, she just seemed to flit from group to group. Jane always thought that Rachel seemed aloof, so maybe that's why she hadn't found her tribe either.

Although Jane tried to project a confident and carefree persona, she did always worry about what people thought about her and the fact that Rachel had asked her for a favour – she said she would be forever grateful – gave her the opportunity to really cement a friendship. A real one, not just a fleeting playground friendship that meant very little.

After four long years of floating and feigning positivity, finding an actual friend would be the icing on her slightly needy cake.

The smell of the cake had obviously drifted out of the kitchen and up the stairs to wake her sleeping husband.

'What you baking?' he asked, as he sauntered into the kitchen rubbing his eyes.

'Oh, it's just for Victoria's Bake Off thing tomorrow evening.'

'Oh!' he looked confused. 'A bake off? I didn't realise you were out tomorrow evening.'

'I'm not, it's for Rachel.'

'Oh!' Ben looked even more confused.

'Just helping out a friend,' said Jane. 'She can't bake so I agreed to help her.'

'So, you do all the work and she gets all the credit?' Ben raised one eyebrow.

'Something like that!' Jane laughed off his comment.

'What's in it for you?'

'Nothing, Ben. It is called being kind,' she gave him a sickly-sweet smile. 'I'm making two though, y'know, just in case... so, I'll give Rachel the best one and we can have the other.'

'Nice to know I'm good enough for the rejects.' He shook his head and flicked the kettle on.

'I know the feeling,' Jane muttered under her breath.

'What's that supposed to mean?'

'Oh nothing,' said Jane, not wanting to get into another argument about him being out at work all the time, while she did everything at home. 'Ben?' She tried to change the subject and held up a tiny bottle in front of his face. 'Does this say *extract* or *essence*?'

Ben moved his head back slightly and squinted at the bottle. 'Extract. Why, what's the difference?'

'Oh, extract is the real deal, that's all. I want the cake to be perfect.'

'Well, it's the real deal.'

'Perfect thanks!' said Jane, as she poured a few drops into the buttercream mix.

'Why don't you just put your glasses on?'

'They don't suit me. I look–'

'You look fine,' said Ben. 'If you need them, you should wear them.'

'I know, I know,' said Jane. 'Anyway, I'm almost done now.'

Ben smiled and made himself a coffee and a couple of slices of toast. He sat down at the kitchen table and yawned.

'Long night?' asked his wife.

'Just the usual,' said Ben. 'Drunken idiots, angry idiots, stupid idiots.'

'So, idiots then?' Jane smiled.

'Honestly,' said Ben. 'If there were less idiots in this country... I'd be out of a job!'

Jane laughed. 'Here's to the idiots!' She raised her mug of cold tea towards him.

'The idiots!' he said, smiling, clinking his mug against hers.

Jane knew that he down-played his job to protect her feelings. He must get involved in some interesting cases or make some memorable arrests, but if he did he never really spoke about it. She appreciated that he was being thoughtful in sparing her the details, but sometimes she wanted them. After all, she had completed her police training too. Maybe she could offer some help and advice, put her training to use, prove that it hadn't been a complete waste of time.

Of course it hadn't been a *complete* waste of time as that is where she had met Ben. And if she hadn't met Ben, she wouldn't have Lottie. She wouldn't have become a mum, and she wouldn't have her perfect family. She loved being a mum and knew she was a good one, but Rachel's comment the other day had made an old, suppressed thought that she sometimes had arise again. It was something that she has always, secretly, thought but never voiced to anyone. Sometimes she wished she wasn't *just a mum*. Sometimes she wished she was something more.

The oven timer went off and snapped her out of her thoughts.

She took the four tins of cake out of the oven and sniffed the air above them. They did smell good. Rachel was going to smash this baking contest and then Jane sandwould have a friend for life.

All thoughts of career opportunities missed wafted away on the delicious smelling air. Jane didn't need to be a police officer to be complete. She was a domestic goddess. Their house and community were wonderful. This was – nearly – all she'd ever wanted.

She turned the cakes out onto the cooling racks and examined them closely to decide which two halves were best. There wasn't much between them. The final cake would be fabulous whichever she chose which meant that, luckily for Ben, the reject would be pretty amazing too. She turned on her electric whisk to finish the buttercream. After all this effort, Rachel would definitely owe her one!

'Oh my God! It's amazing,' said Rachel, peeking under the lid. 'I could never have made anything like this.'

'Well, you are going to have to pretend that you could have,' said Jane, putting the lid back on the cake carrier and glancing around the playground to check no one was watching the covert handover. 'How are your acting skills?'

Rachel shrugged, being careful not to knock the cake. 'I just hope no one else has made her cake namesake too.'

'Nah,' said Rachel. 'People will have gone extravagant rather than classic, I reckon. But I think that this will win her over.'

'And win overall.' Jane smiled.

'Do you think she'll believe that I made it?' asked Rachel.

'Why wouldn't she?'

'I don't know. Maybe you'd better tell me the ingredients just in case.' Rachel spoke with hushed tones, as if Jane was about to tell her a generations-old secret.

Jane laughed. And then realised that Rachel was staring blankly back at her. *She was serious!*

'It's a Victoria sponge,' she said, raising her eyebrows.

'Sugar, butter, eggs, flour, a bit of baking powder... oh, and a splash of milk.'

'And the filling?'

'Butter, icing sugar and a drop of vanilla extract.'

'It's that easy?' asked Rachel.

'It's that easy.'

'Wow, okay fine. I can remember that.' Rachel's phone pinged and she looked down at the screen. 'Ugh,' she said. 'Look at this.' She turned her phone so that Jane could read the direct message.

> Victoria (PTA): I hear you're making a Victoria Sandwich. My favourite, for obvious reasons! I do hope it's good. No pressure... just kidding of course; lots of pressure with that choice!!

Jane's eyes widened.

'How the hell did she hear that?' Rachel rubbed her forehead.

'I think I might have mentioned it to someone a few minutes ago,' said Jane, sheepishly. 'I guess important news travels fast.'

'She's a nightmare!'

'She's not that bad,' said Jane, although she secretly agreed that she was being a bit of a diva about this whole thing.

Rachel's phone pinged again, and again, and again. She couldn't ignore it any longer.

'She... she's winding everyone up,' said Rachel, scrolling through the messages. 'Giving out her orders, telling people what to do. Who does she think she is?'

'She's just excited about her event I guess,' said Jane, diplomatically.

'Do you always see the best in people, Jane?' asked Rachel, getting more and more agitated by the messages that kept arriving to her phone.

Then she went silent. She looked down at her phone in what looked like utter disbelief.

'What's wrong?' asked Jane. 'What has Victoria said now?'

Rachel didn't answer either of these questions and simply replied by saying, perhaps a little bit louder than she should have on the playground, 'I am going to kill her!'

5

———————

RACHEL

Despite her anger, Rachel managed to get the Victoria sandwich cake home in one piece. Whether that could be said of Victoria Sandwich, the person, when Rachel had finished with her, was another matter.

Rachel had been lost for words when she had received the message from her at school pick-up, but the long and short of it was that now, Victoria had told *everyone* to make a Victoria sponge, so that she could compare them properly. The audacity of it. Who did she think she was? Rachel couldn't believe that someone could be so self-obsessed, so full of self-importance. People had spent hours baking – not her – and now they had to start again... again, not her, but it was the principle. She couldn't believe that no one else was even mad about it.

Someone on *Reception Mums #inittogether* had even said, *This is such fun!*

Fun? Rachel had thought. *Funny idea of what fun is!*

It's ridiculous, Rachel had typed on the mum-chat when she finally calmed down enough for her fingers to work.

> Gina (Harry's mum): I think it's supposed to be a bit of fun.

> Rachel (Charlie's mum): It's like a bloody technical challenge. Even Paul Hollywood wouldn't change the rules this close to the deadline.

> Natasha (Freddie's mum): Please don't swear @Rachel. This is a friendly space.

> Rachel (Charlie's mum): I'll swear if I bloody well want to. Who put you in charge?

Rachel wasn't sure why she was getting so irate about this. They were just cakes. This was just a few mums baking. And a dad. She took a deep breath and waited before she typed anything else.

> Rachel (Charlie's mum): Sorry… didn't mean to snap.

> Frankie (Billy's mum): I think I'm going to give it a go.

> Sarah (Mia's mum): Me too!

> Greg (Masie's dad): I'm with you @Rachel I've already made a flippin' red velvet cake, so that's what I'm taking.

'Thank you!' said Rachel to herself. 'Glad someone is talking sense.'

> Natasha (Freddie's mum): I don't think Victoria will be best pleased with that @Greg

> Rachel (Charlie's mum): Which is why you should definitely do it!!

Nothing.

Rachel was starting to take the tumbleweed personally.

Rachel arrived at Victoria's house, sponge in hand, and rang the doorbell.

'Do come through, darling,' said an extremely over-polite Victoria, as she ushered her inside, closing the door with one hand and clutching a personalised champagne flute, encrusted with diamantés, in the other.

'Victoria Sandwich... a Victoria sandwich,' said Rachel, as she held out the cake and stifled a snigger.

'On the table with the rest please. Do help yourself to a glass of fizz. Haven't even managed a sip of mine yet, still, I think you are the last to arrive so we can crack on now.'

Rachel blinked. Victoria was a lot to take in. The red power suit was a bold choice, but Rachel was quietly impressed that she somehow pulled it off.

Despite seeing her flit in and out of various school events, Rachel had never actually spoken to Victoria before. She was taken aback by her captivating blue eyes. The creases at the edges gave away her older years, but they sparkled with a beauty that Rachel had never noticed before, and perhaps explained her over-confidence.

Rachel followed her into the dining room, where there were already several cakes spread out across the table. She put her own down next to them as she eyed up the competition. 'Wow!' she exclaimed in surprised approval.

'Not *too* bad,' said Victoria, eyeing Rachel's cake as she took the lid off.

'Erm, thanks,' said Rachel. 'I think.' She looked around the room to see who else had turned up.

Natasha was there of course. 'I didn't really need to bake a cake,' she said to the room. 'Victoria already knows that I'm a dab hand with a mixer, but I thought I would knock one up anyway. Just to get involved... and to make sure at least something was edible.'

Rachel rolled her eyes.

Gina, the newbie, spoke next. 'I've made one too. I hope it's okay. Please don't feel you have to eat it if it isn't. I won't be offended. I promise.'

Rachel smiled at her, assuming the nerves were on account of the battleaxe in charge of proceedings. She hadn't had a chance to speak to Gina yet, although she admired her braveness at getting stuck in straight away and coming to one of these crazy PTA events when she didn't really know anybody.

'My family all love my Victoria sponge,' chipped in Sarah. 'So, I'm pretty confident you'll like mine. Greg's already had a bite, haven't ya, darlin'?'

She winked. Rachel turned her nose up.

'Yes. Very tasty,' said Greg. 'Very tasty indeed...'

'And the cake wasn't bad either,' added Natasha with a smirk.

No one laughed. Sarah turned pink. The joke would have been funny if it wasn't so uncomfortably close to the truth. Rachel, along with pretty much everyone else in the room, happened to know that Sarah had a bit of a reputation. She also knew that you should never judge a book by its cover, or judge a person by their gossip.

'Is that everyone?' asked Victoria, ignoring the elephant in the room. *And the red velvet cake on the table.* 'If so, perhaps we could get started with the tasting. Debbie, be a love and make sure everyone has a full glass.'

Debbie handed out some much plainer flutes and went around filling all the glasses with fizz.

'She's keeping you on your toes,' said Rachel, quietly, as Debbie got to her glass.

'And don't I just know it,' said Debbie, under her breath.

'Whose is this one?' asked Victoria, pointing to a cake that hadn't been claimed yet.

'Oh yes, that's mine,' said Frankie. 'Hi, I'm here.'

'Well, why didn't you speak up?' said Victoria. 'You'll be no use on the PTA if you can't let yourself be heard.'

Frankie looked down at her toes and seemed to mouth the word *sorry*, although no actual sound came out.

Rachel wasn't surprised people were always so reluctant to get involved in the PTA events if this is how Victoria carried on. These people were volunteering their evening and she was talking to them like she was some sort of army corporal.

'Right, everyone,' announced Victoria. 'Talk amongst yourselves while I try the cakes. I'd like to say they all look delicious, but well, they all look edible and I suppose that's the main thing.'

Rachel raised her eyebrows and shook her head.

She looked around the room as people started to break the stunned silence with their own conversations. Sarah was talking to Greg. Her flirting was off the scale, and although Greg seemed to be enjoying it, he didn't really seem to be reciprocating in any way. Natasha was blathering on about her Instagram account to Gina. 'If you're new to school-mum life, it's a really helpful resource. Mum-hacks, wardrobe advice... it's all there.' Gina nodded politely and Rachel hoped that she hadn't noticed Natasha look her up and down as she'd said wardrobe advice.

Victoria was striding round the table with a cake fork. Debbie scurried behind her taking notes. Which just left Frankie, standing quietly on her own at the edge of the room.

Rachel took a large gulp of her Prosecco and walked over to her. 'Why are we putting ourselves through this?' she asked.

Frankie smiled. 'I guess because we love our kids and want to help the school raise money?'

Rachel nodded. 'Hmm... can't help thinking that there must be an easier way!'

'Maybe robbing a bank or dealing fake gold would be easier?' Frankie suggested with a completely straight face.

Rachel nearly choked on her cheap Prosecco. 'You're a dark horse... I like it.'

'Actually, betting on the horses could work too,' remarked Frankie and Rachel grinned. 'Anything has got to be better than this.'

They watched as Victoria guzzled her way around the table.

'I'm going to take a few piccies for the Gram, if that's okay?' announced Natasha. 'Show people what mumlife is all about and all that.'

'What, cake and Prosecco?' Sarah laughed.

'I was thinking more community spirit,' said Natasha, with just a hint of a scowl.

The mums, and dad, started muttering and murmuring until Debbie dinged her glass to hush everyone.

'Well, I've tried them all,' announced Victoria. 'And I'm still standing.' She tittered and a couple of other people laughed a little bit too, mainly to humour her it would seem. 'First of all,' she continued. 'I would like to raise a glass to say thank you all for coming and for making the effort. That's what it's all about.'

Everyone raised their glasses.

'I'll drink to that,' said Rachel. 'Was not expecting that woman to produce the word *thank you* from her lips, I'll tell you that for free.'

'She should keep people on side if she knows what's good for her,' murmured Frankie in response.

Rachel nodded and then frowned as she digested Frankie's strangely aggressive comment. She opened her mouth to ask her exactly what she meant, but Victoria was already speaking again. *No surprises there.*

'So,' she said. 'Who wants to know which cake I thought was the best? I have to tell you it was an easy decision as the rest were pretty awful but... the winner gets automatic enrolment to the PTA baking team so, exciting times! Drum roll please...'

Greg obliged by drumming his hands on the table.

'The best cake was...' Victoria took a deep breath. 'It was...' She gasped for air again. 'It–' She put her hands up to her throat. 'I.... I can't...'

Rachel laughed and clapped. 'Ha! Very good. We get it, they are all so awful that they've poisoned you.'

'I... I...'

'Spit it out, love!'

'Stop!' Frankie held up her hand to stop Rachel from speaking. She shook her head. 'I don't think...'

'She can't breathe!' wailed Gina.

Rachel stood and stared at her, along with the rest of the room. At first she'd thought Victoria was building her part, adding a bit of drama, but now she could see that she was actually struggling to breathe.

Debbie let out an ear-piercing scream. She clutched her faux pearls, then began nervously twiddling the buttons on her cardigan.

'Someone call an ambulance,' squealed Natasha.

'I will,' said Gina, taking out her phone and dialling.

'Lay her down,' said Greg. 'I think she's having a seizure.'

'I'll grab a cushion,' said Sarah. 'And a blanket. And a glass of water.'

Rachel just stood, staring at Victoria who was now on the floor convulsing. She seemed to be losing consciousness and

Rachel felt herself drifting out of the room too. She wasn't good in these sorts of situations. 'I think I need to sit down,' she said to herself as her knees gave way.

'Here,' said a voice. It was Frankie, who moved a chair behind her so that she could sit.

'Thank you,' said Rachel. She sat down and the dizziness seemed to ease a little. 'What is happening?'

'I don't know,' said Frankie. 'But I don't think we're going to find out who baked the best cake any time soon!'

6

JANE

Jane sat at home, one eye on her phone, fully expecting some updates from Rachel on the Bake Off party.

She scrolled through Instagram wondering where Natasha's photos of her cake being better than everyone else's were.

She opened the various mum-chats and was surprised that there were no updates there either.

Weird.

She shook her phone and held it above her head. *Did she have signal? Was the WiFi down?* Perhaps people were too busy to message or post or comment. *Surely not.*

She decided to make the most of a night alone. Lottie was in bed. Ben was at work. He wouldn't be back for a couple of hours, so she took the opportunity to run a bath.

As she eased herself into the bubbles, she breathed in the mixed aromas of steamy bath oil, scented candles and freshly laundered towels. She closed her eyes and her body relaxed. It was probably as close to heaven as a tired mum could get.

The tranquil calmness was, of course, too good to be true. The water was still piping hot when her phone buzzed the first time. She ignored it. She shouldn't have brought it into the bathroom. Whatever it was could wait. It would be Rachel telling her that her cake went down a treat... or like a lead balloon. Or Natasha saying that the party wasn't up to her standard of hosting.

Or probably, and much more likely than all of those possibilities, was that it was Ben saying that he'd be home later than he thought. That a hen-do got out of control, or a boy racer should never have been given his licence, or some under-aged drinkers got carried away and robbed a corner shop.

Whenever Ben was busy at work she felt a pang of jealousy. Not about the drunken hen-dos or the silly teenagers; she just missed the adrenaline. The closest she got to adrenaline was leaving the house for the five-minute walk to school, with only four minutes to go. *Would she beat the bell? Would she beat the gate? Or would she get a red slip?* The anticipation and excitement kept her on her toes.

Several pings later, and after reading messages from Ben and Rachel, amongst others, Jane found herself staring hard into the mirror, her own expression of disbelief. 'What?' she said aloud to her reflection. 'Victoria is dead?'

She replied to Ben first:

> Jane (Wifey): She can't be?!!

> Ben (Hubby): She definitely is. Matty was at the scene. Sorry love. I know you liked her.

Jane typed her reply: *Yes. She was such fun.* She wondered if that sounded convincing. She had always found Victoria slightly annoying, but that probably wasn't the thing to say when you had just found out someone had died.

> Jane (Wifey): What happened?

Ben (Hubby): Looks like anaphylactic shock. She was allergic to nuts. The cakes have all been taken off for testing.

Jane (Wifey): Ooh that's a nice job for someone. Do they get to taste test too?

As soon as she pressed send she realised that she probably shouldn't make light of such an awful situation.

Ben didn't reply, so she sent another message to confirm she had been joking. But still nothing, so she tapped out a response to Rachel instead asking if everyone was okay.

Rachel (Megan's mum): Bit shaken. Everyone just in shock really. Just walking home. We didn't even find out who made the best cake.

Jane (Lottie's mum): Ben says they've taken the cakes off for testing.

Rachel (Megan's mum): How does he know that?

Jane (Lottie's mum): News travels fast at the station. His mate who was on duty got called to the scene.

Rachel (Megan's mum): Ooh the one who came to the house? He was a bit of all right.

Jane (Lottie's mum): Ha! Steer clear of him... he's a right floozy!

Jane tutted at herself. Someone had just died and she probably shouldn't be making jokes, although it made her feel better that Rachel was too. In any case, in their personal chat, she asked if Rachel herself was okay, just to make sure.

> Rachel (Megan's mum): I'm okay, I think, kind of. Such a terrible thing. Think I'm going to try to get some kip. Got a busy day tomorrow. Need to try and forget about it all and refocus my energy. If I can.

> Jane (Lottie's mum): Oh yes, your interview. Best of luck… you will smash it! Be kind to yourself after tonight.

> Rachel (Megan's mum): Hope so. As long as I can get Victoria Sponge off the brain.

Jane tipped her lukewarm coffee down the sink and poured herself a large glass of wine, whilst pondering whether to correct Rachel on Victoria's surname. She didn't bother, there were more important things going on.

She looked at the Yummy Mummies chat. She didn't know what to do so she just typed: *Gosh!* And then: *Are you okay Natasha?*

Within seconds her phone was pinging.

> Amy (Rosie's mum): Why? What's happening?

> Beth (Oliver's mum): What's going on?

> Trace (Kai's mum): What have I missed?

They were like vultures.

> Natasha (Twins' mum) is typing…

Jane waited with bated breath as Natasha stopped typing, started typing, stopped typing and then started typing again. Finally her phone pinged.

> Natasha (Twins' mum): You won't believe it. It
> was awful. Poor poor woman. I feel
> traumatised. Not sure how I'll get over this one.

> Amy (Rosie's mum): What?

> Beth (Oliver's mum): What the hell?

> Trace (Kai's mum): Are you okay?

> Jane (Lottie's mum): It is such awful news.

> Trace (Kai's mum): What is? You are worrying
> me!

Natasha still wasn't saying anything so Jane thought that perhaps she should fill the others in. Perhaps Natasha really was traumatised and reliving the experience would upset her deeply. Jane didn't want that. She was about to start typing when:

> Natasha (Twins' mum): Well, I can hardly
> believe I am typing these words but Victoria is
> DEAD!

Jane wondered if the capitals were completely necessary. She was about to offer her condolences, but Natasha kept typing.

> Natasha (Twins' mum): There we were,
> standing around chatting, having some fizz,
> laughing and joking, when Victoria eats the
> cakes and BAM! Just like that... she's gone.
> Right in front of all of us.

> Amy (Rosie's mum): That is awful.

> Beth (Oliver's mum): I can't believe it.

Trace (Kai's mum): How terrible for you. What did you do?

Natasha (Twins' mum): We remained calm and called an ambulance. We are mums after all and remaining calm is our superpower.

Trace (Kai's mum): It might be yours, Natasha. But I'd have shit my pants!

Natasha (Twins' mum): 🙈 No need for that, Trace. It was all very high drama, but the police soon arrived to take control.

Amy (Rosie's mum): The police?

Beth (Oliver's mum): Why were the police there? It was just an accident right?

Natasha (Twins' mum): Well, between you and me… don't say anything but… they think someone did this on purpose.

Amy (Rosie's mum): Whaaaaat?!

Beth (Oliver's mum): You are kiddin'?!

Trace (Kai's mum): 😲

Jane felt a bit uncomfortable, like perhaps Natasha was exaggerating and that no one had really confirmed this yet.

Jane (Lottie's mum): I am sure they are just covering all bases.

Trace (Kai's mum): Ooh Jane. You can get the dirt from Ben.

Jane (Lottie's mum): He won't be on the case. Victoria is a neighbour, so it's too close to home.

Natasha (Twins' mum): It was anaphylaxis.

Jane (Lottie's mum): I don't think that has been confirmed.

Natasha (Twins' mum): And the thing is, we all made her cakes.

Jane wondered whether Natasha was ignoring her on purpose.

Natasha (Twins' mum): We all knew she was allergic to nuts. Someone must have deliberately put nuts in their cake. It's the ONLY explanation.

Jane's mind wandered to the fact that Rachel had suggested making a coffee and walnut cake, but then she remembered that she herself had made Rachel's cake, so she knew there were no nuts in that one. Hopefully no one else would remember Rachel's suggestion.

Natasha (Twins' mum): Between you and me ladies, one person did suggest making a coffee and walnut cake...

Oh dear! Trust Natasha to remember!

Beth (Oliver's mum): Really?

Amy (Rosie's mum): Who?

Trace (Kai's mum): Well that's dodgy, isn't it?

Natasha (Twins' mum): Rachel! Megan and Charlie's mum.

> Jane (Lottie's mum): She didn't realise Victoria
> was allergic.

Jane typed the message before thinking she didn't really want to get involved in all this, but it would come out eventually that she made Rachel's cake, so she needed to put out these little fires before they got out of control. Not that it mattered. She knew that cake was nut-free, but it might look suspicious.

> Natasha (Twins' mum): How do you know?

> Jane (Lottie's mum): Well, I was chatting to her. She said she was going to make coffee and walnut, and I advised her to stick to the brief. I told her that Victoria was allergic so she changed her mind and went with a Vicky sponge.

The chat went quiet for a bit before Natasha officially signed off for the evening:

> Natasha (Twins' mum): Right ladies that's me. I need to lie down with a face mask and a glass of cucumber water. All too much for me.

The others all chimed in with various *Sleep wells* and *Take cares*. Jane typed: *Night lovely,* although she wasn't sure how lovely Natasha was being. She seemed to be acting like she was the only one who'd been affected by the evening's awful events. She also seemed to be trying to point the finger at Jane's friend, Rachel, and knowing how influential Natasha could be, that really worried her.

She took a large gulp of wine.

The doorbell rang.

Jane looked at her watch. 9.47pm; bit late for visitors.

She went to the door and peered through the peephole. The

outside light lit up the face that was standing on the doorstep; eyes damp and mascara smudged down her cheeks. She was clutching a half empty bottle of wine.

Jane flung open the door.

'Oh, Rachel!'

7

———

RACHEL

'Are you okay?' said Jane. 'What are you doing here?'

'I... I just couldn't go home,' sniffed Rachel.

'So you thought you'd turn up on my doorstep with half a bottle of wine?' Jane raised one eyebrow.

In the commotion at Victoria's house Rachel had grabbed an open bottle. 'It was full when I took it,' said Rachel, not really sure if that made things better or worse. 'Then halfway home I realised that I probably shouldn't be taking things from a crime scene.'

'Oh, I wouldn't worry,' said Jane, ushering Rachel in, out of the cold. 'It was an accident, wasn't it? Victoria's death, I mean, not you taking the wine. When they realise that, it won't be a crime scene anymore, so don't fret about it.'

'The copper said he smelt almonds on her breath...' Tears were streaming down Rachel's face. 'Someone must have put some in their cake.'

'But no one would have done that on purpose, surely?' Jane frowned. 'Maybe someone didn't realise she was allergic?'

'I guess, I mean I didn't know until you told me... maybe other people didn't know either!'

'Exactly!' Jane put her arm around Rachel's shoulders and led her through to the kitchen. 'Sit down,' she said, and as Rachel took a big swig out of the bottle, she added, 'I'll get you a glass.'

Rachel hovered by the kitchen door. She leant on the door frame and watched as Jane took two glasses out of the cupboard, holding each one up to the light before pouring some wine, from an already open bottle in her fridge, into one of them. *Was this really the time to be worrying how sparkling the wine glasses were?* Jane picked up both glasses, turned around and jumped. Rachel was now standing directly behind her, still holding her bottle of wine.

'Jeez,' she said. 'You frightened the life out of me!'

'Sorry,' said Rachel. She took the empty glass from Jane, poured some wine into it and then took another swig out of the bottle. 'It's just... well, I said I'd make a coffee and walnut cake!'

'But you didn't,' said Jane. 'You made a Victoria sponge, or rather *I* made a Victoria sponge.'

'You know that... and I know that,' said Rachel, taking another big slurp. 'But people are going to put two and two together and make whatever number they feel like!'

Jane didn't say anything for a moment.

'You think I'm right, don't you?' Rachel blurted out following the lack of response.

'I mean...' Jane paused for a moment. 'Let them think what they want, but I've never heard of anyone being killed by a Victoria sponge!'

Rachel stared at Jane. She could feel her cheeks burning red. And then out of nowhere she just burst into laughter. She couldn't control it. 'You're absolutely right,' she said, wiping the tears from her eyes. 'I mean *death by cake*... who has ever heard anything so ridiculous?'

'Exactly,' said Jane, refilling both of their glasses. 'I know you're upset; you've had a shock this evening, but our cake had no nuts in it. So, whether this whole thing was a mistake or on purpose... it definitely wasn't *our* mistake.'

'Thank you,' said Rachel, throwing her arms around Jane and sloshing wine onto the kitchen tiles. Rachel wasn't usually a hugger, but she had drunk way too much.

Jane frowned at the spilt wine and then with a forced smile, she wiped it up. 'Let's sit down,' she said, gesturing to the breakfast bar.

Rachel wobbled her way onto one of the stools and took another large gulp of wine. 'To Victoria Sponge,' she said, raising her glass towards Jane. 'May she rest in peace.'

'Her name is Victoria *Sandwich*,' said Jane.

'Oh yes,' said Rachel. 'What did I say? To Victoria; Lady Sandwich of Lunchbox Lane.'

'I think you might have had enough wine.' Jane reached for Rachel's glass.

'Nonsense!' Rachel thought about saying something about Victoria's weird Bake Off party leading to her untimely death, but she was not sure that she could string a sentence together that wouldn't make her seem rude or uncaring or *guilty*, so she left it at that.

'It's ironic isn't it,' said Jane eventually, 'that she forced people into making cake for her and that one of those cakes killed her.'

Rachel chuckled. 'You have to laugh,' she said. 'The alternative is too depressing.'

Jane smiled back at her.

'Is it just me or is this wine awful?' asked Rachel. 'Trust Victoria to get the cheap stuff. I bet she only gave that to the guests and kept a nice bottle for herself.'

'I've just topped your glass up with *my* wine,' said Jane, looking offended.

'Ah.' Rachel tried to think of something apologetic to say, but Jane saved the awkward silence by asking, 'Do you want some lemonade in it?'

'Yeah, that might do the trick,' replied Rachel.

Jane got up, but her phone rang. 'It's in the pantry,' she said. 'Help yourself. I need to take this.'

Rachel wandered over towards the pantry, past the artistically stacked fruit bowl, past the keys that hung carefully on hooks by the back door and past the wooden cabinet underneath, that Rachel assumed hid a collection of perfectly polished shoes.

As she turned into the pantry, she looked around in awe at the shelves packed full of food and drink. Everything was stacked so incredibly neatly. Kilner jars, wire baskets and ceramic stacking canisters were lined up meticulously along the shelves.

It was all so Instagrammable. Not like the mouldy fruit in her fruit bowl at home or the pile of shoes in her hallway.

'Wow,' she said out loud to herself as she thought about the shelves in her own kitchen cupboards. *Jane has too much time on her hands.* Rachel didn't have a pantry, but she did have a large kitchen cupboard that she could never find anything in because it looked like a jumble sale.

She could hear the faint murmuring of Jane on the phone out in the kitchen. Her eyes scanned the shelves and finally landed on the soft drink section – *it's like being in a swanky bar!* – and as she reached up towards a bottle of lemonade, her top caught on a packet in front of her. She stretched for the bottle but the packet toppled over.

'Shit!' she said as she caught the pack, but it was too late as a cloud of flour exploded in front of her. 'Shit, shit!' She scooped up as much flour as possible and poured it into the bin that was in the corner of the pantry. *Who has a bin in the pantry?* She scrunched the top of the pack of flour together and put it back in its place on the countertop next to the plastic rattan-effect tray.

There were a few items chucked into the tray, which caught her eye as she brushed herself down. It was nowhere near as neat as the rest of the pantry. There was a bag of sugar, a half empty egg box, a pack of icing sugar, a tub of baking powder and a little bottle of flavouring. Rachel remembered Jane listing the ingredients of the cake she had made her, and realised straight away that this was them. She assumed they had been thrown in there ready to put away in their correct place, which Jane obviously hadn't got around to yet.

It was some sort of halfway house for the pantry, like when she left piles of her family members' stuff on the stairs at home, hoping that it would be taken upstairs and put away, and not just stepped over. There was something about the contents of the tray though, that didn't feel right to her, but she couldn't put her finger on what it was.

'Rachel,' Jane called. 'Are you okay in there?'

She rushed out. 'Sorry, Jane,' she said, rubbing her hands. 'Slight flour explosion!'

'Oh, okay,' said Jane, much calmer about the mess than Rachel had been expecting. She had thought that she might get a little bit told off. 'That was Ben on the phone.'

'Everything okay?' Rachel asked, noticing that the colour had drained from Jane's face. 'I mean, y'know, apart from Victoria being dead and everything.'

'He said that the police think it was definitely anaphylaxis. They think that ties in with the officer smelling almonds as she took her last breath.'

Rachel swallowed the lump in her throat, as Jane took a very long sip of her wine.

'You didn't get the lemonade,' said Jane.

'Oh God, no sorry,' said Rachel. 'Got caught up in the flour kerfuffle and completely forgot. I'll just go back and...'

Her voice trailed off as she disappeared back into the pantry. That niggling feeling was back with her. In fact, it had magnified and she suddenly went all Miss Marple, headed straight over to the tray of cake ingredients and started rifling through them. She had always thought a spot of amateur sleuthing would be fun, but she felt sick as she picked up the little bottle of flavouring and stared at it with wide eyes.

She staggered back into the kitchen holding the bottle.

'I don't think that's lemonade,' laughed Jane. 'Try looking for a slightly larger bottle.'

Rachel didn't laugh.

'Is everything okay, Rach?'

'No,' said Rachel. It wasn't lemonade and everything *wasn't* okay. She held up the tiny bottle. 'This is *almond* extract. Not vanilla.'

8

———

JANE

'Where did you find that?' asked Jane. 'Oh God! Not in that basket thing on the side?'

'Yes,' said Rachel. 'Is that the stuff you used to…?'

'Make the cake,' Jane finished her question for her. 'Yes. I hadn't got around to tidying it away. I was thinking about getting some containers, you know, nice glass ones – airtight – to put all the sugars and flours and stuff in.'

'Never mind the containers,' said Rachel. 'Why was this in there… with the cake stuff?'

She held up the small bottle. *Who did she think she was, Jessica Fletcher?*

'I didn't put that in the cake, I used vanilla extract, I checked. Ben checked the label too. I remember because I couldn't find my glasses so he had to read the label for me. Ask him, he said he'll be home soon.'

'It's not that I don't believe you, Jane, but why is it in the tray, with the other stuff you used for the cake?'

'I don't know. I… I don't know.'

Jane and Rachel both sat down at the kitchen counter and took a large swig of wine. Rachel seemed to have forgotten about the lemonade she had been wanting to add, and the fact that she had said the wine was awful.

'What are we going to do?' she asked, her knees shaking. 'That was my cake. My cake killed Victoria.'

'We don't know that,' said Jane. 'Plus *I* made the cake, so if anyone should be worried it's me, but I'm not, because I checked the label.'

'How can you be so calm?' said Rachel, with fear in her eyes.

Jane didn't see the point in letting something like this stress her out. She had enough to worry about, after all, she'd just let another mum in her pantry when she had forgotten to tidy everything away. Rachel would think that she was a complete slob, and that was somehow worse than her thinking she was a murderer. Anyway, like she'd already said, if it was the cake that killed her, it hadn't been done on purpose. It was a mistake. She *knew* that she had checked the label with Ben. She remembered asking, *extract or essence?* Oh! Hang on. She had asked, *extract or essence,* but had she checked whether it was *almond or vanilla?*

She decided not to mention that.

'Listen, Rachel. Whatever happened, this was an *accident.* No one wanted to *kill* Victoria, everyone *loved* her.'

Rachel raised one eyebrow.

'Okay well, maybe *love* is a strong word.' Jane nodded. 'But no one wanted her dead. She is just a mum like the rest of us... not a mafia boss or a drug lord.'

'Yeah, because they're the only people that get murdered,' said Rachel, pressing her lips together and raising her eyebrows even higher.

Jane tried to think of something helpful to say, but she was all out. Luckily she was saved by the bell. *Ben had forgotten his keys.*

'Sorry, love,' he said, kissing her on the cheek and hanging up his jacket in the hallway. 'It's been a long night.' He rubbed his eyes and Jane noticed how red they were.

'Have you been crying?' she asked.

'No. Of course not. It's work, love. I'm just tired.'

Jane always told Ben that when he got home from work he could show his emotion, that it was healthy to let it out, but he rarely did.

'How are *you* doing?' he asked, to take the focus away from himself Jane presumed. There was a sympathetic tone to his voice. 'Oh!' His eyes fell on Rachel. 'How are you *both* doing?' he asked, nodding to Rachel as Jane ushered him into the kitchen.

'Holding up,' said Jane. 'I'll put the kettle on. I think we *all* need a cuppa.'

'Not for me,' said Rachel. 'I should really get going.'

'Something I said?' joked Ben.

Rachel managed a small smile.

'She's panicking that her cake killed Victoria,' said Jane, breezily. 'I've told her not to be silly.'

'*Our* cake,' said Rachel as she stood up.

Jane frowned.

'*Your* cake?' Ben held his stomach.

'It's fine,' said Jane. 'Our cake had nothing to do with it.'

'Just get some sleep,' said Ben, the calm copper. 'The autopsy is scheduled for tomorrow. We will know more then. No point worrying about anything until we know for sure.'

Rachel sighed and Jane gulped. The word *autopsy* suddenly made it all feel very real. Jane was police trained, so she knew to just remain calm and be honest about silly mistakes that may become important evidence, but still, she had that feeling of dread. And the way Rachel was acting was very peculiar.

Jane gave Rachel, who was breathing heavily and clearly

starting to panic, a hug and told her that everything would seem a bit better in the morning; Victoria would still be dead, but hopefully the autopsy would clear things up a bit. Maybe she had accidentally eaten a peanut earlier on and the whole thing would not be pinned on their cake.

'Nightmare,' said Jane, as she returned to the kitchen after letting Rachel out.

'Why has she got her knickers in such a twist?' asked Ben.

'Oh, the cake I helped her bake for the Bake Off party. I might have accidentally put *almond* extract in it, instead of vanilla.'

'Accidentally?'

'Of course, Ben! It was the tiniest of drops and I didn't think...'

'Don't worry about it. Just wait until tomorrow. Wait until the autopsy. I've got a sneaky suspicion that it's not worth driving yourself nuts over.'

Jane raised one eyebrow.

'Pardon the pun,' added Ben.

'The thing is,' said Jane. 'Rachel was making jokes on the mum-chat about baking a coffee and walnut cake for Victoria, plus she was being super weird this evening... snooping around in the pantry, *and* only yesterday she said to me, when talking about Victoria, "I'm going to kill her."'

Ben sprayed out his tea. 'She said *what?*'

Jane nodded.

'I'm guessing she was joking?' Ben patted down his uniform with some kitchen roll.

Jane shrugged her shoulders.

'Okay,' said Ben with a deep breath. 'Let's get some sleep, shall we?'

It was going to be a long night and a long day tomorrow,

waiting to find out what killed Victoria. Jane knew she would be unable to think about anything else.

Her phone pinged and she knew before she looked at the screen that it would be the Yummy Mummies chat.

> Natasha (Twins' mum): Any news @Jane?

> Jane (Lottie's mum): I thought you were getting an early night?

> Natasha (Twins' mum): Oh I can't sleep. Not with all the upset and drama. Thought your hubby might've got the lowdown @Jane? Surely even the police gossip!

> Jane (Lottie's mum): I'm afraid not.

> Amy (Rosie's mum): Shame.

> Beth (Oliver's mum): Never mind.

Jane suddenly realised that she was missing out on an opportunity to become very popular within this group of mums. If she could find out nuggets of information for them she would be idolised by this gang of gossip-vultures. Unfortunately, at that moment, she didn't really have any nuggets, at least none that didn't make *her* look bad. She would have to work on that.

> Jane (Lottie's mum): If I find out anything, I'll let you know.

> Natasha (Twins' mum): Good girl!

How did Natasha always manage to make people feel about an inch tall? Jane didn't respond. She was about to put her phone down when another message pinged through.

> Natasha (Twins' mum): I wonder who will organise the Bake Sale now that the chair of the PTA is, you know, unavailable?

Jane started to type out a reply saying that perhaps there were other priorities right now but the other ladies beat her to answering, so she decided not to bother.

> Amy (Rosie's mum): You'd be amazing, Natasha.

> Beth (Oliver's mum): Already our baking queen.

> Trace (Kai's mum): Dull Debbie will do it won't she? She's vice chair.

Jane switched off her phone. Victoria Sandwich was not even cold and they were already discussing bake sales and replacing her. She went up to bed and snuggled down under the covers. She shut her eyes and took a deep breath, hoping she would drift off to sleep. She knew it was unlikely. Her head was like a cake mixer, thoughts swirling around. Had she read the label incorrectly? Had that been what killed Victoria? Would she get the blame or would it all be on Rachel? Would that mean Rachel would hate her? Or... was that all irrelevant? Who out there wanted Victoria dead?

The thoughts came and went but oddly, the one thought that she couldn't shake at all, was that she really fancied a slice of coffee and walnut cake.

9

———

RACHEL

When Rachel's eyes opened the following morning, her first thought was why had she drunk so much wine? Her head hurt.

Her second thought was why on Earth had she decided to bake a cake for Victoria's baking party? Why on Earth had she joked about baking a coffee and walnut one? And why on Earth had she got someone else to bake the cake for her?

Her third thought – assuming that the previous three counted as one – was what the hell did her children need to wear to school today? Was it PE kit? Or uniform? Or wear something blue or red or green? Or wear a number? Dress as a book character? Wear odd socks? Or wear what the flippin' 'eck you want to?

Then she remembered it was Saturday and let out a long, relieved breath.

When she finally allowed herself to breathe back in, she smiled at the smells that were rising from the kitchen. Coffee and pancakes. She crept downstairs and watched through the open kitchen door. Phil had taken control of breakfast, and Megan and Charlie were beaming with joy as they poured lashings of honey and sugar and chocolate sauce and sprinkles all over their stacks of fresh pancakes.

She breathed it in. Not just the smells but the whole scene. A normal family breakfast. She wondered if this would be her last for a while. Her loving family, blissfully unaware that their wife and mother has just been involved in someone's accidental death. Unaware that their wife and mother accidentally made a joke of said accidental death, before it accidentally happened. Unaware that although she may be smiling, their wife and mother was panicking inside.

'Good morning!' She breezed into the kitchen, not allowing the weight on her shoulders to get her down. 'Something smells wonderful.'

Phil smiled. 'I've just put some bacon on too.'

'You are spoiling us,' beamed Rachel.

'Well, you deserve to be spoiled.' Phil put one arm around his wife's waist whilst holding some tongs in the other oven-gloved hand. He kissed her on the cheek. 'How was last night?' he asked. 'Did your cake knock 'em dead?'

Rachel felt her face drop.

'What's the matter?' asked Phil. 'You've gone as white as a sheet!'

Rachel widened her eyes and swallowed. 'I... I didn't make a cake,' she said, eventually.

'Good choice,' muttered Megan under her breath.

'Megan,' said Phil. 'That's not...'

'*What?*' said Megan, before rolling her eyes. 'No one wants one of Mum's cakes... they're... they're always burnt.'

'Megan!'

'I'm going to my room,' said Megan, ignoring her father.

Phil shook his head. 'You like Mummy's cakes, don't you, Charlie?'

'Um...' Charlie considered his answer carefully. 'They're

okay... I suppose, although I'd rather have a biscuit. Can I go and play now?'

Phil sighed. 'Yes, okay.' Charlie had already disappeared. 'Well, that wholesome family breakfast lasted all of five minutes.'

'You tried your best,' said Rachel, sitting at the breakfast bar, cradling her freshly made coffee.

Phil sat down next to her.

'I need to tell you something,' said Rachel, taking a big sip of coffee.

'Okay,' said Phil. 'Sounds serious.' He picked up the TV remote and pointed it at the screen. He started to turn the volume down, but then he stopped and said, 'Hey, isn't that...?'

Rachel looked up. A photo of Victoria filled the screen.

Phil turned the volume back up, higher than it was to start with, and the reporter filled him in on what Rachel had been trying, but failing, to say.

'A local woman collapsed at a small gathering at her house last night. Initial thoughts were that the woman had had an allergic reaction to something she had ingested, but a forensic team has been working through the night and preliminary tests indicate that the woman, identified as Victoria Sandwich, was poisoned. A murder investigation has been launched.'

'What?' said Phil, staring at the screen and then at Rachel.

'Fuck,' said Rachel. 'Thank God!'

'What do you mean *Thank God?*' Phil frowned at her in amazement.

'I mean thank God it wasn't our cake,' said Rachel. 'I was literally about to tell you that Jane and I made a cake. Well, Jane made it, but I asked her to. And I thought we'd given Victoria an allergic reaction. I thought we had killed her, Phil.'

'What?! Why didn't you say something? You should've told me. You should've woken me up last night. Oh, Rach.'

Her eyes filled with tears. 'I really thought we'd killed her.'

Then the sobbing started.

'But you didn't,' said Phil. He still seemed shocked, but he managed to put an arm around his wife. 'She was murdered!'

'Fuck,' said Rachel again. *She really should work on controlling her potty mouth, but now was not the time.*

'No wonder you look so pale, Rach,' said Phil, suddenly looking concerned. 'Why didn't you say anything?'

'You were asleep.'

'You should have woken me up, Rach, when you got in last night.'

'I just needed some sleep... plus I didn't know what to say.'

'Oh, Rach!' Phil put both his arms around his wife and held her tight.

'I was so scared,' she hiccupped. 'I really thought we'd killed her.'

'Your cakes aren't that bad.' Phil laughed.

Rachel just about managed the tiniest of smiles. 'She was allergic to nuts,' she sniffed. 'And Jane accidentally put almond extract in the cake and I took it to the party and...'

'None of that matters,' said Phil. 'They just said she was poisoned.'

'But her dying breath smelt of almonds, the police said so.'

'Rach,' said Phil. 'Have you never watched Poirot? Every murder mystery fan knows that there's a poison that smells of almonds.'

'But...' Rachel was lost for words. Who would have poisoned her? Victoria was an annoying woman, but annoying enough to murder?

If she was poisoned, it must have been someone at the party. She thought about who else was there. Natasha; but she and Victoria were friends, weren't they? They had certainly acted as though they were. Gina, the newbie; she barely spoke and she hardly knew Victoria, so what reason could she possibly have for wanting her dead? Sarah; she's a bit of a floozy, known for snogging other people's husbands, but Victoria was divorced... no husband to snog! Greg, the only dad there; he was miffed that the dads hadn't been invited in the first place, but *surely* that wasn't a motive for murder? Frankie; again didn't say a lot although Rachel got the feeling that there might be more to her than meets the eye. And Debbie; she has wanted to be the chair of the PTA for a long time now... and with Victoria never looking like she would ever step down, maybe murder was the only way.

Rachel laughed out loud that these ridiculous motives were even crossing her mind. 'There's no one,' she laughed. 'I can't think of anyone with an *actual* reason to want Victoria dead.'

'And yet she is,' said Phil.

'And yet she is,' repeated Rachel.

10

———

JANE

Jane's phone pinged and as expected, it was the Yummy Mummies chat.

> Amy (Rosie's mum): Have you seen the news?

> Beth (Oliver's mum): No, still in bed.

Still in bed? thought Jane. She had been up for hours. She'd made Lottie breakfast, put dinner in the slow cooker, dusted the entire house and done three loads of washing.

> Amy (Rosie's mum): They reckon Victoria was murdered.

> Beth (Oliver's mum): What?! I thought the cake killed her!

Despite all this talk of murder. Jane was still worried that actually, maybe, the cake *did* kill her... the cake that she had made!

Amy (Rosie's mum): They're saying she was poisoned.

Beth (Oliver's mum): Well, that's what happens when you trust amateur bakers!

Jane huffed. It wasn't her amateur baking that was the problem, it was her eyesight, but she refused to start wearing glasses. Some people could really pull glasses off, but Jane just didn't think that they went with her look.

Amy (Rosie's mum): Poisoned deliberately they reckon!

Beth (Oliver's mum): Wow! So that makes everyone there a suspect, surely?

Amy (Rosie's mum): Yep!

Jane felt glad that she hadn't been there.

Beth (Oliver's mum): Even @Natasha?

Natasha (Twins' mum): Don't be ridiculous. Victoria was my friend, everyone knows that.

No one typed anything for a minute. Jane wondered whether the silence spoke volumes.

Amy (Rosie's mum): Of course, you are great friends!

Beth (Oliver's mum): We all know that @Natasha. I wasn't suggesting anything.

Natasha (Twins' mum): If you ask me, there was only one person there who was acting shifty. One person being rude on the mum-chat beforehand. And there was only one person there making sarcastic comments, rolling her eyes and generally not getting into the spirit of the evening. And that was the same person that joked about making a coffee and walnut cake.

Jane (Lottie's mum): What? Rachel?!

Jane had been trying to keep out of this conversation, but she couldn't help herself.

Natasha (Twins' mum): Oh yes sorry @Jane! Forgot you two were bum-chums!

Jane (Lottie's mum): We are not bum-chums… I just don't think she would do something like that… that's all.

Jane's heart was thumping. She wasn't used to standing up for herself to Natasha. Usually what Natasha said went, so Jane was a little uneasy.

Natasha (Twins' mum): Well, I am just saying what I saw.

Amy (Rosie's mum): There is something odd about her.

Beth (Oliver's mum): And she never usually gets involved in school stuff… why did she suddenly want to help with the cakes?

Trace (Kai's mum): I heard that she's always had beef with Victoria.

And that was the moment that Jane really had to say

something, but that something wasn't what she had expected to say. She was about to jump in and defend her friend, but something stopped her. She didn't know where it came from but if her cake had even the slightest involvement in all of this, she'd need a tribe behind her.

She didn't want to gossip. She didn't want to get involved. She knew that Rachel wasn't capable of murder and she knew that Rachel had no real reason to want Victoria dead, but she wanted the Yummy Mummies to like her. She wanted to be part of the group, to be respected, to be loved. She didn't think for one minute that Rachel had anything to do with Victoria's murder but she wanted to be part of the chat and she knew getting on the wrong side of Natasha was a bad idea, so she typed...

> Jane (Lottie's mum): Actually, I don't know if I should mention this but...

> Natasha (Twins' mum): Mention it @Jane, whatever it is, mention it!

> Jane (Lottie's mum): It's just... she did say to me, the other day before the Bake Off party, that she was 'going to kill' Victoria.

Again there was silence.

Jane was sure that as each mum looked at their screen they would have fallen silent too. Not saying anything. Not doing anything. No tapping of fingers, feverishly typing out a reply. The only sound would be the distant hum of a washing machine, the ping of an oven timer or the cries of 'Mum, can I have...?' or 'Mum, what's for lunch?' but to all of the Yummy Mummies this background noise would become a muffled blur of sound as they processed the words they were reading.

As Jane predicted, Natasha was the first to eventually reply.

Natasha (Twins' mum): Well, there you have it.

Amy (Rosie's mum): Have you told the police @Jane?

Natasha (Twins' mum): She's married to the police.

Amy (Rosie's mum): Have you told Ben?

Beth (Oliver's mum): Surely Rachel didn't mean it. She must have been joking.

Trace (Kai's mum): People often hide their true feelings within humour.

Beth (Oliver's mum): Did you read that on a fridge magnet @Trace?

After taking a deep breath and making a decision, Jane tapped out her response.

Jane (Lottie's mum): I don't think I need to report it to the police. Like @Beth says, it was just a flippant remark. Rachel would never actually kill someone.

Natasha (Twins' mum): Jane. I don't want to sound patronising, but you know as well as I do that if you don't tell them, you are technically withholding evidence.

Jane swallowed hard. *Why was Natasha so determined to drop Rachel in it?*

Jane (Lottie's mum): And if I do tell them I could be wasting police time.

Natasha (Twins' mum): That is for them to decide.

Jane knew she was right. In fact, she knew deep down that that's why she had mentioned it. She knew she wouldn't be able to keep it to herself knowing that by not telling anyone she was technically lying. Well, not lying exactly, but withholding the truth.

She sighed.

> Jane (Lottie's mum): I know you are right. It's just that she's…

> Natasha (Twins' mum): Your bum-chum?

> Jane (Lottie's mum): I was going to say 'my friend'.

> Natasha (Twins' mum): Well, no one needs a friend that's a murderer.

Jane wondered why Natasha had to be so annoyingly self-righteous all the time, but on this occasion she knew Natasha was right.

And she also knew what she had to do.

11
————

RACHEL

Reception Mums #inittogether

> Gina (Harry's mum): Oh my God, have you seen the news?

> Frankie (Billy's mum): They think it was murder!

> Sarah (Mia's mum): Who would want to murder Victoria?

> Greg (Masie's dad): Very good question, I mean apart from being like the army commander version of Mary Berry, she seemed like a lovely lady.

> Jo (Millie's mum): I'm glad I didn't go.

> Natasha (Freddie's mum): To answer your question @Sarah, I've already heard some rumours. Just rumours of course but you know what that say; no smoke without fire.

> Rachel (Charlie's mum): It's awful, isn't it? To think that we were all there, and that someone in that room was a murderer.

Nothing.

Rachel wondered if she should add this to her CV; specialist skill, being able to stop a group chat dead with one inane comment.

She poured herself a coffee and went and sat between her children on the living room sofa. As she allowed herself a brief moment to breathe, it sunk in that she had seen somebody die. Another mum. A mum who would have snuggled on the sofa with her own daughter when she was small. A daughter who must be in a lot of pain right now.

Her moment of reflection was shattered by a tinny, high-pitched American voice that filled one ear as it gave instructions on how to do something that Rachel had never heard of in her life before. Either Charlie was learning a foreign language or it had something to do with Minecraft. The other ear filled with short bursts of various pop songs. Just as Rachel's brain told her what track she was listening to it would change to something else, that she would rack the depths of her memory to identify, to no avail.

'Just pick a song, Megan,' she said.

'I'm mixing it up,' replied her daughter, without looking up from the screen.

Rachel sighed. 'You two don't know you're born.' Now she really sounded like a mum. 'Do you know that when I was a kid, back in the eighties...?'

'The 1980s or the...?'

'Yes, Charlie, the 1980s!' *How old did he think she was?* 'In the 1980s, there was only an *hour* of kids' TV a day.'

'What did you do after that...?' asked Megan. 'Watch your tablet?'

Rachel didn't know whether to laugh or cry. She didn't like the amount of time her kids spent staring at a screen – she was sure that Natasha's kids and Jane's daughter were currently at home doing some sort of wholesome family activity like baking oatmeal cookies or making bird feeders from old teacups – but sometimes Rachel just needed to reset her brain, and keeping the kids busy for a few minutes gave her half a chance of doing that.

The weekday business of her brain having to remember where everyone needed to be, what they needed to be wearing and what they needed to be fed sometimes got too much. Sometimes she felt more like a PA than a mum. *Perhaps that's what being a mum is?* She didn't know what her excuse was today though; it was Saturday and nobody needed to be anywhere...

'Shit!'

'Mum, stop saying that word in front of Charlie,' said Megan.

'Sorry, love.'

'I asked Miss Williams what it meant,' said Charlie, with a big grin.

'I hope you didn't,' said Rachel.

'What's the matter anyway, Mum?' asked Megan.

'I just remembered that I have an interview this afternoon... I was going to wash my hair.'

'Who does interviews on a Saturday?'

'Someone who is very busy and important and is in need of a super-duper spangly PA to organise their diary, so that things don't fall on a Saturday. Not one who forgets to wash her hair and would have forgotten to go to the interview had some random thought not reminded her.'

'Well, you'd better get ready then,' said Megan as she turned back to the video on her screen of two people dancing in sync, and then falling about laughing about the fact that they were dancing in sync.

'What's a PA?' asked Charlie.

Rachel looked at him for a second, then looked down at her watch – deciding whether or not she had time to explain – before eventually saying, 'Ask Miss Williams.'

When Rachel got back from the most disastrous interview in the history of interviews, she looked at her phone to see that there were still no messages in the *Reception Mums #inittogether* chat.

Something wasn't right.

Surely someone else would have said something by now? This wasn't just an *everyone is busy on a Saturday* silence, this was a *something is up* silence. Something other than the fact that a local mum just got poisoned.

Rachel shook her phone and wafted it in the air in case it was her lack of signal that was stopping the messages.

Eventually she typed...

> Rachel (Charlie's mum): Was it something I said?

Natasha was typing within seconds. *Of course she was.* That woman was surgically attached to her phone. Rachel wondered how she showered.

> Natasha (Freddie's mum): I'm afraid it was!

Oh, thought Rachel. She had assumed she was being paranoid, but it seemed she had *assumed* wrongly and *been paranoid* rightly.

> Natasha (Freddie's mum): Something you said on the playground the other day, about wanting to kill Victoria. Your voice isn't as quiet as you think Rachel and well, as you know… now she's dead!

'Shit!' Rachel really needed to broaden her vocabulary. 'Fuck!'

> Rachel (Charlie's mum): C'mon guys. I was stressed about the cake debacle. You can't honestly think that I actually wanted to kill her? It was a joke.

> Natasha (Freddie's mum): Normally jokes are funny, Rachel.

She had a point. It wasn't funny. Rachel knew it was a stupid thing to say, and now Victoria was dead.

She closed the Reception Mums chat and messaged Jane: *Are you free? Need to talk! xx* And before she could say, 'Well this is a total balls-up,' she was in the pub, with a glass of wine in hand being given sympathetic eyes by Jane.

'They think I did it,' said Rachel, knocking back half the glass of wine in one gulp. 'They think I poisoned Victoria Sponge… on purpose!'

'It's *Sandwich*,' said Jane. 'And, why would they think that?'

'Because they heard us talking, on the playground the other day. They heard me say I was going to kill her. They think that I *actually* was.'

Jane blinked back at Rachel. 'Surely they don't,' she said eventually. 'Everyone says silly things like that, no one ever actually means it.'

'Well, someone did,' replied Rachel. 'Someone meant it and someone killed her.'

Jane sighed.

'You have to help me,' said Rachel. She was panicking now. She was desperate. 'You have to help me prove that it wasn't me. I didn't kill Victoria. You believe me, don't you, Jane?'

Jane took a sip of wine and didn't say anything.

12

JANE

Of course Jane believed her.

She also knew how bad *trial by mum-chat* could get. She'd been there when a missing jumper had turned up in someone's laundry pile weeks after the desperate pleas to find it. She'd seen mums being hunted down for unpaid raffle tickets or missing Tupperware, and she'd witnessed the aftermath of someone not inviting the whole class to a birthday party. Jane wanted to do whatever she could to protect her friend from that, especially because she felt guilty for being the one that told the other mums what Rachel had said.

The wave of relief that came over Jane when she realised that Rachel somehow thought that they had all overheard it, had been only slightly dampened by the guilt. She felt awful for lying to her about how the other mums had found out, but it was for the best.

This swirling mess of heartfelt belief in Rachel, plus the guilt for lying and the relief that her secret was safe, were the reasons why, despite knowing she should tell the police what Rachel had said, she instead wanted to help her.

'The thing is, Rachel,' she said, pausing briefly to sip her wine. 'I *do* want to help you. It absolutely goes without saying that of course I do, but I don't really know how I can.'

'That's easy,' said Rachel. 'There's only one way to prove I didn't do it.'

'Which is...?' asked Jane, having a horrible feeling that she already knew the answer.

'To find out who did!'

'I thought you might say that.' She took another, much larger, gulp of her wine.

'This is perfect for you,' said Rachel, beaming. 'You have police training and everything.'

'That was a long time ago...'

'It wasn't *that* long ago, and surely you want to put it to some use.'

Jane took slight offence to the insinuation that she hadn't put it to any use, but of course the main reason she took offence was because it was true. As soon as they'd had a child all her ambition had gone out of the window and been replaced with the desire to be a perfect little housewife, to a perfect little family, where everything was perfect, and if it couldn't *be* perfect, she could at least make sure that it *looked* perfect from the outside.

Her mind wandered to the flowers that she'd left strewn on the kitchen counter. Ben had popped out earlier, under the pretence of getting bread and milk, and returned with flowers.

'What are these for?' she'd asked, immediately suspicious.

'Um, I'm not really sure,' Ben had stammered. 'I think I thought that you might be upset, that they might cheer you up or something.'

'Oh,' Jane had said, feeling guilty for questioning his motives. 'Well, thank you. They have.'

The truth was that she hadn't really been upset. Shocked yes, but she wasn't friendly enough with Victoria to classify it as being upset. Still, she appreciated the flowers and had been carefully arranging them in a vase when she had received Rachel's panicked message and dashed straight to the pub. *Of course, all real emergencies need an urgent trip to the pub.* She should have realised that emergency was stretching it and at least finished sorting the vase of flowers before leaving.

'Well, don't you?' Rachel snapped Jane out of her thoughts.

'Erm, okay,' said Jane, trying to remember what she was agreeing to.

'Great,' said Rachel. 'First we need to go through the suspects.'

Ahh, yes the murder, Jane remembered. Putting police training to good use. *How could she forget?* She looked at her watch. 'Isn't it getting a bit late for...?'

But Rachel had already taken a notebook and pen out of her bag. 'So, are you in agreement that it had to have been someone at the party?'

'Well, yes,' said Jane. 'From the timings, and assuming the autopsy confirms it was poison, it is likely to have taken effect quite quickly... so I guess we can safely assume that the poisoning took place at the party, yes.'

'Assume makes an ass out of you and me,' said Rachel, and Jane raised her eyebrows. 'Sorry, I don't know where that came from.'

'It's true though,' said Jane. 'You're right, it can be really dangerous to make assumptions in a murder case. You have to look at all the evidence, but we also have to start somewhere and the party guests seem like a logical place to get going.'

'Right,' said Rachel, taking the lid off her pen.

'Remind me who was there,' said Jane, trying to show willing.

'Well,' said Rachel. 'Other than Victoria and myself, there was Natasha.'

Jane laughed. 'I mean she can be a bit of an uppity bitch but she wouldn't murder anyone.' She took a sip of her wine, hoping that Rachel hadn't noticed the slip in her polite demeanour.

'She might break a nail,' agreed Rachel, as she wrote the next name on the list. 'Gina.'

'We don't know a lot about her,' said Jane. 'Maybe she has some deep dark secrets.'

'Deep dark secrets that lead to you poisoning someone at a PTA Bake Off event?'

'You never know!' Jane smiled and shrugged. 'Who else?'

'Sarah... but she only ever pissed off women with husbands!'

Jane rolled her eyes. 'Presumably Debbie was there? She's been gunning after Victoria's job for years.'

'Yeah, but murder?' asked Rachel. 'Over a voluntary position?' She carried on scribbling on the notepad. 'Greg was there, representing the men-folk.'

'Bit of a cliché for the man to be the murderer,' smirked Jane.

'He was hacked off that the dads weren't invited. I think he thought it was sexist. I reckon he only went to prove a point.'

'Is that everyone?' asked Jane.

'Just leaves Frankie,' said Rachel

'Oh yes, I've met her before.' Jane racked her brain to try and remember where. 'She wouldn't say boo to a goose,' said Jane. 'I mean she never speaks. That's a weird saying, isn't it? I mean who would say boo to a goose? What a weird thing to do...' Jane trailed off.

'She spoke to me,' said Rachel.

'When?'

'At the party.'

'What did she say?'

Jane looked at Rachel, waiting for her to answer, and could see that she was replaying the conversations from that evening in her head. She focused on her wine and stayed quiet, allowing her to remember.

Eventually Rachel spoke. 'She said that Victoria should keep people on side if she knows what's good for her!'

Jane swallowed her wine quickly, which made her cough. 'She said *what?*'

Rachel nodded.

'Well, I think we know where to start,' said Jane. 'That's suspicious as hell!'

'Hmm,' said Rachel. 'Although don't forget why I'm in this mess. I said something equally as flippant and incriminating.'

'Yes,' said Jane. 'But you're my friend, and I *know* you are innocent. We know nothing about this Frankie... well apart from her dubious remarks. Oh, and that she's quiet. You know what they say: it's always the quiet ones.'

Jane said all this with such conviction that she convinced herself. Even though she knew never to make assumptions, here she was, assuming the worst about someone new in order to protect her friend.

Friends were like gold dust after all. *Why else would you bake a cake for them?*

Okay, so maybe Jane didn't always agree with Rachel's haphazard and disorganised approach to mum-ing, or her allowing people to bake competitive cakes on her behalf, but she knew that Rachel was genuine; a real friend.

Her friend smiled. 'We need to talk to Frankie.'

13

FRANKIE

Frankie sat drawing silly stick men – and silly stick women – and Billy laughed.

It was a habit that she'd got into to do something with her son that didn't involve his tablet, or him getting cross, or him getting bored. She would ask him to draw something – anything, whatever he liked – and then she would add stick people to the drawings, doing hilarious stuff like riding a T. rex or being eaten by a shark.

Doodling had become an accidental hobby recently, too. Frankie found that it helped her to relax. Although she had started with silly doodles for Billy, she had gradually moved on to drawing funny, or annoying, or outrageous things that grown-ups said and did. She still called them grown-ups because she still didn't really feel like one herself. Even though she technically *was* a grown-up, and a wife, and a mum, she still sometimes couldn't get over some of the ridiculous things the other mums, and wives, said and did. So she drew them.

She'd been feeling anxious again since the horror that was the Bake Off party. God only knows why she had decided to go, but something deep – *very deep* – inside her, told her to make the effort, to get to know people, to stop lurking in the shadows like she had done in the pre-school queue.

Billy handed her his latest drawing and Frankie placed the piece of paper down in front of her, covering her doodle of an angry mum holding a cake, dripping with red jam, like it was a dagger, with the words *death by cake* scrawled underneath. As she drew a laughing face on the stick person that was sliding down the tail of a brachiosaurus – she had initially thought it was a diplodocus but according to Billy, you could tell it was a brachiosaurus because of the ridge above its eyes – her anxiety slid down the tail and whooshed off into thin air. *It's cheaper than therapy!*

She let out a contented sigh. And then her phone pinged.

It was Rachel, another mum from Billy's class.

> Rachel (Charlie's mum): Could we pop round?
> Just got a few questions. Rach x

Frankie wasn't sure who *we* meant, and she wasn't sure what kind of questions Rachel meant either, but she'd never had another mum over before and thought that maybe it might be fun. It was very out of the blue, especially considering the whole Bake Off saga, but *what the hell...*

I'll pop the kettle on, she replied, hoping she sounded breezy, spontaneous and fun.

Then she rushed around, shoving things away in drawers and cupboards, wiping the surfaces, snapping at Billy to, 'Get dressed!' and dashing upstairs to get changed herself.

'Sorry,' she said, stroking Billy's cheek as he whimpered, not used to being ordered about on a Sunday morning. 'I just don't want anyone to think that we live in a mess.'

Frankie's wife Amanda was in the army and worked away for long periods of time. While she was away, and particularly on a Sunday morning, Frankie's house was the exact opposite of a military operation. It was chilled, it was slow, it was messy.

Subconsciously Frankie wanted to keep Billy's life as relaxed and carefree as possible, to counteract the harsh realities of war and the danger that his mother's job brought with it, so she tried to be the laid-back mum. Inwardly, her anxiety was through the roof, but outwardly she was as calm as a millpond, not allowing the outside world to see the whirlpool that was circling underneath.

She took a deep breath.

'Hi,' she said, opening the door. 'Come on in.'

Rachel and Jane stepped into the small hall, and Frankie was relieved when they both flicked their shoes off. The thought of having to ask them to filled her with dread, but she would not have been able to relax had they kept them on. *It is my home after all,* she reminded herself, *my safe space that they have invited themselves into.*

'Can I get you a drink?' she asked.

'Ooh, I'd love a cuppa,' said Rachel, with a warm smile.

'Me too,' said Jane. 'Tea would be lovely.'

Although she smiled too, Frankie could feel Jane's eyes wandering around her small and ordinary home. The piles of stuff waiting to be put away, the wilting flowers in a vase on the table, the lingering smell of the toast she had burnt at breakfast. Nothing like Jane's perfect Instagram home. Instagram was the only place Frankie had seen Jane's home, of course. This social visit was not a usual occurrence at all, and as Rachel began to speak, Frankie got the feeling that it was not a *social* visit at all.

'So,' said Rachel, and Frankie swallowed. 'We wanted to talk to you about Victoria.'

'Oh,' said Frankie.

'Is that okay?'

'I mean, I guess so.' Frankie took a deep breath. 'I don't really know what I can tell you though.'

'Anything you can tell us will help,' said Rachel.

The ladies sat down, around the kitchen table, as Frankie handed out the mugs of tea.

'Something to eat?' she asked, suddenly feeling nervous, although she wasn't sure why. 'I can offer you, um...' She scanned her kitchen for anything suitable to offer. She literally had nothing in, she had forgotten to order an online food shop and she had been meaning to go to the local shop but somehow, just hadn't got around to it. 'A jam sandwich?'

Rachel and Jane giggled and it lightened the mood.

'We're fine,' said Jane.

'I'm guessing you've seen what they are saying on the mum-chat?' Rachel asked, clearly eager to crack on.

'Uh-huh.' Frankie nodded.

'Well, it's not true,' said Rachel. 'And Jane is going to help me prove it.'

'I am,' agreed Jane. 'So, we just wanted a chat really. We are going to talk to everyone else who was there too, y'know, at the Bake Off party.'

'Have you started with me?' asked Frankie, in a sudden moment of realisation.

'Well, yes, but only because...' Rachel paused.

'No reason,' said Jane. 'We had to start somewhere.'

Frankie took a large gulp of tea, from her chipped *Best Mummy* mug. 'So, what do you want to know?'

Rachel got a notebook out of her bag and took the lid off a pen. Frankie raised her eyebrows. Despite Rachel's scruffy mum-bun and baggy sweater, she was the one who had brought a notebook. It made Frankie smile that the flawlessly put together Jane had nothing, and instead sat restlessly picking the skin by her manicured fingernails.

'You don't mind, do you?' asked Rachel.

'I guess not.'

'I just have a terrible memory and if I don't write stuff down, I...'

'It's fine. Let's just get on with it.'

'Okay, so you were there on the night it happened?' asked Jane.

'You know I was.'

'She was,' confirmed Rachel. 'Did you think anyone was acting suspiciously?'

Frankie laughed.

'What's funny?' asked Rachel.

'Nothing,' said Frankie, swallowing and taking a deep breath. 'I guess you just have to laugh...'

Rachel tapped her pen on the blank page.

Frankie thought for a moment and then began speaking. 'I guess I don't really know if anyone was acting suspiciously, because I guess acting suspiciously would be acting differently to normal, and I don't really know what any of those people *normally* act like. I don't tend to go to those sorts of events and if I'm honest and, *murder aside*, this one didn't really sell them to me.'

'What made you go to this one?' asked Rachel.

'Pardon?'

'You said you don't normally go to these events... why did you decide to make an exception?'

Frankie felt her cheeks flush as she breathed out. 'I... I dropped off Billy on the first day of school and stood alone on the playground as he skipped in. I looked around at all the other mums chatting and laughing, and thought to myself, *I can't stand alone on the playground every day for the next seven years.* So, when I saw the message about the Bake Off thing I thought, well, that would be one way to meet some other mums. I might even make some friends and y'know have them round for a cuppa.'

She looked down at her cup of tea and laughed nervously.

Jane smiled.

Rachel did too. 'Was this not what you had in mind?'

'Well, I'd kind of imagined we might talk about the weather, how tiring kids are and where to get our nails done.'

'We can get to that,' said Rachel, which put Frankie at ease slightly.

'For the record,' said Frankie. 'I didn't think it was you, when they said it on the mum-chat. I thought, *There's no way!*'

'Well, thanks,' said Rachel. 'That means a lot.'

Frankie smiled and thought about whether to tell them that she was suspicious of Debbie. *Could she trust these ladies or should she keep her cards close to her chest?* They seemed genuine, well apart from the whole Rachel being accused of murder thing, but more importantly than that, she liked them. She could talk to them, enjoy spending time with them, hang out with them and be herself.

She took the longest of breaths inwards and then blurted out, 'My money's on Debbie, I mean, not that we're betting or anything.'

Rachel and Jane looked at each other, and then back at Frankie.

'Go on,' said Jane.

'Well, she's desperate to be chair of the PTA, everyone knows that, even me, so having Victoria out of the way means instant promotion.'

'Is promotion into an unpaid job enough motive for murder?' asked Jane.

'Who knows?' Rachel shrugged. 'The whole class thinks me finding Victoria a bit annoying is enough motive, so...'

'A *bit* annoying?' asked Jane.

'Okay, a *lot* annoying,' said Rachel, and Frankie agreed with a grin.

'But then there's also the fundraising money,' said Frankie

'Fundraising money?'

'Yeah, a load went missing last year and Victoria reckoned Debbie had been helping herself. Debbie denied it but Victoria told her at the Bake Off party that if she didn't confess she was going to take it to the school governors.'

'Gosh,' said Jane.

'How do you know all this?' asked Rachel. 'You are always so quiet and unassuming.'

'It's amazing what you hear when people forget you are there.' Frankie felt herself blush again.

'Wow, well that is very interesting.' Rachel looked at her watch and then held her stomach. 'Perhaps I might go for that jam sandwich now, if it's still on offer?'

14

RACHEL

Rachel definitely wasn't getting any *murderer* vibes from Frankie.

'She's making us jam sandwiches... that doesn't really scream *killer*, does it?'

Jane raised one eyebrow. 'You can eat yours first.'

Rachel laughed. 'You don't really think?'

'Of course I don't, but you said yourself, you can't make assumptions in this game. In fact, you said something about it making you an arse!' Jane somehow kept her serious face on. 'You have to weigh up the evidence.'

Rachel nodded. 'Still, this dirt on Debbie sounds promising.' She rubbed her hands together.

'Don't jump to any conclusions,' said Jane.

They both sat looking around Frankie's small kitchen. It wasn't as tastefully decorated as Jane's or as chaotically stylish as Rachel's. It was just a plain little kitchen.

Rachel picked up a notebook on top of a small pile of papers at the end of the table.

'What are you doing?' hissed Jane.

'Snooping,' whispered Rachel.

'You know we're not *actually* coppers,' said Jane. 'We're here as friends.'

'We barely know her! Anyway, if we *are* friends then I'm being friendly, taking an interest.' Rachel smiled. 'These are great,' she said, flicking through the pages of the notebook.

The pages were full of doodles. Doodles about motherhood; about losing your identity; about coping with life as a mum; about the chaos of having kids; about the loss of the person you were before kids. It was like her life story had been illustrated. Rachel could relate to almost every single one.

She heard footsteps in the hallway and quickly put the notebook back in its place.

'Billy wants one too,' said Frankie, breezing back into the kitchen. 'So, four jam sandwiches coming up.' She smiled.

Rachel and Jane smiled back, and Rachel wondered how forced Jane's smile was.

'Great,' said Rachel.

'I can't remember the last time I had a jam sandwich,' said Jane.

'What?!' said Rachel. 'I guess it's all hummus and cucumber on rye bread in your house?'

'Ha ha,' said Jane. 'I'm not that bad.'

Frankie placed a pile of jam sandwiches in the middle of the table and gave them each a small side plate.

'Billy,' she called. 'Lunch is ready.'

Less than thirty seconds later – why did Rachel's kids never come that quickly when they were called? – Billy walked into the kitchen.

'Oh,' he said.

'We have some guests for lunch today, Billy. Say hi!'

'Hi,' said Billy, quietly, giving them half a smile as he sat down at the table.

'Hi, Billy,' said Jane.

'Don't worry, we haven't eaten them all yet,' added Rachel, nodding towards the tower of jam sandwiches.

'A little treat for you, Billy,' said Frankie. She turned to the others. 'Please don't think I give him jam sandwiches all the time.'

'We had them yesterday,' said Billy. Frankie dropped her head into her hand.

'Hey, no judgement here.' Rachel held her hands up. 'Jam has fruit in, doesn't it? So, it's one of your five-a-day!'

Frankie's cheeks returned to their natural colour, and Rachel smiled as she watched her carefully put some grapes and crisps and a jug of water on the table too, before she sat down.

'This is nice,' she smiled, 'having people over for Sunday lunch.'

Rachel and Jane chuckled.

'I'll do a roast next time!'

Next time? thought Rachel, and she couldn't help feeling a bit sorry for Frankie. She seemed genuinely delighted to be having jam sandwiches with her and Jane. For most people, them popping over would have been at worst an inconvenience and at best a mundane occurrence, but for Frankie it seemed to be quite the occasion.

They ate and chatted about school and Lego. Rachel was desperate to ask Frankie about the notebook, but for some reason she got the feeling that doing so in front of Billy might be awkward, so she waited patiently.

'Please may I get down, Mummy?' asked Billy, during his last mouthful of jam sandwich.

'Lovely manners,' said Rachel.

'Although you could have emptied your mouth before asking,' tutted Frankie.

'Sorry,' said Billy. 'May I then?'

'Yes,' said Frankie. 'Off you go.'

He trotted off and Frankie smiled as she watched him go.

'Nice lad,' said Rachel.

'Very polite,' added Jane.

Frankie's smile widened. 'He's a good boy.'

'So, my question is,' said Rachel, slurping down another cup of tea and hoping that they weren't outstaying their welcome. 'Does Debbie know that you heard what Victoria said to her?'

Frankie scrunched her face up as if it would help her to think. 'I don't think so,' she said eventually. 'I mean, I'm not sure, but well, would it matter if she did?'

'Yes,' said Rachel, spraying a bit of tea across the table.

'You could be next on the list.' Jane nodded.

'List? You mean...' Frankie gulped.

'Look, we're not trying to worry you or anything,' said Rachel. 'We are just saying *take care*; keep your wits about you. If Debbie killed Victoria to keep her quiet, and now you know what she knew, then...'

'Shit!' said Frankie. 'That hadn't even crossed my mind.'

'But we won't let that happen,' said Jane.

'We've got your back,' added Rachel.

'Thanks,' said Frankie. 'That means a lot.' She took another sip of tea. 'So, what's next?'

'Next?'

'Are we going to talk to Debbie?'

'We?' Rachel tried to hide her confusion, she didn't want to seem rude after all.

'I thought I could help you,' said Frankie. 'You know, be part of the team.'

'The Jam Sandwich Detectives?' laughed Jane, scoffing one last mouthful of jam and bread.

'I like that,' said Rachel.

Jane raised her eyebrows. 'I was joking. You're not seriously thinking...?'

'Chill out, Jane,' laughed Rachel. 'I'm not going to get it printed on T-shirts or anything.'

Jane looked relieved.

'Mugs, maybe!'

'Do you think that was a good idea, Rach?' asked Jane, as they walked home together. Rachel was relieved that they had finally been able to tear themselves away from the pile of carbs and sugar.

'Probably not, I am going to feel bloated in the morning and...'

'I didn't mean the sandwiches,' laughed Jane.

'Oh! What did you mean then?'

'I meant welcoming Frankie on board. How do we know we can trust her?'

'There's no way Frankie's the murderer, Jane. She's just a mum, like you and me.'

'We're *all* just mums.' Jane frowned. 'But someone did it! Plus, if we let everyone we vaguely trust onto our little team of detectives... we are going to end up with a murder squad!'

Rachel laughed. 'You're right! The Jam Sandwich Murder Squad doesn't have quite the same ring to it, does it?'

15

———

JANE

Jane couldn't shake the niggling feeling that she'd had in the back of her mind ever since they had left Frankie's house.

She knew that Rachel was right, that Frankie didn't seem capable of murder, but she was worried about letting her into, what was now, their little trio. It wasn't that she was jealous, she didn't even know Rachel that well herself – not really – they weren't like best friends or anything. They always chatted on the playground, but they hadn't spoken for the whole summer. She guessed that some friendships were like that, out of sight, out of mind, but with everything that had happened already this term, they already felt a lot closer.

And sometimes you need a mum ally.

But would Frankie throw that off-kilter if she joined the team?

Jane didn't want to be a snob, but she wasn't sure that Frankie was quite one of them. *I mean, who has jam sandwiches for Sunday lunch?* She knew full well that everyone *mum-ed* differently – some worked full time; some stayed at home; some followed their dreams; some did whatever they could to earn money; some spent money on

94

expensive schools; some spent money on holidays and clothes – and who was she to say which way was the right way? She wished the cliques and the judgement didn't exist, and she was old enough to deal with it all now, but she still tried to look her best and be the best, all of the time. That didn't mean she wasn't genuine.

She had just been starting to relax in Rachel's company. Jane had always felt like she was competing against the other mums. Who is 'mum-ing' the best was a weekly competition, judged on the following criteria:

- School-run attire – full hair, make-up and catwalk-ready clothing is required for the three minutes spent in the presence of the other mums at drop-off.
- Neatness of kids' appearance – they will come out of school looking like they have done three rounds of wrestling with the Gruffalo, but that doesn't matter. It is how they arrived at school that counts. Only you – and possibly one other mum – will have seen this. The class teacher, sure as hell, will not notice or care... but if your child arrived with even a hair out of place, it'll be all over the mum-chat before you know it.
- Whether you have remembered the weekly extras. As the name suggests, this changes on a weekly basis – just to keep you on your toes – and can include (but is not limited to) seasonal things such as: a pound coin for mufti, a tin of food for the harvest festival or a pumpkin for the Halloween display.
- How much homework your kid has done / you have done for them – no one else will know or care about this, but if your child has done any, you are entitled to feel smug about it.

- How Instagrammable your house is despite having three children and a dog. If you can post a mid-week picture of a tidy living room, this is worth serious bonus points. Oh, and if you have an Instagrammable husband who is willing to pose for *I love him so much* photos on Valentine's Day, birthdays or at other humdrum events, then even better.
- Please be aware that points can and will be deducted for:
  - Sending a child in wearing PE kit when it is not a PE day.
  - Sending a child in wearing uniform when it is a PE day.
  - Sending a child with a thin coat on a cold day or a thick coat on a hot day.
  - Forgetting to tie long hair back for; PE/science/art or all of the above.

Every day was like the Mum-Olympics, and Jane was a gold medallist. It took a lot of effort. But with Rachel, Jane could finally relax; she wasn't putting on an act, she was able to be herself. And it felt nice.

She was worried that Frankie entering the mix would ruin all that, take away her friend, her buddy, her... no, she needed to remember why she was doing all this. It wasn't about her. She was trying to help Rachel prove her innocence. If Frankie knew stuff that would help and was on their side, then they had to give her a chance. They had to let her in. They had to let their guard down, for the moment at least.

She opened her phone and tapped out a message to a freshly created group. She scrolled through her image search for the right photo, named the group *The Jam Sandwich Detectives* and sent the message.

> Jane (Lottie's mum): Well done ladies, today's chat was really helpful. Any suggestions of who to talk to next?

No one replied straight away, which meant that either they were busy or they thought the group or the question – or both – were ridiculous.

Jane started to panic. Maybe she should delete the group or delete the question, but then...

> Frankie (Billy's mum): ...is typing...

Jane waited.
And waited.
And then...

> Frankie (Billy's mum): Thanks for letting me help, ladies. Rachel, we will prove you had nothing to do with this awful murder. We are with you every step of the way. Whoever is responsible will be sorry they ever messed with The Jam Sandwich Detectives.

Jane smiled. She should never have doubted her.

> Jane (Lottie's mum): Hear hear!

> Rachel (Megan's mum): Thanks ladies. Lots of love.

Lots of love? thought Jane to herself. *Wow!* Rachel was quick to dole out the love. She had never said that to *her* before. She knew that this *lots of love* was technically aimed at both herself *and* Frankie, but she was a bit peeved that Frankie had been the one to earn it. Jane needed to up her game. She needed to prove that *she* was the friend that Rachel needed; that Rachel couldn't live without.

She started typing again, but this time the message was to Debbie.

> Jane (Lottie's mum): How are you doing, Debbie? I know you were close to Victoria. You must be going through a lot. Can I help in any way? Keep an eye on the PTA accounts for you? Relieve some of the load?

Before Jane had put her phone down on the table in front of her, it pinged.

> Debbie (PTA): No.
>
> I mean, no thank you.
>
> I'm fine.
>
> But thanks for the offer.

Well, that has got guilty written all over it, thought Jane. But guilty of what? Guilty of fiddling the books, doesn't necessarily mean guilty of murder, does it? But, it was something. Something she could report back on. Admittedly it was something that Frankie had pretty much already said, but Jane now had it in writing. *Well, sort of.*

> Jane (Lottie's mum): Would you like to come over for a coffee, Debbie? After school drop-off tomorrow? I'll bake a cake?

Jane wondered why she had typed the last bit. Not only was

cake baking a bit of a touchy subject at the moment, but also she now had to spend her Sunday evening baking a bloody cake.

> Debbie (PTA): That would be nice.
>
> Sorry for snapping before.
>
> It has been a difficult few days.

As Jane was typing out a very thoughtful reply, her phone pinged again.

> Debbie (PTA): Chocolate is my favourite.

Cheeky cow!

> Jane (Lottie's mum): No worries. See you tomorrow then.

Bloody hell! Now she had to tidy the house, bake a cake *and* wash her hair, but first she needed to message the girls. Ooh *the girls*, she liked that.

> Jane (Lottie's mum): Tomorrow morning. After the school run. Prime suspect interview.

16

RACHEL

Ugh, Monday! Rachel hadn't slept a wink.

The thought of walking onto the playground made her feel sick, but when her alarm went off she got up, made herself a coffee and put on her mum face.

'Mummy!' squealed Charlie, skidding into the kitchen and throwing his arms around her. For the briefest of moments, his unconditional love made her forget about the nightmare.

'Darling,' she replied. 'All set for school?'

'What? I have to go to school *again?* But I went last week.'

Rachel laughed. 'I'm afraid you have to go to school every week now.'

'Every week?!'

'Every week,' said Rachel. 'Well, apart from the holidays.'

Charlie shook his head. 'When are the holidays?'

'Not for a while,' said Rachel. 'We've only just had the summer.'

The thought made her take another big swig of coffee. Parenting meant being busy all year round, but term time had the added stress of remembering what was happening, and on which days, checking the right clothes were washed and dry, and making sure children were in the right place at the right time for their array of *very expensive* extra-curricular activities. It was exhausting.

Now, she had to do all that as well as proving that she wasn't a murderer! Although, surely no one actually believed that she was capable of murder. *I mean, how would she have time for a start?* No, she was sure she was worrying about nothing and that no one *really* thought that she had anything to do with it. It would be one of those things where everyone jumps on the mum-chat bandwagon, throwing accusations about, but no one would take them seriously. It was Monday morning; a new week. Any outrageous allegations would be long forgotten.

Once breakfast was shovelled down, clothes were thrown on and hair was brushed as much as the screaming would allow – the sound of Rachel brushing Megan's hair may well mean she was already on some sort of police watch-list – they grabbed their bags and coats and lunchboxes and headed out on the school run. Rachel swore that she was never as stressed leaving for a two-week holiday abroad as she was setting off on a Monday morning, hoping that the kids were all dressed appropriately, with everything they needed for a whole six and a half hours at school.

The sun was out, the sky was blue and the gentle breeze cooled Rachel's warm cheeks as she rushed her children towards the school gates. As they approached the school and began to hear the distant murmur of the playground, a brief glance at her watch told Rachel that they had time to spare, so she slowed down and breathed in the crisp autumn air as the leaves crunched beneath her feet. She smiled and stepped onto the playground, and in that split-second, her moment of calm vanished into the breeze.

A hundred pairs of *eyes* were on her as the playground fell silent. The oblivious children still ran in circles and squealed with laughter, but the murmur of grown-up chitter-chatter had dropped to zero.

Rachel stopped, taken aback.

'What's wrong, Mummy?' asked Charlie.

'Why is everyone staring at us?' said Megan.

'No one's staring, love,' said Rachel, disobeying her number one rule of not lying to the children. 'Right, the door's open. Have you both got everything you need?'

'I dunno,' said Charlie, shrugging before kissing Rachel on the thigh and running off into school, not waiting for her to bend down for a proper hug.

'Yes,' said Megan, as if she knew her mum had enough on her plate without adding to it with a last minute realisation that it was *cookery day* or *bring in a book about Ancient Egypt week*. 'All sorted.'

Rachel smiled and kissed her daughter on the top of her head, realising that she wouldn't be able to do so for much longer. Megan was growing fast, in both height and maturity, and despite the monotony of house chores and the mundanity of mum admin; time was flying by.

'Bye, Mum,' said Megan, and she walked off towards the school door, but glanced back over her shoulder, as if for reassurance that her mum was, actually, okay.

Rachel waved, ignoring the whispering that had started around her, and although she wanted the ground to swallow her whole, she turned confidently, with so much gusto that she bumped straight into Natasha.

'Do watch where you are going,' said Natasha, brushing down her way-too-fancy-for-the-school-run black dress. 'We don't want any more *accidents!*'

Great, thought Rachel. If she didn't have Queen Natasha on side then she had no hope. They may as well lock her up now and throw away the key.

She slipped through the crowds of parents as quickly as she could with her head down, avoiding eye contact with anyone, until a friendly face said, 'See you in a minute.'

'Frankie,' said Rachel. 'Boy, am I glad to see someone who doesn't think I'm Jack the bloody Ripper.'

'Tough morning?' asked Frankie.

'I've had better.'

'Well, a cuppa and a slice of Jane's homemade cake will cheer you up.' Frankie smiled. 'She's bound to have gone all-out for our little chat with Debbie.'

Rachel forced a laugh. 'It was Jane's flippin' cake that got me into all this trouble in the first place.'

'Jane's cake?' asked Frankie.

'Oh, shit yeah, that was supposed to be a secret,' said Rachel.

Frankie scrunched up her forehead in confusion.

'Jane helped me out with my Bake Off entry,' admitted Rachel. 'I can't bloody bake!' She lowered her voice. 'And then when they thought it was anaphylaxis and I found out that Jane had put flippin' almond extract in it, I nearly had heart failure... y'know, 'cause I'd joked about making a coffee and walnut cake and everything. Anyway, thankfully they realised it was poison, not Jane's baking, so I was off the hook. At least I thought I was, but apparently I'm still suspect number one for some reason.'

'Oh,' said Frankie, and Rachel realised that she wouldn't blame her if she turned and ran a mile. 'It sounds like you need something stronger than a cup of tea.'

'I do!' Rachel nodded, with a twinkle in her eye. 'Got any whisky?'

Frankie smiled, slightly nervously.

Rachel was more grateful for that smile than Frankie would ever know.

Her phone pinged and Rachel looked down at the screen.

> Jane (Lottie's mum): Oh my goodness, we've got no milk.

> I am the worst host ever.

> It's Lottie and Ben, they drink it by the gallon.

> I'm so sorry, could one of you...? I mean I hate to ask...

Rachel read her reply out loud as she typed. 'It is fine. I'll pick up some milk... and I won't even mention it in the TripAdvisor review.'

Frankie's smile relaxed a bit and she giggled.

'Right,' said Rachel. 'Time to play detective.'

'Once you've bought some milk.'

'Once I have bought some milk! I bet Poirot doesn't have this trouble.'

17

FRANKIE

Frankie and Amanda had never adhered to gender stereotypes.

Who is like the mum and who is like the dad? had always been a ridiculous question in their eyes, but if she had to answer it, lately, Frankie had started to feel more and more like *the mum* in their relationship.

Their jobs were probably the main reason. Amanda was away a lot, serving in the army – definitely taking on the *man's* role – whereas Frankie had a job that was *perfect for mums.*

Freelance graphic design was a pretty gender-neutral job, if you ignored the fact that the latest project she had been working on was designing the pretty patterns for sanitary pad covers, but it was more about the flexibility. She could easily work from home and fit in her hours as and when she had time, which meant she was mostly left with the childcare. *Is it called that when it's your own children?* At first she had resented this automatic role assignment, and for the whole time Billy was at pre-school, she had refused to get involved in any *mum* activities. *Why should mums have to do all the fundraising and organising of playdates and pretending to be sociable?*

As she walked along with her new *mum* friend, heading for

coffee and cake at another *mum* friend's house, she actually found herself not hating the mumlife for once. She decided that it might even be fun, especially if they got to play detective.

'I'll pay for the milk,' she said, as Rachel placed it on the counter of the local shop.

'You don't need to,' said Rachel.

'I'd like to,' she said, and not wanting to sound too needy, added, 'I mean, if you don't mind?'

'I don't mind,' laughed Rachel. 'I'll take you with me next time I do my weekly shop!'

Frankie giggled, but secretly thought that might actually be fun.

They strolled towards Jane's house and Frankie felt content. She wasn't sure if it was the interrogation she was looking forward to or the hanging out with some other mums. Amanda would laugh her head off if she knew Frankie was about to conduct an interrogation – albeit an amateur one – as she was more the interrogating type, whereas Frankie had always been laid-back. Until they had Billy that is. Since becoming a mum, Frankie was in panic mode twenty-four seven. It was all-consuming.

Maybe that was why she wanted to do the investigation so much, why she wanted to be part of The Jam Sandwich Detectives; so that she could prove to Amanda – and to herself – that she was more than just an anxious mum.

'Are people actually going to answer our questions?' asked Frankie. 'I mean, we are not the police. They could tell us to F-off.'

'I'd be disappointed if they didn't!' laughed Rachel. 'But to be fair, they could just as easily tell the police to F-off too!'

'Hmm,' said Frankie. 'Fair point.'

'I am fully expecting to be greeted with a few middle fingers on our travels,' said Rachel, with a massive grin.

Frankie got the feeling that all Rachel's laughing and joking was a big ruse, and that actually, underneath she was extremely worried about the whole debacle. *I would be if it was me,* she thought. Maybe that was what being a mum was all about, constantly pretending that everything is okay. That you are fine. That you are in control.

'Are you okay?' she decided to ask eventually.

'Sure,' said Rachel. 'Why wouldn't I be?'

'I dunno. It's just, well, playground gossip can be hard at the best of times, let alone when people think...' She stopped herself.

'Let alone when people think you are a murderer?'

'Well, I wasn't going to put it quite like that but, yeah!'

Rachel took a deep breath. 'I just figure, at least I'm doing something about it, y'know. Like, if I just sat worrying, I'd go mad, but you and Jane standing by me and helping me prove that I had nothing to do with it... well, I appreciate it. And after all this, I will owe you a large drink. Or fifty.'

Frankie smiled. 'You're welcome.' Rachel hadn't actually said *thank you,* but Frankie knew what she meant.

Rachel smiled. 'C'mon,' she said as they turned into Jane's street. 'I can already smell the freshly baked cake.'

Frankie sniffed the air. 'Mmmmmm. And the coffee in the pot.'

Jane's street was one of the prettiest in the village. Her street was like being on Main Avenue at the Chelsea Flower Show, with the neat gardens, window boxes and beautiful flowers tumbling out of hanging baskets. But Jane's house was definitely the winning display. No silver gilt in sight; Jane's was a gold medal all the way.

Frankie had gnomes outside her front door at home. Two little lady gnomes, with rainbow hats, sitting on a log together. They were cute. Frankie loved them to bits, but they would lower the tone of Jane's garden for sure. The only statues in Jane's garden were classic metal sculptures. A swirl of bronze complementing the flora. Not a pointy hat or fishing rod in sight.

It was worlds apart from anything that Frankie was used to, and suddenly she was little bit daunted and out of her depth, but sometimes you needed to take a step out of your comfort zone. After all, there was a murder to solve... and murderers don't care whether or not you've got gnomes in your garden.

———

As Frankie and Rachel waited on Jane's doorstep, under the last of the season's wisteria flowers, they both stood in silence reading the latest email from school.

'Just the seven emails so far this morning,' Frankie had said as it pinged through.

'You'll soon get used to it,' said Rachel. 'You can ignore most of them.'

They didn't ignore this one.

Dear Parents,

Due to unforeseen, and very sad, circumstances we have been left without a chair of the PTA, but I am pleased to announce that the vice chair, Debbie Davis, has kindly offered to step up into the role for the foreseeable future.

Please find attached a short statement from Debbie. We do hope you will all support her efforts in memory of a dear friend and supporter of the school, Victoria Sandwich.

Kind regards,
Mrs Wright

Head Teacher of Castle Upperhill Primary School
Attached – Message from Acting Chair, Debbie Davis:

I am deeply saddened by the death of my dear friend Victoria and I am also devastated by the loss of a really strong chair so hope you will join me in fundraising for a new one.

Like all of us, Mrs Wright was shocked at the news from the recent PTA Bake Off party and sat down with a little too much vigour, causing her office chair to break. Just like the children, a head teacher needs to be comfortable at work, so we must all do our bit towards helping to replace it.

Our annual coffee morning will therefore go ahead as planned next week and as we do not yet have a new team of PTA bakers in place, we are asking for cake donations from any willing volunteers. In light of recent events we ask that you do not make a Victoria Sandwich cake as we do not feel that it would be appropriate, plus we do not want to be inundated with one type of cake.

Please note:

All cakes must adhere to the PTA guidelines. As I am yet to appoint an Acting Vice Chair, please contact myself for approved recipes.

All cakes must be nut-free, gluten-free, sugar-free and dairy-free.

All cakes must be brought in named containers. Unnamed containers will be disposed of.

All cakes must be pre-cut into eight equal slices.

In my new role as Acting Chair I have also decided to rebrand our PTA. From now on it will be called the Friends of Castle Upperhill Primary School. I think this sounds more welcoming and friendly, and I am looking forward to this new chapter.

The show must go on… Victoria would not have taken a day off to mope and neither will I.

Kind regards

Debbie Davis

Chair of the FoCUPS

'Am I actually reading these words?' asked Frankie, with raised eyebrows.

'It's heartless!' said an open-mouthed Rachel.

Frankie shook her head. 'It most definitely does not exude innocence.'

The latch clicked as Jane's front door swung open and a waft of sweet, freshly baked aromas filled the air.

'Anyone thinking of joining the FoCUPS?' asked Jane, beaming as she folded up her pinny.

'No chance,' said Rachel. 'I'm in enough of a fuck-up as it is right now, thanks.'

18

RACHEL

Debbie looked as awkward as Rachel felt, as she walked into Jane's kitchen. She tucked her short bob behind her ears and straightened out her M&S knitwear.

'What's all this?' she asked, raising her eyebrows.

Rachel, recalling all the eyes on her in the playground this morning, realised that Debbie was feeling something similar.

'Oh, just a little something I threw together,' said Jane, ushering Debbie towards the table that was proudly displaying a cake stand with four varieties of homemade sponge cakes, some shortbread and several macarons. 'No one has a nut allergy, do they?'

Rachel rolled her eyes as Debbie shook her head and let out a little whimper.

'Oh, I didn't mean... I mean, I didn't think,' stuttered Jane.

'Don't worry,' said Frankie softly. 'We know what you meant.'

Debbie sniffed loudly and finally sat down. 'Well,' she said. 'This is a lovely gesture. It has been a tough few days.'

The three other ladies nodded and Rachel realised that Debbie had been brought here under false pretences. She was clearly expecting *cheer-me-up-cake* and what she was actually going to get was *laying-into-me-macarons* but maybe that was the right tactic. Softly does it. Still, they needed to crack on.

'So, you were close to Victoria?' asked Rachel.

Jane frowned, and widened her eyes at Rachel who took a large gulp of tea and pretended she hadn't noticed.

'Yes,' sniffed Debbie. 'She was my best friend.'

'You didn't seem too cut up in the school email just now,' said Rachel, wincing as she felt Jane's foot on her ankle.

'I was trying to remain professional.' Debbie's tears had now dried. 'Plus, I said I was *deeply saddened.*'

'Not as saddened as you seemed to be about a bit of furniture,' said Rachel, under her breath, before taking another large slurp of tea.

'I saw you arguing at the Bake Off party,' said Frankie.

Rachel spat the tea out across the table and Jane dived straight in with a cloth, as Rachel mouthed, 'Thanks!' *Wow!* she thought. *Get straight to the point!*

'Oh, that was nothing,' said Debbie.

'It was about money,' said Frankie.

Rachel hid her proud smile by wiping the tea spray from her lips. She was thrilled to have this super-sleuth on the case.

'Well, yes...' mumbled Debbie.

'Some was missing?' asked the super-sleuth.

'Yes,' said Debbie, with a mouthful of macaron. 'I was just a bit worried as we had to present the annual accounts to the school governors, and we were quite a large chunk short.'

'And Victoria was onto you?' asked Rachel.

Debbie finished her mouthful of cake. 'I see what this is,' she said, wiping her mouth with a serviette from the pile carefully displayed in the middle of Jane's table. 'You are looking for someone to shift the blame to. All eyes are on you so you want to get them looking at someone else instead. Someone who has just lost her best friend.'

'A best friend who was about to drop you in it for stealing money,' said Rachel.

'What exactly are you accusing me of?' asked Debbie, her eyebrows rising to meet her neat fringe.

'Nothing,' said Rachel. 'I am merely pointing out that having Victoria out of the way has done you a favour, hasn't it?'

'She was my best friend,' said Debbie, sniffing away a tear. 'You think you are oh-so clever, but you've got it all completely wrong.'

'Then enlighten me!'

Rachel met Debbie's glare.

'Ladies,' said Frankie. 'We are all adults here, let's talk about this like grown-ups, shall we?'

'I'll make some more tea,' said Jane, scurrying off. Presumably to keep herself busy, and out of the firing line.

The room fell silent, as if everyone was too involved in their own thoughts to know what to say.

Rachel looked at Debbie and felt a sudden wave of guilt that she had moved the weight from her own shoulders and was trying to place it all on hers. She still couldn't quite comprehend why everyone was convinced that *she* had killed Victoria. Okay, so she'd got a bit annoyed with her and might have said she could kill her, but that was a figure of speech. People say that stuff all the time, it doesn't mean they are actually going to commit murder. There's a thing called motive. What would Rachel's motive be? That Victoria got on her nerves? Hardly worth killing her over.

Debbie on the other hand was in deep shit. If the school found out she was fiddling the books, they'd report her to the police and she would be in a lot of trouble. And the one person who knew everything and could drop her deep into this steaming turd of a situation was dead. Now *that* was a motive.

Jane returned to the table with a tray of fresh tea and a plate of homemade biscuits. Rachel wondered how she had time to bake backup-biscuits in the middle of a crisis.

The four women each picked up a mug and took a sip whilst the uncomfortable silence hung in the air.

'I suppose I should be honest,' said Debbie eventually.

'Might be an idea,' said Rachel.

'We are here to help you,' said Frankie, and Rachel scrunched her eyebrows at her. 'We just want to get to the truth.'

Rachel sighed, feeling like she was in some sort of good cop, bad cop duo with Frankie, although as Debbie put down her mug and looked like she was about to begin talking, Rachel realised that good cop might be the way to go.

'Honesty is always the best policy.' She gave Debbie an encouraging smile.

'It was Victoria,' said Debbie.

Rachel, Jane and Frankie looked at each other with puzzled expressions.

'Victoria took the money. I was covering it up for her, y'know fiddling the books, but then she started taking too much. It was getting harder to hide and I felt sure that someone was going to notice.'

'Wait, Victoria was stealing money from the PTA?' asked Rachel.

'Well, yes,' said Debbie. 'But that night, at the Bake Off party, I told her she had to stop, that I couldn't – *wouldn't* – cover it up anymore.'

'Why the sudden change of heart?' asked Frankie.

'This is my kids' school. My kids were losing out because of Vic's selfishness.' Debbie exhaled. 'At first she had needed the money – she was desperate – so I had agreed to help her, but by the end she was getting greedy, and it wasn't fair.'

'Well, that's very noble of you,' said Rachel, hoping it hadn't sounded quite as sarcastic as she'd meant it. 'So, she was upset I take it?'

'That's an understatement!'

'But at the Bake Off party...?' Frankie eyes flickered, like she was trying to work out how what she had heard fitted into Debbie's version of events.

'She said that if I mentioned it to anyone, she would deny the whole thing and say that I had taken the money,' said Debbie.

'So, your best friend was going to drop you in it and make you take the flack for it?' *It still sounded like a motive to Rachel.*

'Yes,' said Debbie. 'Yes, she was.' Her voice was so quiet Rachel could barely hear it.

'I bet that made you angry,' said Frankie, which seemed to snap Debbie out of the trance she had fallen into.

'Yes, it bloody well did, but I know what you're thinking and that doesn't mean that I killed her.'

'Would solve the problem though, wouldn't it?' asked Rachel.

'You could pin the missing money on the dead woman and get away with it,' added Frankie.

'No,' shouted Debbie. 'I'm not pinning anything on anyone. Victoria took the money and someone killed her. I don't know anything about who or why. My only crime here is covering up what she was doing and I wish I never had. I would go to the police and admit everything, but no doubt they would jump to the same conclusion that you all have.'

'Who would?' asked Ben, sauntering into the room and rubbing his eyes. 'What's all the shouting about?'

The four ladies fell into a now familiar silence, until

eventually Jane cleared her throat and spoke. 'Debbie has some information that might be relevant to Victoria's death.'

'What?'

Debbie looked at the floor and then up at Ben. 'Should I tell you?'

'No,' snapped Ben. 'Don't tell *me*. It's nothing to do with me, I mean it's not my case.' He breathed out slowly. 'I'm being kept off it because I live in the village. They reckon I'm too close to it all... and it sounds like they're right.'

'Ben!' Jane gave him some wide eyes.

From his expression, Ben had seen them many times before. 'But you should probably talk to the police,' he said, in a calmer tone.

'I... I'm scared they won't believe me,' said Debbie. 'Will you ladies help me?'

Rachel, Frankie and Jane looked at each other.

'Us?' asked Rachel.

'I will tell the police, I promise, but I just want to get things straight in my head first.'

Debbie opened her bag and rummaged around in it. 'Here,' she said, handing over a thick envelope.

Frankie took it and looked inside. 'What's all this?'

'They are all Vic's receipts. She gave them to me before the party and told me to use them to cover up all the money she'd spent.'

'What are they for?'

'I haven't had a chance to look through them since, well you know, since she died,' said Debbie. 'I just can't seem to bring myself to do it, but maybe they will help in some way.'

'It's fine,' said Jane, placing a kind hand on her shoulder. 'We can have a look at them for you, and if there is anything of importance, you can decide whether or not to go to the police.'

Rachel opened her mouth to speak and then changed her

mind. She looked around the room and saw that Ben had managed to slip away unnoticed. Either he was diligently trying to steer clear of a case that wasn't his, or he agreed with Rachel's inkling that the receipts would be a complete waste of time.

After Debbie had left she finally said what she had been wanting to say. 'Surely it doesn't matter what the receipts are for. The point is that they are *not* for anything to do with the school or its fundraising. They are for Victoria's own stuff.... whatever that is, it proves she was pinching the money, and if she was going to pin it on Debbie, then as lovely as Debbie seems, I'm afraid it gives her motive for murder.'

'Let's just take a look at them,' said Frankie. 'These things are often not that black and white. They may tell us something we hadn't even thought about.'

Rachel smiled. 'Sorry, Miss Marple.' She chuckled.

But the smile soon disappeared from her face when Frankie replied, 'Who?'

How young is she?

19

FRANKIE

For some reason, Frankie offered to take a look through the receipts.

Did she really want to make friends that badly?

There was a whole pile of them – in fact they wouldn't even stay in a pile, there were so many. They toppled over every time she tried to take one – and she didn't *really* know what she was looking for.

'You'll know when you see it,' Jane had said. 'That's what they always said at police training. Sometimes you don't know what you're looking for until you find it.'

Frankie didn't have a lot of work on at the moment, so at least it gave her something to do. Something that wasn't housework.

She made herself a cup of coffee and put the slice of cake that Jane had carefully tucked in a little cardboard cake box for her earlier this morning onto a plate. Frankie had nearly choked on her mouthful of Earl Grey tea – and not just because of the flavour – when she'd seen the cake boxes. It was like another world. *Who has cake boxes? Who is that organised? And who has the confidence to know that their cakes are so good that people will want to take more home with them, in a fancy little box?* The answer to all of these questions was *Jane*.

Frankie didn't feel like Jane had been quite as friendly towards her as Rachel had been. Of course she had been charming and couldn't do enough to make Frankie welcome, but it didn't seem sincere like it did with Rachel. There was some underlying *thing* that was making it awkward. Jealousy maybe? Did Jane see Frankie as a threat? Sometimes women do feel threatened by things that you wouldn't expect.

Frankie, for example, was threatened by stunningly beautiful women who looked amazing with no effort. Jane and Rachel were both beautiful, but Jane clearly made a *lot* of effort. Rachel less so, but she pulled off the bedraggled-mum look pretty well. At least Frankie still had youth on her side – she hadn't asked, but she was pretty sure she was five, maybe ten years younger than Rachel and Jane – but she never felt like she had any style. She wore a *mum uniform* of jeans and a sweater. Sometimes she thought about going on a shopping spree and splashing out on a whole new wardrobe, but where would she wear any of it? On the school run? No, she'd leave the school-run catwalk to Natasha.

She flicked through the receipts and got her mind back on track. There was nothing remotely interesting. A pair of shoes, a couple of bottles of wine, some lipstick, her TV licence renewal, some key-cutting, a new keyring, a kettle and a cuddly toy. It was like *The Generation Game*. A totally boring list of items. Dull as dishwater. And talking of dishwater, Frankie groaned as she remembered the pile of washing-up. She should do it now, then she could relax for a couple of hours before the school run sprung back around again.

Her coffee had gone cold, so she popped it in the microwave. This was standard procedure. Since becoming a mum, she could count on one hand the mugs of fresh and hot coffee she had drunk. Billy was at school though, so she couldn't even blame him for this one. It had become a habit to let coffee go cold, then heat it up, and then probably let it go cold again.

The microwave pinged and she took out the steaming mug. She sat down on the sofa. *That was the first mistake.* She would just drink the coffee and then do something productive. She took out her phone – *mistake number two* – and automatically began scrolling. She scrolled through photos of people that she either barely knew, or didn't know at all, until one caught her eye. It was Natasha.

Still looking chic whilst mourning a loved one, the caption read.

'For fuck's sake,' she said out loud to herself and her cup of coffee. She took a sip. 'Shit!'

She'd forgotten what drinking a hot cup of coffee felt like. She patted her bottom lip and when she looked at her finger, saw a red mark from the lipstick she had forgotten she'd put on this morning. *Still hanging in there,* she thought and immediately felt guilty. *What was she thinking, wearing red lipstick on the school run when another mum had just been murdered?* But then she looked down at Natasha's photo again and her red lippy paled in comparison.

What the hell was Natasha doing swanning around the school playground in full mourning gear? Frankie wondered if talking to Natasha should be next on their list. It was like she was overcompensating. Almost putting on the grief for show. I mean sure, everyone deals with these things in different ways, but posting about your grieving outfit on Instagram was an unusual move. *Even for Natasha.*

Was she trying to prove to everyone that she was sad? Devastated by the loss of her good friend, someone she absolutely, definitely would *not* have murdered!

Frankie stared at the picture on Instagram, obsessing over

what Natasha was wearing. Obsessing over how many likes it had and what people were commenting, and as she stared she became fixated on one thing. The red lipstick that Natasha was wearing. There was something about it that made her feel uncomfortable. Was it her own guilt for wearing lipstick today? Or was it something else? She flicked back through the receipts.

There it was, a red lipstick from Chanel. Forty-two quid. Not cheap. Victoria had been wearing a much paler shade at the party. But Natasha often wore red. She had even mentioned *#chanellippy* on her Insta grid, possibly even on one of the mourning posts. Yes, there it was: *Brightening up a difficult day with #chanellippy and newly shaped #mumbrows.*

She had better tell the others that they needed to talk to Natasha sooner rather than later, although Frankie was pretty sure that the promise of a cuppa and cake wouldn't have quite the same allure that it had for Debbie. No, they needed to be a bit more creative with Natasha. Maybe a cocktail evening would entice her? There was no way Natasha would put up with being questioned by three amateur sleuths, but she seemed like the type of woman who would struggle to turn down alcohol and a bitching session, so a low-key cocktail night would surely go down a storm.

20

RACHEL

Rachel peered at The Jam Sandwich Detectives chat on her phone.

Rachel (Charlie's mum): Mum brows?!! Since when did sculpting eyebrows become such a thing? I don't even have time to pluck mine… I'm too busy plucking my chin!

Frankie (Billy's mum): 😄

Rachel (Charlie's mum): Anyway, nice idea 🍷 but someone else will have to invite her. There is no way she'll come if I do!

Jane (Lottie's mum): Whyever not?

Rachel (Charlie's mum): Um, well maybe because she thinks I murdered Victoria. You know her supposedly really good friend Victoria… the one she's going round dressed as Morticia Addams for.

Frankie (Billy's mum): 😇

Oh hang on, I meant 😿

Jane (Lottie's mum): Fair point, Rachel. Frankie, why don't you invite her? It was your idea after all.

Frankie (Billy's mum): I barely know her. I don't think she'd come.

Rachel (Charlie's mum): It needs to be a Yummy Mummy, Jane.

Frankie (Billy's mum): It needs to be you, Jane.

Jane (Lottie's mum): Oh, well maybe I could host a little something.

Rachel (Charlie's mum): I would be forever grateful, Jane. I need to prove I had nothing to do with this. I need to get my life back.

Okay, so maybe Rachel's last message was a little dramatic. It wasn't like her life was over. So far she was basically carrying on as usual and other than a few more people than normal avoiding her on the playground, not a lot had changed.

Jane (Lottie's mum): Okay then. When were you thinking?

Rachel (Charlie's mum): Tonight?

Jane (Lottie's mum): Tonight?! 😮

No time like the present.

Rachel (Charlie's mum): Too soon?

Jane (Lottie's mum): Umm… could work. Ben's out so should be fine. Nothing I can't handle.

Rachel (Charlie's mum): That's the spirit, Jane! School night cocktails… love it!

Frankie (Billy's mum): Great. Looking forward
to it.

Rachel got the impression that this was the highlight of
Frankie's social calendar. A couple of cocktails with a couple of
other mums that she barely knew. One who had been accused
of murder. One who hadn't yet but that they were secretly going
to question. And one that was bound to go overboard on
planning a few impromptu *Monday* night cocktails.

Rachel (Charlie's mum): I'll bring the umbrellas.

Frankie (Billy's mum): Why? Is it supposed to
rain?

Rachel (Charlie's mum): I meant cocktail
umbrellas.

Jane (Lottie's mum): Bit tacky, Rach… I'll sort
the decor.

That was Rachel told.

'She's printed menus,' whispered Frankie under her breath.

'Yeah,' nodded Rachel. 'That is very *Jane*.'

Frankie raised her eyebrows and then smiled as Jane
waltzed over with two fancy glasses and handed them one each.

'Let's go easy,' said Rachel. 'We want to remember what
Natasha says don't we?'

'Oh, they're not that strong,' laughed Jane, as Frankie
winced while taking her first sip.

'Who are you kidding, Jane?' Rachel took a sip of hers too
and it nearly blew her head off. 'That's cleared some cobwebs.
Are you trying to get us drunk?'

Despite their strength, the first cocktails slipped down easily. Rachel almost forgot why they were there and the three ladies laughed and joked as the contents of their glasses rapidly disappeared.

'I'll go and make some more,' said Jane, collecting up the glasses. 'Do you want to pick, or shall I work my way through the menu?'

'Um, it is a Monday night,' said Frankie. 'We should probably slow down a bit.'

'Nonsense,' said Jane, as she flitted back into the kitchen.

'Where has Natasha got to?' asked Frankie. 'Do you think she's coming?'

'Sure,' said Rachel. 'Fashionably late... that's Natasha all over.'

The doorbell rang.

'Oop, speak of the devil,' said Rachel, and she called, 'I'll get it, Jane. You've got your hands full.'

The cocktail had gone straight to her head. She toppled towards the door and flung it open, with an enthusiastic, 'It's cocktail time, Natashaaaaaaaaa!'

'Not for me, thanks,' said Ben. He was dressed in his police uniform. 'And why exactly are you answering my front door, Rachel?'

'Jane's busy,' said Rachel. 'And more to the point, why are you ringing the doorbell of your own house? Does Jane not let you have your own key?' She giggled.

'I was trying to be discreet,' said Ben, without smiling. 'But as you've answered, I may as well just come out with it. Phil told me I'd find you here. Can you come with me to the station please, Rachel? You are wanted for questioning in relation to the death of Victoria Sandwich.'

'Me?'

'Yes, you!'

'But, why? We're having cocktails,' said Rachel. 'Can I possibly pop down another time?'

'How many have you had?' asked Ben. 'Are you drunk, Rachel?'

'Gosh no! We're just getting started.'

'Well, in that case I would advise you to come with me,' said Ben. 'It is best to co-operate. They will be interviewing everyone who was at the party, but they want to start with you.'

'Why me? I haven't done anything wrong.'

'I don't know why you, Rachel, but if you refuse to co-operate it will look like you have something to hide.'

Rachel took a deep breath.

'You do have the right to a solicitor,' Ben added.

'A solicitor?' Her voice rose and she almost swore. She lowered it and tried her best to appear sober. 'Why would I need a solicitor? I haven't done anything wrong!'

'They just want to ask you some questions, Rach.'

'But I'm not, I mean I– okay fine. Let me grab my stuff. I'm allowed to do that, aren't I?'

'Yes, you are,' said Ben.

Jane appeared in the hallway. 'What's going on, Ben?'

'He's arresting me,' slurred Rachel.

'He's what?' asked Jane. 'You're what, Ben? We are trying to have a cocktail evening.'

'Well, I'm sorry, love, but this is a murder case. And, I'm not *arresting* her, she can leave at any time, but she really should come with me.'

'A murder case? I thought you weren't *on* the murder case?'

'I'm not, I'm just bringing her in. I offered. I thought it might be less daunting for Rachel than an officer she doesn't know. Y'know, a friendly face and all that.'

'Well, thank you, Ben,' giggled Rachel. 'You do have a friendly face.'

'This is ridiculous,' said Jane. 'We're trying to have a nice evening and...'

'Jane,' said Ben, not smiling. 'Rachel needs to come with me.'

Rachel realised that he wasn't messing about and his serious tone sobered her up slightly. 'It's fine, Jane, I won't be long. You carry on and I'll be back before you know it.'

Rachel felt her stomach tie into a knot, and it wasn't related to the cocktails. *This is it.* This was what she'd been worried about. This was why The Jam Sandwich Detectives were investigating; proving her innocence.

'We knew this was going to happen,' she said to Jane. 'It's the whole reason we are–' She paused and looked at Ben.

'Whole reason you are what?' He raised one eyebrow.

'Nothing,' said Jane. 'You get off. We'll wait for Natasha.'

'Natasha? Since when have you been friends with–'

'We're trying to make her feel better,' Rachel interjected. 'She's really upset about Victoria.'

'We all are,' said Ben, which struck Rachel as a strange thing to say. She assumed he was just trying to be kind and not say what most people were thinking, which is that they are not actually that upset at all and that she was an annoying and bossy cow.

'Yes,' said Rachel, wiping a tear from her eye.

A real tear.

She knew that the tear would seem forced but it wasn't. It was from the heart. Not because Victoria was dead, but because she was starting to feel her life unravelling. And as much as she moaned about her life – the mundanity and the stress – she would be heartbroken if it all fell apart.

21

———

JANE

Jane was fuming.

What the hell was Ben thinking, taking Rachel in for questioning in the middle of her cocktail night? Surely he could have called her first, and surely it could have waited until the morning.

She poured herself another drink.

'Perhaps you should slow down a bit,' said Frankie. 'Natasha will be here in a minute and we don't want–'

Jane cut her off. 'I can't believe him. He's completely ruined the evening and now Rachel will probably hate me forever.'

'Of course she won't,' Frankie assured her. 'His actions aren't yours, Jane.'

Jane knew she was right but even so, it just made her more determined to help Rachel. To prove her friend's innocence. 'You're right.' She sighed. 'I suppose he's only doing his job,' she said through gritted teeth.

'Exactly.'

The doorbell rang. Jane took a deep breath and a swig of her cocktail. 'Here goes nothing,' she said to Frankie, disappearing off down the hall. Then, as she opened the door, 'Natasha! How lovely to see you. Do come through. Have you met Frankie?'

Jane was in full *putting it on* mode. Sometimes she didn't even realise she was doing it, but today she knew full well. It was the only way to get through the evening.

They walked into the kitchen.

'What's all this in aid of?' asked Natasha, gesturing towards the table full of bottles, glasses and little dishes full of chopped up lemon, lime and mint.

'Just thought we needed a bit of cheering up,' said Jane, attempting to sound breezy.

Natasha eyed her suspiciously for a second, but then she smiled and said, 'Good idea!'

Jane was relieved when the three women relaxed into polite conversation, occasionally mentioning Victoria in passing and pausing as they each searched for the right words.

Eventually Frankie said, 'So, were you and Victoria close, Natasha?'

Jane took a long sip of her drink and waited to see Natasha's reaction which, to her surprise, was calm and controlled.

'We were,' said Natasha. 'She was a great friend.'

'Did she ever help you out financially?' asked Frankie.

Jane coughed as she swallowed her mouthful of cocktail.

'I beg your pardon,' said Natasha.

'It's just...' said Frankie, '...well, we've heard that she was in a spot of money trouble. That she'd been buying things for other people, but struggling herself.'

Natasha looked affronted. 'Well, I have absolutely no idea where you've got that from. Perhaps you shouldn't believe every bit of tittle-tattle that you hear on the playground.'

'So, did she?'

Jane remained silent as Frankie kept on digging.

'Did she what?'

'Buy you anything?'

'Absolutely not,' Natasha folded her arms.

'Not a Chanel lipstick?'

Natasha touched her lips; she looked taken aback. 'Well, actually yes she did buy me this lipstick. It was a birthday present. How the bloody hell did you know that? What *exactly* is going on here, ladies?'

Jane suddenly decided that honesty was the best policy. 'We're just trying to help Rachel.'

'I've just seen her go past in a police car. Is that related to Victoria's murder?'

Jane and Frankie looked at each other, but didn't say anything.

'I knew it! Wait...' Jane could almost see the cogs turning in Natasha's head. 'You're *helping* her? The finger has been pointed at Rachel, so she's desperately trying to point it anywhere else, and she's roped you two in to help... that's what this is all about! You think I–'

'No,' said Jane weakly, but Natasha didn't let her speak.

'You think I murdered my friend over a lipstick?'

'Of course not,' said Jane.

'It was a present,' said Natasha.

'We just wondered if it was bribery for something?' Frankie chipped in.

Natasha looked at her for a moment and then burst into fits of hysterical laughter. 'Ladies,' she said. 'I think you two need to find yourselves a hobby. Maybe running, or tennis, or jigsaw puzzles? Why don't you leave the Miss Marple-ing to the police.'

'It's just...' Frankie was undeterred. 'Well, if someone knew something about me that I didn't want them or their fifty-thousand Instagram followers to know, then I would be super-duper nice to them, and maybe even, y'know... buy them the odd expensive gift.'

'I don't have to stay here and listen to this,' said Natasha, slamming her glass down onto the table, but then moving it slightly so that it was on the coaster properly. 'Enjoy your cocktails, ladies.'

She strutted off towards the door and Jane followed her.

'I'm so sorry,' said Jane. 'Frankie is getting a bit carried away. We've all had a drink and well–'

'Be careful, Jane.' Natasha stopped at the front door. 'All this detective work... you might end up finding out something that you didn't want to know.'

'Where did that all come from?' Jane asked Frankie, as she returned to the kitchen, trying not to let Natasha's parting remark get to her.

'Call it a hunch,' said Frankie.

'A hunch? All that was a hunch?'

'Kind of.' Frankie grinned. 'It just came to me so I tested the water and I'm not being funny but Natasha's reaction tells me that there is definitely something to it. You don't react like that unless you've got something to hide.'

Jane nodded. 'But, why would Natasha kill the source of her Chanel lipsticks?'

'Maybe she'd threatened her,' said Frankie. 'The bribery thing was a stab in the dark but I think it might have been close to the money. The question is, if Victoria was bribing her and Victoria is dead, then why is Natasha still keeping the secret?'

'Good point,' said Jane. 'Perhaps it's not that after all.'

'Unless, there's someone else involved in the secret too.

Someone new to bribe. I mean all those expensive outfits she parades around in won't pay for themselves.'

'We need to be careful, Frankie... Natasha is a force that we don't want to mess with.'

'And so are The Jam Sandwich Detectives,' said Frankie.

Jane smiled. 'Oooh, what a brilliant idea.' And she got out the bread, and the butter, and a jar of strawberry jam.

22

RACHEL

Rachel sat alone in the grey room.

It wasn't as dank as she had expected. It was plain and dull but not unpleasant. If she let her mind wander she could pretend she was waiting for a job interview, not a police one. Of course this job interview would be for a much less glamorous company than the one she'd had a couple of days ago. The one that she was still waiting to hear back from. The one that she had probably messed up by using 'organising lifts to my kids' various clubs and activities' as her example of good diary management. What was she thinking? Had being a mum wiped all previous knowledge and experience from her brain?

The office she had sat waiting in then had a coffee machine. It had expensive looking artwork on the walls, and plants dotted around in a seemingly random way that someone had probably spent hours planning. It had upholstered chairs and a table set up with matching glasses, and a contemporary-style water jug with ice and cucumber bobbing about in it.

In front of her now was a paper cup of tepid water.

There was nothing to look at except a clock, but looking at that just made time go even slower. No posters or notices on the walls. No window to gaze out of and pretend she was somewhere else. The only thing that caught her eye was the fire exit sign above the door and she started to think about what she would do if there was a fire. Was she free to leave or was she locked in? Buildings had to have fire exits, she knew that, but how did it work for prisoners?

Not that she was a prisoner – although she felt like one. She hadn't even been arrested, just asked to accompany Ben to the station for some questioning.

Wondering whether she was locked in this grey room was suddenly overwhelming, so she got up and walked over to the door. Her heart was pounding and as she pushed down the handle, relief flooded through her as the door opened.

'Going somewhere?' asked Ben, making her jump. He was standing outside in the corridor, talking to another officer.

The bright lights of the corridor made Rachel squint. 'Oh, I, er,' she stumbled. 'I just needed the loo.'

'Down the hall on the right.' Ben nodded in the direction he had indicated. 'Don't be long. DI Harding will be ready to interview you shortly.'

'DI...? I thought you were going to...?'

'You are friends with my wife, Rach,' said Ben. 'I can't interview you in a murder investigation.'

Rachel swallowed and the lump in her throat slowly worked its way down to her chest. It was making it hard to breathe, as though the air had been sucked out of the room. As she stepped out into the sterile corridor the waft of cool air on her face was a welcome relief. She made her way towards the toilet that she didn't need. What she did need was to escape for a moment.

She splashed her face with water. *That's what people do on TV, right?* This was all suddenly very real. The chatting about suspects over tea and jam sandwiches felt a million miles away from this. And she was terrified.

Back in the grey room, DI Harding put Rachel at ease fairly quickly. She spoke to her like a grown-up and asked her questions like she had done this a zillion times before, which she probably had. 'So, you were at a social event at Ms Sandwich's house on the evening of her death?'

'Yes, it was a Bake Off party. Seeing who made the best cakes ready for all the bake sales and fundraising events that were coming up.' Rachel realised how ridiculous her words sounded within the four walls of a police interview room. A room that had probably had drug dealers, armed robbers and *actual* murderers in it previously, and she was now sat there discussing a cake baking contest.

DI Harding looked at her over her glasses and Rachel found herself wondering whether she was a mum too.

'It was just a bit of fun really... you know, until Victoria was murdered.' Rachel giggled nervously.

'How well did you know Ms Sandwich?'

'Oh, not very well at all really,' fumbled Rachel. 'Knew *of* her really more than anything else.'

'So, she was popular?'

'No!' laughed Rachel. She cleared her throat. 'I mean, not exactly. I think the word is *formidable*. People respected her but she was hard to say no to, hence us all spending our Friday evening comparing cakes at her house.'

'I see. So, you didn't like her?'

Rachel swallowed. 'Not especially.'

'And did you say... let me see,' DI Harding looked down at her notes. 'That you wanted *to kill her?*'

'No! I mean, yes.'

'Which is it, Ms Walker?'

Rachel touched her forehead. It was wet so she wiped it

with her sleeve. 'Yes, I think I did say something along those lines, but I was joking, of course. The woman had us all at her beck and call: be here at this time; make this, make that; she was like a school bully. The messages were so condescending and some of them were just rude. She was just so annoying.'

'And were you annoyed enough to…?'

'Absolutely not! No way! Yes, okay, she was a complete nightmare, but I am not going to kill someone over bloody cake!'

DI Harding bit her bottom lip. Rachel couldn't tell whether she was deciding what to say or holding in a little smirk.

'And just to clarify,' Rachel added. 'I wouldn't kill anyone over anything else either.'

DI Harding nodded. 'Did anyone else at the party have any reason to want Ms Sandwich dead?' she asked bluntly.

Rachel laughed. *Where do I start?* she thought.

'We have plenty of time,' said DI Harding.

Rachel looked up at the clock on the wall, then back down at DI Harding and the other officer, who hadn't spoken yet, and wondered if they had kids to get home to. It was getting late. Phil still thought she was round at Jane's. Although the visit from Ben in uniform asking where she was might have got his mind working overtime. Rachel had declined various offers from police staff to give him a call, but if this wasn't over soon she would have to call him and explain what was going on.

'Not that I know of,' said Rachel eventually. 'I don't know anyone that would want to kill Victoria.'

Her head was spinning. That was her moment, her moment to drop other people in it. To take the heat away from her. To tell the police that Debbie had been helping Victoria fiddle the books and that there had been something weird going on with Natasha. But she couldn't bring herself to do it. Not until she had some actual evidence. She knew how it felt to have all eyes on you for some silly little reason and she didn't want to inflict that on anyone else. These were all busy mums, they had enough going on without being the suspect in a murder investigation because of some, probably unrelated, possible fact.

'Well,' said DI Harding. 'If you think of anything, please let us know.'

'Of course.'

'One last thing,' added the detective. 'Do you know who Bee is?'

'Bee?'

'Beatrice maybe?'

Rachel mentally scanned the playground but couldn't think of any mums, or kids, called Beatrice.

'I don't think so. Why do you ask?'

'For the tape, I am showing Ms Walker a copy of item C12.' DI Harding placed a piece of paper in front of Rachel on the table. It was a photograph of a calendar. One that hangs on a wall. The thought of Victoria with a Country Companions wall calendar made Rachel smile, although she tried to hide it. The world had gone digital but Rachel, too, still liked to have a calendar hanging on the wall.

'There are several mentions of Bee,' said DI Harding pointing at the photo. 'Any help in working out who she is would be much appreciated.'

Rachel scanned the photo, reading through the dates where Bee was mentioned but also taking in what was noted on some of the other dates too.

'Bee,' she said. 'No, I don't know anyone called Bee or Beatrice I'm afraid.'

'Okay,' said the detective snapping the piece of paper away. 'That's all for now.'

'For now?'

'We are just at the initial questioning stage,' DI Harding

explained. 'We may well need to get you back in when we have more of a picture of what happened.'

The detective started shuffling her papers and Rachel sat still in her chair.

DI Harding looked over at her. 'Is there anything else you want to tell me?'

Rachel knew she should mention it, but she also knew that it would throw Jane under the radar, so she hesitated.

'Ms Walker?'

'It's just, well, I should probably tell you that I didn't bake my cake,' Rachel mumbled, confessing her dark and heinous Bake Off sin. She felt like DI Harding was going to throw her in jail for cheating at baking.

DI Harding's hard exterior dropped for a second and she laughed. 'I'm not Paul Hollywood. I'm looking for a murderer, not judging the baking.'

'But, one of the cakes was poisoned,' said Rachel. 'So, I thought...'

'No,' said DI Harding. 'No cyanide was found in any of the cakes. The only trace was in Ms Sandwich's glass.'

'Oh!' Rachel's mind was spinning. *This is good news, surely? The cake didn't kill her!*

'Did you see anyone near Ms Sandwich's glass before she drank from it?' asked DI Harding.

'No,' said Rachel. 'I think she had it in her hand when I arrived.'

Rachel's mind shot back to the party, then she looked at DI Harding's takeaway coffee cup with her name scrawled in Sharpie on the side. 'Victoria's glass had her name on it!'

'Yes,' confirmed DI Harding. 'So, it looks like the poison was definitely meant for her. Unfortunately, as lovely as her special personalised glass was, it just made things easier for the murderer.'

23

———

JANE

'We need to talk,' said Rachel from underneath her hoodie.

'Good morning to you too!' Jane looked Rachel up and down. 'Also, what *are* you wearing?' She glanced around the playground.

'Are you more embarrassed to be seen with someone wearing a hoodie or someone who is a murder suspect?' Rachel spat out.

She's stressed, Jane thought. 'Good point,' she said aloud. 'Keep it on.'

Rachel rolled her eyes and Jane realised that she should probably show some concern. 'How did it go?'

'It was very helpful,' Rachel whispered.

'Helpful?' Not a word Jane had expected her friend to use to describe being questioned about a murder.

'For our investigation. I found out some good stuff.'

'You do know that you were being questioned by the police...?'

'Shh, keep your voice down.'

Jane glanced around the playground and lowered her voice. '...Not having an intelligence gathering meeting with them.'

'Well, yes, but Di was very helpful.'

'Di?'

'Di Harding.'

Jane laughed. 'D...I... is her title, detective inspector, not her name!'

'Oh, I know,' said Rachel. 'But as soon as she introduced herself I just couldn't get Di Hard out of my head, so that's what I'm calling her.'

'Not to her face, hopefully?'

'Of course not.' Rachel smiled.

Jane loved Rachel's playful nature. She would never have the guts to casually refer to a police detective by such a silly – and potentially offensive – name, even behind their back. She was also in awe of how calmly Rachel was dealing with being questioned by the police – well, apart from skulking around in a hoodie – she would be a nervous wreck.

'What have you come as?' said a jovial voice behind them, making them both jump. 'Are you trying to look like a criminal?'

'It's not funny, Frankie,' said Rachel sternly.

Jane exchanged looks with both Frankie and Rachel, before all three women burst into laughter. The whole scenario was kind of crazy when you really thought about it.

'It must be nice to be able to laugh at such a difficult time,' said another voice. Natasha was still dressed in black. This school-run mourning was getting out of hand. She turned to Rachel. 'Let you out for good behaviour, did they?'

'Just some routine questions,' said Rachel, taking down her hood.

'Glad to see some proper detectives are doing their job.' Natasha walked off.

'What a snooty cow,' said Frankie.

'Everyone grieves in a different way,' said Jane, not sure why she was sticking up for her.

Jane noted that Rachel and Frankie raised their eyebrows.

'Anyway,' said Rachel. 'I've got a lot to fill you in on, and you ladies need to tell me what happened last night after I was whisked away by–'

'By my husband,' said Jane, her cheeks getting hot. 'I feel like I need to apologise.'

'Don't be silly,' said Rachel. 'He was only doing his job, and like I say, it was a very interesting chat. I learnt a few things that will help The Jam Sandwich Detectives out no end. So, when can we catch up?'

'I've got a bit of housework to do this morning,' said Jane. 'But I'm free other than that.'

Frankie laughed. 'Your house is spotless, Jane. Surely you can have a day off from chores?'

Jane felt her cheeks flush again. She didn't want to seem square, but she also wanted to keep on top of the housework; if she let that slip then everything else would follow. 'I suppose I could, but if I keep having days off, we'll be living in a pigsty.'

'Welcome to my world,' said Frankie.

'I'd rather be living in a pigsty than in jail,' said Rachel.

Jane knew she was right. She had to help her friend and the truth was that she'd rather hang out with Rachel and Frankie than worry about what her house looked like, which was a big step for her.

'I'm as free as a bird,' said Frankie.

'Quick coffee at mine then?' asked Rachel. 'And then you can both go off and do all the cleaning you like while I squelch about in my pigsty.'

'Sold,' said Jane.

'I'm in,' said Frankie. 'I'm just going to pop home and get my notebook and I will be right over.'

'That's what I like,' said Rachel. 'A proper detective always takes notes.'

Jane suddenly felt like Frankie was doing better at detective-ing than her. What could she bring? What do detectives need? She thought about all the cop shows she'd ever seen on TV.

'I can bring doughnuts,' she said out of nowhere.

Rachel laughed. 'As long as they're jam ones.'

Jane smiled. 'Naturally.'

'Doughnuts and detecting for breakfast,' said Frankie. 'Sounds perfect.'

'So, what have we got?' asked Frankie, taking the lead as the amateur sleuths sat around Rachel's kitchen table, coffee and doughnuts in hand.

Jane didn't mention that she had had to drive around to three different shops to find the doughnuts, nor that she had snapped at the man in front of her in the queue at the last shop, after he had done eenie-meany-miny-moe to decide whether he wanted jam or custard.

'Some people would actually prefer the jam ones if you are at all interested,' she had said, as his finger landed at random on one of the three remaining jam doughnuts in the glass counter.

His face had turned pink and he turned back to the shop assistant and said. 'On second thoughts, I think I'll go for custard.'

'No bother at all,' said Jane breezily, when Rachel and Frankie thanked her for the doughnuts. 'We were so lucky, there were exactly three left in the very first place I popped to.' She wasn't sure why she was lying.

'It was meant to be then.' Rachel smiled.

'Well, in that case, I'll just have to force one down.' Frankie giggled.

'So,' said Rachel now, wiping the sugar from her lips. 'First things first. Does anyone know a Bee or Beatrice? I had a quick look at Victoria's Facebook friends and couldn't see one.'

Jane tapped her bottom lip and Frankie scrunched her mouth up.

'I have a feeling Victoria's sister is called Beatrice,' said Jane, after a moment. 'She sometimes visits her, if my memory serves me correctly.'

'Well, she had been visiting her a lot recently if Victoria's calendar was anything to go by,' said Rachel.

'You've seen Victoria's calendar?' asked Jane.

'Yep,' said Rachel smugly. 'Well, a copy of a photo of it.'

'Should the police be showing you evidence?' asked Frankie.

Jane realised that Frankie was looking at her for an answer but she wasn't sure she had one.

'They must be really desperate for leads,' she said, eventually.

There was a brief silence.

'Strange not to be friends with your sister on Facebook,' mused Frankie.

'Not everyone is on Facebook,' said Jane.

'I sometimes wish I wasn't,' said Rachel.

'So,' asked Jane. 'What else was on this calendar?'

'Well,' began Rachel, rubbing her hands and flicking bits of sugar off her fingers.

Jane had the urge to wipe it up, but held it in as she was eager to hear what Rachel had to say.

'I only got to see it for a few seconds, but I did spot a couple of interesting things.'

'Like...?' Frankie looked at Rachel in anticipation.

Jane took a deep breath. 'Don't keep us in suspense.'

'Well,' said Rachel, seemingly enjoying having control of the floor. 'There was a note scribbled on last Tuesday I think, saying "Gina – five hundred pounds".'

'Gina?' asked Jane.

'One of the other new mums,' said Rachel.

'Oh, yes,' said Frankie. 'She's on the Reception chat… and she came to the Bake Off thing.'

Rachel nodded. 'She did.'

'And?' said Jane. 'You said you spotted a couple of things.'

'Oh yes,' said Rachel. 'This one will make you laugh; a couple of Saturdays ago it just said "Greg – trim bush"!'

Jane nearly spat out her coffee.

'Haaaaa!' squealed Frankie. 'That is bloody brilliant!'

'You don't think…?' began Jane, but she couldn't bring herself to finish.

'Well, either Greg was popping round to do some gardening for her,' said Rachel. 'Or Victoria was doing a spot of topiary herself, to get ready for a visit from Greg!'

Jane put the jam doughnut, that she had just picked up, back down on her plate; she had suddenly lost her appetite.

24

FRANKIE

Frankie opened her notebook.

'Your drawings are so great,' said Rachel.

Feeling her cheeks flush, Frankie quickly flicked the page over to a blank one. 'Oh, they're just doodles.'

'Well, they look like fun.'

'Yeah.' Frankie laughed. 'It kind of helps me relax.'

'I'd love to look through them sometime.' Rachel smiled.

Frankie's heart raced. 'Oh no, they are just for me. I've never shown them to anyone. They're just silly really.'

Frankie wasn't really sure why the thought of someone looking through her drawings filled her with dread. She definitely didn't think of herself as an artist – the pictures were very simplistic; stick people and basic doodles – but it wasn't the drawings themselves that she was so overwhelmingly embarrassed about. It was the honesty. She drew things that she felt: her angers, frustrations, annoyances, and if someone looked at them, they would be seeing her thoughts. Reading her mind.

She changed the subject quickly. 'So, the next step is to talk to Greg and to Gina, they are both already on our list anyway so it makes perfect sense to. They were both at the party and...'

She hoped that if she kept talking maybe Rachel would forget about the doodles and stop asking her questions about them and, actually, had she even asked any actual questions? Maybe not, but it seemed to be working as Rachel wasn't looking at her notebook anymore. 'And we need to track down Beatrice. I mean, we know it couldn't have been her, as she wasn't at the party, but it still might be useful to chat to her.'

'Oh yes, that's the other thing I needed to mention.' Rachel paused for dramatic effect.

'Yes?' asked Jane impatiently.

'The cake wasn't poisoned... it was her glass; they found traces of cyanide in it.'

Frankie and Jane both widened their eyes.

'Rachel!' Jane raised her voice, which was very unlike her, but this information changed everything. 'Maybe you could have started with that?!'

'Sorry, I–'

'I've been having sleepless nights over that bloody cake I made you!'

'But we already knew that the cakes themselves had nothing to do with it.'

Frankie nodded. 'She's right, Jane, the bakers have been off the hook for a while, in terms of their cakes at least.' Frankie couldn't deny that she'd had a similar worry at first; what if her cake had been tampered with? Poisoned... but by who? If someone else had interfered with her cake then that wasn't her responsibility. She thought about her doodle of the knife-wielding cake and smiled. Her unwanted thought flittered away.

'I guess you are right,' said Jane. 'Sorry!' She paused for thought. 'I just think this information should have been higher up the pecking order than Victoria waxing her bits for a visit from Greg!'

The phrase waxing her bits nearly made Frankie spit out her now cold coffee, but she managed to hold it in – just about – and she wiped the corner of her mouth with her sleeve.

Jane didn't seem to notice, and continued undeterred. 'So, when you say her glass... you mean *her* glass?'

'The naff one with her name painted on the side?' asked Frankie.

Rachel nodded. 'Yep.'

'Well, that's one way of making sure the right person drinks it,' said Jane.

'Exactly,' said Rachel.

'Where would someone even get hold of cyanide from?' asked Frankie, as the thought popped into her head.

'Well, that's a good question and one we should definitely look into,' said Rachel. 'Anyway, this all tells us two things. Firstly, this was definitely no accident and that Victoria was one hundred per cent the intended victim; and secondly, the killer might not even be on our list.'

'How do you figure that?' asked Jane

'Our list is everyone at the party, everyone who had opportunity... but if the poison was in her named glass, then they could have dropped it in before the party started. Maybe even days before.'

'Shit,' said Frankie. 'You're right.'

Jane nodded. 'But she lives alone. Who else would have had access to the glass?'

'We need to talk to this Bee,' said Frankie.

'We had better get busy,' said Rachel, and Frankie rolled her eyes with a smile. 'Anyway, talking of Bees, what happened when you talked to the Queen Bee the other night? Obviously I missed the whole thing.'

Frankie looked at Jane.

'Um,' said Frankie.

'What does um mean?'

'She went off in a strop!'

'I think she knew that we were trying to help you,' Jane added. 'You know, to prove your innocence by...'

'...by throwing her under the bus?' said Rachel.

'Basically, yes,' said Jane with a grimace.

'But, it wasn't her,' said Frankie, matter-of-factly.

'Oh?'

'The lipstick was a birthday present. Yes, Victoria was sucking up to her by buying her an expensive gift, and yes, she was potentially funding such extravagant purchases from the PTA kitty, but Natasha wasn't asking her to. She's a bitch, but if anything, I think she actually felt sorry for Victoria.'

Jane and Rachel nodded in response.

'Okay, good work, Frankie,' said Rachel.

Frankie smiled and tucked her hair behind her ear. Gaining Rachel's approval felt good.

She wondered if perhaps she should aim higher than a suspected murderer as her new friend, although that was kind of irrelevant as Frankie knew that Rachel didn't do it. Rachel was just a mum; just like she was and just like Jane was too. Admittedly Rachel was a mum who said she was going to kill someone and then, suddenly, that someone was dead, but mums say things that they don't mean a hundred times a day: eat your dinner or there will be no treats for a week; if you don't start behaving I'll cancel the holiday; anything left on the floor in your bedroom is going in the bin.

In fact Frankie did nearly stick to the last example on one occasion. And she would have done had there not been most of a brand new Lego set that cost £54.99 in amongst the debris.

The truth was that she really liked spending time with Rachel and Jane. Although they were a bit older than her and neither of them were very much like her, they did have one big thing in common. Being mums had taken over their existence and they were all now, suddenly, relishing having a hobby. Something to focus on other than their kids. Something important. And it was important. It might keep her friend out of jail. Rachel couldn't go to prison over some flippant remark she made on the playground... could she?

'We need to get cracking,' said Rachel. 'If Natasha's on the warpath, thinking we were trying to stitch her up, then it's only a matter of time before she does the same to me.'

'Okay,' said Frankie, ready for action.

'We need to crank this investigation up a gear,' said Rachel. 'Let's split up. Frankie, you talk to Gina. You're both newbies after all, so she might open up to you.'

'No problem,' said Frankie. 'I'll arrange a playdate.'

'Excellent! The perfect setting for some murder chat,' smirked Rachel.

'I'll be subtle.' Frankie blushed.

'Jane, you see if you can find out anything else about Victoria's sister, Beatrice.'

'Sure,' said Jane, going quiet for a moment and tapping her lip with her finger. 'I'll talk to Ann in the Post Office.'

'Why?' asked Frankie. 'Do you need some stamps?'

'Oh, the Post Office is the hub of the village news, darling!' said Jane. 'Ann always knows who's who and what's what.'

'Oh,' said Frankie. 'Well, good to know.'

'Great,' said Rachel. 'And I'll pay Greg a visit.'

'Need a tidy up do you?' Frankie grinned.

'Don't even go there!' Rachel laughed, and Jane blushed.

'Shall we finish our doughnuts first?' asked Frankie.

'Obviously,' said Rachel. 'I'll put the kettle on.'

25

———

JANE

Jane stood at the back of a long Post Office queue.

Five people may not seem that long, but Ann liked to chat to every customer with an enthusiasm, knowledge and genuine interest that Jane was in awe of.

She'd known Ann for years. She trusted her. The postmistress was genuine and kind and reliable, and most importantly, Ann remembered details, and details were what Jane needed right now. She also knew that although Ann tried to stay out of village gossip she took it all in and if you thought the mums on the playground were bad, it was nothing compared to the stories you could hear in the village Post Office.

At the front of the queue was Margery. She wanted to get some cash out. Jane missed cash. She liked the feel of it in her hands, the counting out of the notes and coins, but she wouldn't be keeping up appearances if she went around paying for things by cash rather than with her phone – which drove her mad – so she continued the cyber-struggle.

Margery couldn't remember her PIN number, but not to worry as Ann had a list pinned up, just out of view, behind the counter, so, before you could say 'please don't mug an old lady,' Margery left the Post Office with two hundred pounds in ten pound notes, stashed in her bag-for-life... and the entire queue knew about it.

Next, one of the other mums from school was returning some parcels. Jane couldn't remember her name but she was sure that Ann would.

'Morning, Gemma.'

Oh yes, Gemma. Jane always thought that Gemma looked nice – nice without looking like she'd tried too hard – and now Jane knew her secret. Buying clothes online and sending half of them back. A practice that Jane had never got into – she would end up keeping everything and spending a small fortune – but she could see the benefits; plenty of time to try everything on without the pressure of a shop changing room queue.

The Post Office queue didn't cause quite the same stress, for a start the selection and difficult decisions had already been made, plus half the queue were just there to kill time anyway. Like Gerald who was next.

'Could I have a form to apply for a new passport please, Ann?' said Gerald.

'Of course,' said Ann, flicking through her folder of forms. 'Going somewhere nice, Gerald?'

'No, no,' said Gerald. 'But it's always best to be organised.'

'It is.' Ann smiled, before nodding along to Gerald's analysis of the current weather.

'Have you heard about this murder?' said the next lady in the queue.

'Yes,' said Ann. 'Funnily enough, you are not the first person to mention it.'

'Well, what do you know, Ann? Should we be worried?'

'I don't think so, Enid. It's just one of those things.' Ann smiled. 'Can I get you anything, or was it just the local news you were after?'

'I just like to know what's going on,' replied Enid.

'Well, if it's all the same to you, I am going to keep my nose out of it,' said Ann. 'Who's next please?'

She looked over Enid's shoulder and the old lady behind her admitted that she was just there for an update on the murder too. 'But I'll take this paper,' she added. 'Look, it's all over the front page.'

When Jane finally arrived at the front of the queue, she was worried that Ann might be hacked off at the realisation that Jane was also there to quiz her about something murder-related, so she asked for a book of stamps.

'Six pound eighty please,' said Ann.

'Oh, just eight please, Ann, and second class is fine,' said Jane.

'That is for eight second class.' Ann smiled.

'Gosh!' said Jane. 'That's a bit bloody dear.' She felt her cheeks flush. 'Pardon my French, but they have shot up.' Jane couldn't remember the last time she'd bought stamps.

'Sorry,' said Ann. 'I don't control the prices.'

'No, I know,' said Jane, as she tapped her phone to pay, and then tapped it again because, of course, it didn't work the first time. 'Listen,' she lowered her voice and briefly glanced back over her shoulder as the person behind her huffed. 'Do you know anything about Victoria's sister, Beatrice?'

'Not you as well, Jane.'

'I'm not gossiping,' said Jane. 'I promise. We're trying to get to the bottom of all this... I'm helping a friend, and... and this mysterious sister has been mentioned. That's all.'

She scrunched her face up, pleading with Ann to help, and she did. 'Victoria used to come in all the time to send letters or parcels to Bee, she'd draw little bumblebees on the envelopes.'

'That's sweet,' said Jane, as she thought about the bumblebee vase that Ben bought her years ago that is still on their kitchen windowsill.

Ann nodded. 'I think she lives in Scotland from memory.'

'Oh,' said Jane. 'Quite a way then. Did she visit often?'

'Not that I know of,' said Ann. 'I mean, of course Victoria didn't tell me everything going on in her life, but she came in nearly every week to send Bee a letter or pick up a parcel from her.'

'Wow!' Jane raised her eyebrows. 'Every week?'

'Pretty much,' said Ann. 'Although, now you come to mention it. I don't remember seeing her for a couple of weeks before...'

She didn't seem able to say the words.

'Before she died,' Jane helped her out.

'Yes,' said Ann, with an exaggerated sniff that was either intended to stop any stray tears, or pretend there were any stray tears to stop.

Jane nodded in thanks as the woman behind her coughed loudly.

'Right,' said Jane. 'I'd better be off. Thanks, Ann, you have been really helpful.'

'Anytime,' said Ann. 'Although maybe when there's less of a queue next time.' She winked.

Jane laughed. 'Sorry.'

'And, Jane,' Ann added, as Jane turned to leave. 'I hope this is all solved soon. Victoria was a lovely woman. Sometimes she hid it well, but she didn't deserve this.'

Jane realised that Ann was right. Victoria Sandwich may have been a bit bolshie but she didn't deserve to be murdered. A single tear ran down Jane's cheek and took her by surprise, so she wiped it away.

She nodded sympathetically. It was obvious that someone

disagreed. Someone thought that Victoria deserved it, and sooner or later The Jam Sandwich Detectives would find out who.

26

RACHEL

As luck would have it, Greg was out gardening when Rachel casually strolled past, hoping to bump into him.

'Hey, Greg,' she called. 'Nice day for it.'

'It is,' he replied, with a friendly smile. Men are different creatures to women. Rachel didn't detect the raised eyebrows or the judgemental stare that she'd had from most of the women on the playground.

'Do a lot of gardening, do you?' she asked, stopping, and leaning on the front wall. As Greg wiped the sweat from his forehead with his forearm, Rachel got a glimpse of why Sarah and some of the other mums flocked round him. The arms of his white T-shirt neatly hugged his biceps and his thighs fitted snugly into his ripped jeans.

'Um, I guess so,' said Greg. 'It's cheaper than the gym... although actually, my garden centre loyalty card would probably disagree with that.'

Rachel laughed. 'I heard you did a bit of gardening for Victoria from time to time.'

Greg eyed her suspiciously. 'You heard correctly.'

'Okay.' Rachel was unsure where to go from there.

'You saw what she was like with the cake night; she's hard to say no to! I just trim her shrubs and mow the lawn occasionally, although I guess I'm out of a job now.'

Rachel nodded, and they both took a moment, allowing the silence.

'It was just to earn a bit of extra cash,' Greg said eventually. 'Times are hard. Don't get me wrong, I love being a stay-at-home dad, but I just wanted to be able to treat the kids occasionally and I hate asking the wife for money all the time. I feel like I'm getting pocket money.'

Rachel smiled. She knew that feeling oh-so well. 'You have absolutely no need to explain yourself to me, Greg, I get it.' Rachel paused. 'I just wondered, well, as you have been, y'know, around the house – Victoria's house, I mean – whether you have, well, seen anything?'

'Such as?'

'I don't know,' said Rachel. 'Strange comings and goings, unusual visitors, someone sneaking in the back door with a bottle labelled *poison*!'

Greg laughed. 'Why don't you leave the detective work to the detectives?'

'Because they've already questioned me, Greg, and half the playground think I did it... but I didn't. So, I need to find out who did.'

Greg fell silent for a moment then, with a kind smile, said, 'Don't worry about what people on the playground think. You just said yourself that you didn't do anything, so that's all that matters.'

'Easy for you to say, you are not looking at life in prison!'

'Oh, life is never life these days,' teased Greg.

Why did men say such stupid things? Rachel took a deep

breath, unsure whether to laugh or cry. 'Well, thanks for that,' she said. 'That is very reassuring.'

As she walked home, she wondered whether Greg's answer was a little bit *too* rehearsed.

If you were having a fling with a dead woman and someone asked you why you'd been at their house, trimming bushes and mowing lawns would be a solid cover-up.

Rachel decided to take a little detour past Victoria's house. The police had gone. The only sign that they had ever been there was a bit of blue and white tape hanging from a bush in the front garden. It had obviously been missed in the clear-up.

The bush was, however, neatly trimmed, and sure enough the grass looked like it had been mowed fairly recently too. She couldn't imagine Victoria out there with a mower and a pair of shears, so, perhaps Greg was telling the truth. House-husband turned handy man.

She stood and looked at the house for a moment, thinking about that awful evening. It had been pretty bad before the murder, so that was just the icing on the cake. The image of Victoria falling to the floor and gasping for breath still haunted her.

Something made her push the gate, and it opened. She walked down the path glancing over her shoulder to make sure no one was watching, then she walked up to the front door and peered through the small glass pane. She couldn't see a lot, but she could see a pile of post, lying on the mat.

She wondered for a moment, who would come and sort through all the post? Who would sort through Victoria's house? Who would organise the funeral? It was the first time these thoughts had occurred to her. She'd been so focused on who had killed Victoria that she hadn't considered these basic logistics. And it made her wonder, was there a will? Who would inherit her, presumably fairly modest, fortune?

There was this possible sister named Bee... and then she remembered that Victoria had a daughter who, from memory, was away at university. Had someone told her? Of course they had! They must have.

Rachel snuck around to the back of the house so that she could have a quick look through the dining room window. She had no idea what she was looking for. Clues, she presumed. As she looked through, she could see half empty glasses and plates dotted around the room. Left as they were on Friday night, like some sort of morbid still-life painting. A few flies buzzed around some of the half-drunk champagne flutes. Surely they would let someone in to clean up soon? Victoria would not be happy about the state of the room.

She sighed and then remembered that this was not her problem. Her problem was being accused of causing this. She turned to go, but heard the crunch of a foot on some crispy fallen leaves. Someone else was there.

Shit!

She looked around. Where had the noise come from? Would she be able to sneak back around and leave without being seen, or should she hide and wait for whoever it was to leave?

She heard more crunches and realised that she had no time to make a decision. She couldn't see anywhere good to hide so she turned to walk as quickly as possible back the way she came, but she immediately bumped into...

'Jane!' she breathed. 'What the hell are you doing here?'

'I might ask you the same question,' Jane hissed back. She, too, seemed on edge.

Shit! thought Rachel. She was supposed to be proving her innocence, not making herself look more guilty. But before either of them could explain themselves there was a loud crash and the two women darted out of the garden quicker than you could say, 'cat knocking over a recycling bin'.

27

FRANKIE

'That would be lovely,' Gina had said when Frankie invited her over for a coffee and a playdate.

Frankie had immediately felt guilty.

Guilty, but also kind of brave.

Why was organising playdates more daunting than actual dating? At least if you asked someone on a proper date, all cards were on the table. Both parties knew where this was heading. Okay, so one person might be after marriage and babies and one could want a quick fling but generally, both people wanted some sort of romance.

Playdates were a whole new ball game. Did the other mum actually want to come for coffee and a conversation that was not about *Peppa Pig,* or were they secretly hoping to drop and run, so that they could get an hour or two of housework done, or some actual work, or an hour or two of sleep?

Whatever Gina wanted, Frankie was overrun with guilt. It had crept up on her. She had been too busy all day, trying to get some work done and frantically making the house look presentable before school pick-up. Billy had only that morning asked her why the school day was soooo long, and maybe to a kid it was, but to a grown-up, who had to fit a million things into their day, those six short hours flew past.

It was the false pretence of it all that hit her as she and Gina walked back to her house from school, the two excited boys trotting along in front of them. This innocent coffee was actually an interrogation. The playdate was a ruse and those poor kids were being used to trick Gina into said interrogation.

The plus side was that they didn't care. They got to make the sofa cushions into a fort and eat half a plate of biscuits each while their mummies chatted, both too polite to shout at either child and tell them not to make a mess or fill themselves with sugar.

When Billy said, 'Can Harry come and play in my room?' Frankie saw her chance and said, 'Of course, darling. If that is okay with Harry's mummy.'

They all looked at Gina. Harry's mummy didn't seem to have a lot of choice.

'Pleeeeeeeeaase,' said Harry, fluttering his eyelashes. 'Billy has got the whole set of Paw Patrol cars and the lookout tower.'

'Oh, well in that case,' grinned Gina, 'how could I say no?'

'Yes!' chorused both the boys, and they disappeared off upstairs, giggling as they went.

'Another cuppa?' asked Frankie, giving Gina the most friendly – *of course I don't have an ulterior motive* – smile that she could manage.

'Yes, please,' said Gina. 'We won't stay too much longer though, you probably want to get your dinner ready.'

'Oh, stay as long as you want... it's fish finger night!'

The two women laughed.

'Oooh, I love a fish finger sandwich,' said Gina. Her eyes twinkled and her ponytail bounced as she laughed. She was quite a young mum. Frankie thought she might even be a bit younger than she was, and she wondered for a moment how she coped so seemingly well with the chaos of mumlife.

'Me too,' said Frankie.

As they sat on the sofa and sipped at their too-hot teas, Frankie's eyes wandered around the room spotting toys that she should have put away and shelves that she should have dusted. She hoped that Gina wouldn't judge her for it. She started to think about how she could wind her way to the subject that she was trying to arrive at, when she noticed Gina unfold her arms and sit back slightly in the chair. Maybe her non-perfect living space was relaxing her a little bit. She hoped that it was, so she dived right in.

'Awful about Victoria, isn't it?'

'Awful,' agreed Gina.

'To think that we were all there, just hanging out and then... boom.'

Gina put her tea down on the coaster in front of her and leaned towards Frankie. 'I heard that Rachel has been questioned by the police,' she almost whispered.

'Yes,' said Frankie. 'But she didn't have anything to do with it. And they said they were questioning everyone.'

'Well, they haven't questioned me. How are you so sure she's not involved?'

Frankie thought for a moment, and realised that she wasn't. There was no way she could be completely sure that Rachel was innocent, but she liked her and wanted her to be, which is maybe why she had offered to help. 'I just know,' she said, eventually.

Gina nodded. 'It's not nice, is it? Having one of the mums at school accused of murder? To think, our little ones are playing with hers every day.'

'I'm sure they'll be fine,' said Frankie, looking up towards the pattering of feet through the ceiling above. 'If we don't find out who did it soon, we will have to get the Paw Patrol on the case.'

Gina smiled. 'Might not be such a bad idea.'

'Are you kidding?' said Frankie. 'Those dogs are a bloody nightmare!'

Gina giggled.

'Did you know Victoria well?' asked Frankie, hoping that it seemed like a passing question.

'Not really,' said Gina. 'She was quite kind to me, I think maybe because she was a single mum too, she knew how hard it can be.'

Frankie nodded, but stayed silent, hoping that it would allow Gina to open up.

'I first met her over the summer,' said Gina.

This is good, thought Frankie, giving her interested nods.

'I was sitting in the park while Harry was playing. He plays quite nicely by himself. He's used to it, I guess. Anyway, Victoria sat down beside me, we got chatting and when she found out that it was just me and Harry she told me that if I ever needed anything, anything at all, to let her know.'

'And did you?' Frankie asked. 'Did you ever ask her for help?'

Gina went quiet and chewed on her bottom lip as if she was considering how honest to be. Frankie just looked at her, as kindly as she could, knowing that if she pushed her, she would close up like a dandelion at night.

'No,' said Gina, eventually. 'Not really.'

'Okay,' said Frankie, thinking about her next move.

Gina looked down at her toes as her heel shook up and down. 'We should probably get going.'

'But you haven't finished your tea.'

Gina picked the mug up and her hand was shaking.

'Is there something you're not telling me, Gina?'

'Of course not,' Gina tried to steady the mug with her other hand.

There was nothing else for it, Frankie was going to have to bulldoze in and just ask her. 'Did she give you some money, Gina?'

'What? Where did you...? How did you... how did you know?' she crumpled her shoulders and brought her knees up to her chest.

'I saw it on her calendar.' Then Frankie told a white lie. 'When we were at the party.'

'Oh shit,' said Gina. 'So, other people might have seen it too. The police might have seen it... they are going to think that I...'

'Did you?'

'Of course not,' shouted Gina, and the footsteps upstairs stopped abruptly. 'Of course not,' she repeated in a whisper. 'But people might jump to that conclusion.'

'So, what was the money for?' Frankie asked.

Gina sighed. 'There's just so much stuff... Kids need so much stuff,' she said, her eyes filling with tears showing Frankie just how much she must have struggled. 'I thought the baby years would be the most expensive but people buy you stuff, don't they? My parents bought me loads: a pram, a cot, a change table... and people buy you gifts like clothes and blankets, but it fizzles out and...'

'Your friends and family wouldn't help you out anymore?' Frankie asked.

'It's not that they wouldn't. I didn't like to ask. I wanted them to think I was capable, that I could do it on my own and I didn't need help. But uniform, and school bags and all that stuff adds up. Then Harry wanted to start drum lessons and...'

'Well, you can definitely say no to that one,' said Frankie. 'For the sake of your ears, if not your wallet.'

Gina smiled.

'But I know what you mean,' said Frankie. 'It's a lot.'

'I feel like every penny I earn goes on Harry and, don't get me wrong, I love spending money on him but, well, I just wanted to treat myself for once.'

'Oh?'

'An old friend invited me on a spa weekend and it was just what I needed. It sounds silly, but I just really needed some time for myself, a reset and a catch-up with a friend, but it was so expensive... I happened to mention it in passing to Victoria one time – I think I must have bumped into her when the friend had just text me – and she... well, she insisted.'

'That was very generous of her,' said Frankie, with raised eyebrows.

'I know! And I was going to pay her back, but then...'

'She was murdered,' said Frankie.

'I know how it looks,' said Gina. 'But I wouldn't murder someone over five hundred quid. I mean, the spa weekend was nice and all that, but it wasn't worth killing for!'

Frankie nodded. 'I believe you,' she said.

And she did.

28

———

JANE

'You're out with that lot *again?*' Ben asked, as Jane ran him through the dinner instructions.

'Yes, is that okay with you?' Her tone was sarcastic. 'And technically, last night I was *in* with them!' The investigation had given her confidence. A sense that she had the right to do things for herself. To not feel guilty if she had a social engagement that left Ben looking after their daughter. Looking after their daughter like she did whilst he was off having her dream career or going out with the boys.

If Ben had a night out, things just carried on as normal. But for Jane to go out, she had to tell him what to cook for dinner, organise or instruct him on any lifts to and from clubs and check that tomorrow's clothing was clean, dry and hanging in Lottie's room ready to put on in the morning.

She knew that his job was stressful and that it put food on the table; she also knew that it was her choice to take care of their child rather than following that path, but sometimes the mental load of being a mum was a lot to place on one woman's shoulders.

When they had first talked about starting a family, Ben had

been really good about it and said that it was entirely her choice. When it came to deciding what to do about work, he had always been on board with whatever she decided, and she was grateful for that, but this never seems to be a choice that men have to make. It is just assumed that they will go out to work, whereas a woman has to decide whether she wants to keep her career, and if she does, how to balance that career with her children.

Jane had appreciated the opportunity to choose, but she also slightly resented the fact that men completely avoided the guilt that came with whichever choice she made.

Jane had decided that having two parents in the police force; working shifts and putting themselves in harm's way on a daily basis was not what she wanted for her child, but that didn't stop the guilt. Whatever a mum decides, there is guilt. Guilt at working; guilt at not working; guilt at spending less time with the children; guilt at not being able to provide them with as much; guilt at not inspiring your child into believing that they can be whatever they want to be and guilt at the insinuation that being *just a mum* is not enough.

She wondered if Ben ever felt any guilt.

Jane had always known that whatever she chose to do, there would be guilt, but what she hadn't been prepared for was that there was never an acknowledgement that she had missed out on her own career. The assumption that she was fine with it, and the fact that her wanting children somehow justified this assumption, niggled away at her. Eventually it had led to resentment and generally feeling a little bit stale.

That was exactly how Jane felt, stale, like an old slice of bread, but The Jam Sandwich Detectives had given her a new lease of life and she refused to be the stale bread that let them down. The excitement and fun that she had unknowingly been craving, had been met by hanging out with Rachel and Frankie.

So, yes she was off out with them *again* and no, she was not about to start apologising for it.

'No problem,' said a defeated Ben. 'Well, erm, have fun.'

Jane smiled, she could tell he knew that there was no point in arguing and that if he did attempt it, he wouldn't win. 'I will,' she said.

<hr>

As Rachel poured three large glasses of wine, Jane wasn't sure that her head could take another night of drinking.

Just one glass, she thought initially, but before long Rachel was topping up all three glasses again.

With the small talk out of the way, Rachel launched in, 'So, lots to catch up on. Who wants to go first?'

Jane looked at Frankie, and before either of them had time to speak...

'Fine, I will,' said Rachel, and dived straight in. 'Well, Greg's story checks out. He reckons he's her gardener and sure enough her bushes have been trimmed. I checked. No sign of any *double entendre* there I'm afraid.'

'Gina's too,' said Frankie. 'Not the trimmed bushes part, but the story checking out! Seems like Victoria felt sorry for her so gave her some money. I think they kind of bonded over being single mothers, or something.'

Rachel sighed. 'This is no good. We are supposed to be leading the suspicion away from me, not proving everyone else is innocent so that I'm the only one left who could have done it.'

'Sorry,' said Frankie.

'Tell me you had more luck, Jane,' said Rachel. 'I've not had a chance to ask you what you were up to at Victoria's yesterday.'

Wasn't a woman allowed any secrets?

Jane nearly said, *I could ask you the same question, Rachel!*

but she took a deep breath and stopped herself. 'Well, I spoke to Ann at the Post Office and she confirmed that Beatrice is Victoria's sister,' said Jane. 'And not only that, but Victoria used to write to her nearly every week until recently when she stopped, suddenly!'

Jane wasn't sure whether Ann had actually said suddenly, or whether she was just adding it in for dramatic effect, but she went with it.

'Interesting,' said Rachel.

'So, you think someone killed her sister too?' said Frankie, with wide eyes.

'No,' said Jane. 'I think that maybe Beatrice had visited her, so Victoria hadn't needed to send a letter, and maybe while she was visiting…'

'She dropped some poison in her sister's favourite glass,' said Rachel with glee. 'That's brilliant, Jane. It all adds up.'

'Does it?' asked Frankie.

'It's pretty circumstantial,' said Jane. 'I have absolutely no evidence to back it up.'

'We can look for some,' said a newly enthused Rachel.

'That's why I was poking around,' said Jane. 'I was trying to see if there was any evidence of a recent visitor, but then that bloody cat put the wind up us and we scarpered.'

Rachel laughed. 'God, I hope no one saw us legging it from the crime scene.'

'Gosh, me too,' said Jane. 'I hadn't even thought of that.' A sudden bolt of panic shot across her chest. Jane wondered if this was how Rachel had been feeling ever since this whole thing happened.

'I'm sure we'd have heard on the playground grapevine or seen on some mum's Instagram account if you had been caught red-handed,' said Frankie. 'But maybe we should learn from this and start being a bit more careful.'

'Agreed,' said Rachel.

'I second that.' Jane nodded.

'So, what now?' asked Frankie.

'I think we need to go through everything we've got so far, think about it logically, think like proper detectives,' said Rachel. She took a large slurp of wine. 'But I think I've had too much to drink right now, so it might have to wait until the morning.'

The ladies agreed and Jane suggested that they meet up after the school run in the morning.

'I've got an old pinboard,' said Frankie. 'We can stick up mug shots and pin on bits of string to connect the dots.'

Rachel laughed. 'Sure, if you think it will help.'

'I think it's essential.'

Jane smiled. 'I think there's an old whiteboard in our playroom, you know on an easel... that might be good too.'

'Excellent,' said Rachel. 'Thanks, girls... I knew I could count on you both.'

Jane smiled. She was one of the girls and Rachel could count on her.

29

RACHEL

Rachel opened the front door, flicked off her trainers and saw Charlie's school shoes sitting neatly on the top of the shoe rack. This was strange because firstly, they were never where they should be. They were usually upside down on the floor in the kitchen, or shoved under the console table in the hall, in fact often they weren't even in the same room as each other, and secondly, Charlie was at school. Rachel had just got back from taking him.

'Shit!'

'What's up?' asked Frankie, as she followed her through the door.

'Charlie's school shoes... he walked to school in his wellies and I forgot to take them with me.'

'Don't worry.' Frankie smiled. 'It's PE today, so he doesn't need them.'

'Double shit,' said Rachel. 'He's in his uniform... I totally forgot it was PE.'

'Oh,' said Frankie.

'I'd better run his PE kit in,' said Rachel. 'He won't be impressed if he has to do it in his vest and pants.'

'I'm pretty sure they don't do that anymore. There'd be uproar.'

'Still, I'd better pop it in. I'm really sorry. Are you okay to stay here in case Jane arrives? She said she just had to pop home for something.'

'Sure,' said Frankie. 'Shall I get the boards set up?' She grinned and shimmied the old corkboard that she was holding.

'Yes, great,' said Rachel. 'Jane dropped the whiteboard round first thing... it's in the lounge.' She gestured towards the doorway. 'Help yourself.'

Rachel ran upstairs and frantically hunted for Charlie's PE kit, hoping and praying that it was clean. Or that it smelt clean at least.

'See you in a bit,' she said, as she ran back downstairs and started putting her shoes on.

'Have you got his trainers?' asked Frankie.

'Shit! No.' Rachel rolled her eyes at herself. 'What would I do without you?'

She grabbed the trainers and started running to school. PE was normally first thing and she knew Charlie would throw a paddy as soon as he realised he was in the wrong attire. Her running soon slowed to a jog, which slowed to a hobble, then a limp. It may be her married name, but she was most definitely a Walker not a Runner. The *Couch to 5K* app still sat downloaded, but unused, on the home screen of her mobile phone. A gentle reminder of the exercise she could be doing. The other thing that she should add to her daily to-do list.

She hobbled into the school entrance just as the receptionist was picking up the phone, apparently to dial her number. 'Oh, thank goodness, Mrs Walker, Charlie has been a bit upset.'

'Mummy!' yelled Charlie, from the comfy chair in the school foyer. His face quickly turned from delight to anger. 'Why didn't you put me in the right clothes, Mummy?'

'Sorry, dear, I just... Well I don't really know. I guess I just got muddled up,' said Rachel. 'But I'm here now, and I have the right clothes. Here.'

She held out the carrier bag towards Charlie. He took one look inside and then pulled out a white T-shirt. He held it up in front of him. It was clearly too big and had a slight frill on the sleeves.

'This is Megan's!' he said in dismay.

'Is it?' asked Rachel. 'Well, I'm sure it will be fine.'

'It's for a girl.' He frowned.

'C'mon, Charlie,' said Rachel. 'There's no such thing as a girl's T-shirt. Boys and girls can wear whatever they want.'

'Well, I don't want to wear this.'

'Leave it with me,' said the receptionist, clearly wanting to get rid of the erratic mother from her own list of things to deal with. 'I'll sort something out.'

'Thank you,' said Rachel. 'And sorry I–'

'You don't have to explain,' said the receptionist, pressing the button to release the door lock. 'I know you have a lot on your mind.'

Bloody great, thought Rachel, as the reason she was being ushered out of the door as quickly as possible suddenly became crystal clear. Of course, why wouldn't the school secretary know she'd been questioned for murder? The playground gossip had obviously spilled in through the front door of the school. She needed to get this thing wrapped up and sorted as soon as possible, before she was banned from the playground altogether.

Although on second thoughts, a few weeks off from the school run would be bliss.

As she walked home, as quickly as possible, occasionally looking up from her screen full of mournful posts from Natasha or sweeping accusations in the mum-chats, she spotted Jane crossing the road ahead of her.

'Wait up, Jane,' she called.

'Oh, Rachel,' said Jane, a little flustered, but still looking flawless. 'I thought you'd be at home already, I was just on my way.'

'I had to pop back to school. PE kit mix-up. Don't ask!'

'Easily done,' said Jane kindly, although Rachel doubted that Jane had ever made such a basic mistake in her entire parenting career.

'Where have you been?' asked Rachel, realising that Jane wasn't coming from the direction of her house. 'I thought you had to pop home.'

'Oh, er, not home,' said Jane. 'I had to pop to the shop... I just thought we might need a little treat to get us through.' She grinned and held up a pack of Jammie Dodgers. 'Sorry they're not homemade, I just haven't had a spare moment.'

'Who *makes* Jammie Dodgers?' laughed Rachel, but felt bad about it when Jane blushed, so moved on swiftly. 'This investigation is not doing a lot for my waistline.'

'Best to build up the reserves, just in case,' joked Jane, and Rachel's face dropped.

'In case what?'

'Oh, sorry. It was a joke, I didn't mean, I just meant...'

'In case I go to prison?' asked Rachel, her stomach clenching.

Jane looked at the floor. 'Forget I said anything.'

Rachel could feel herself turning red as the anger boiled up inside her, but she didn't want an argument. 'I'm not going to prison,' she said firmly. 'I didn't do it.'

'I know,' said Jane, blushing again, but this time Rachel didn't feel bad about it. 'Sorry.'

Rachel released a long, slow, puff of air. 'It's fine,' she said. 'Just help me prove my innocence and I will forget your silly joke.'

'Deal,' said Jane, with an apologetic smile.

They walked the rest of the way to Rachel's house in a tense, awkward silence.

As they arrived at the front door, Jane put her hand on Rachel's arm and said a very sincere, 'Sorry.'

Rachel smiled. 'It's already forgotten.' She put her key in the lock and opened the modern front door. It didn't really go with the house, but Rachel had really wanted it, despite Phil's reservations. As they walked into the lounge both of their jaws dropped. Frankie was in full-on investigation mode. She had mug shots of everyone at the Bake Off party pinned to the corkboard, with red string connecting them to various bits of paper and pictures that were pinned all over the rest of the board. She also had a list of notes bullet-pointed on the whiteboard and a file labelled *Evidence* in thick marker was propped up next to it.

'Wow,' said Rachel. 'Hercule Poirot is in the building.'

Frankie smiled. 'Just a little something I put together.'

'I love it,' said Rachel.

'Yes,' said Jane, with her eyebrows raised. 'It's wonderful. We'll be sure to catch the killer now.'

Rachel shot her a look. She hoped that wasn't a hint of sarcasm, because, in her humble opinion, this was bloody brilliant, and Frankie was an absolute genius!

30

FRANKIE

'So,' Frankie began, as she took them through her suspects' board. 'There were seven people at the Bake Off party…'

'Well, eight technically,' said Jane. 'I mean, it started with eight.'

The three ladies went quiet until Frankie broke the uncomfortable silence.

'Yes,' said Frankie. 'Good point.' She paused and took a deep breath. 'So, there were *eight* people at the Bake Off party…'

'Rocking party!' smirked Rachel.

'*Eventful* party,' said Jane, and they both nodded.

Frankie ignored their comments and pointed at the whiteboard, like a teacher carrying on with a lesson while the children at the back giggled amongst themselves. 'These are the seven *remaining* people and therefore the seven suspects. I have also added Beatrice as she probably has a key, you know being Victoria's sister and all, so in theory she could have slipped in and poisoned the glass. We now know that the glass was poisoned so it must have been someone at the party or someone who had access to the glasses beforehand.'

'Does anyone else have a key?' asked Rachel.

'Not that we know of, but that is something we should probably look into.' She glanced around expectantly.

'I can do that,' said Jane.

'Great,' said Frankie, not sure why she suddenly seemed to be in control.

'Would her ex-husband still have a key?' asked Rachel.

'I doubt it,' said Jane. 'From what I hear he is *very* ex, as in expat. Lives in France. They barely hear from him. I don't know if her daughter even sees him.'

'Ahh, yes,' said Rachel. 'What about her daughter?'

'Yeah, she must have a key,' agreed Jane. 'I'll try and track her down, and she might know if anyone else has one too.'

'Great, so unless we can find anyone else with a key we have our eight suspects... Well, nine, I suppose, if you count the daughter.' Frankie tapped her pen against the whiteboard.

'Grace wouldn't kill her mum,' said Jane.

'We can't rule anyone out at this stage,' said Frankie, as she added a square to the whiteboard next to the photos, drew a girl's face and wrote *Grace – daughter* underneath.

'Except me and you,' said Rachel. 'That takes us down to seven.'

'Well, yes,' said Frankie, 'but I'm leaving us up there for now because well, I don't want to mess up the board!'

'Where did you get all the photos from?' There was always that one kid in class who asked irrelevant questions and made the lessons go off on pointless tangents. Here, that kid was Rachel.

'Facebook.'

'Okay, explains why Sarah's holding a cocktail and Greg is dressed as a sausage roll.'

'Yeah, a couple of them didn't have much of a selection...

Natasha on the other hand; I had about three-million photos to choose from.'

'Anyway,' said Jane. 'Shall we crack on? I'm getting my nails done at twelve.'

'Yes, sure sorry,' stuttered Frankie, sensing Jane's impatience. 'I'll go through each suspect and let's recap what we know.'

The other two nodded in agreement.

'Natasha.'

'She got very defensive when we spoke to her,' said Jane. 'And she has been really hamming up the mourning, but I'm not really sure what her motive would be.'

'Okay,' said Frankie. 'Needs looking into. Do you want to give that a go, Rach?'

'Sure, as I missed out on all the fun last time!'

'Okay, great. Debbie next,' said Frankie. 'She knew about Victoria's dodgy bookkeeping but why would that make her want to kill her? The other way round would be more likely!'

'Maybe, that's it,' said Rachel. 'Maybe she was worried that Victoria would do her in, so got in there first.'

'Maybe.' Frankie tapped her chin. 'But she was so helpful in giving us those receipts that I just can't see it.'

'I agree,' said Jane.

'Okay, let's park her for now. Gina.'

'Poor Gina,' said Rachel. 'I can see why Victoria felt sorry for her.'

'Yeah,' agreed Frankie. 'She seems to be the one person Victoria was actually nice to, so I think we can safely rule her out.'

The others nod.

'Greg next.'

'His story checks out,' said Rachel. 'I don't think he was

having it off with Victoria. Plus, if he was, why would he kill her?'

'Maybe she was going to tell his wife?' said Jane.

'Good point,' agreed Frankie.

'But, I really don't think he was copping off with her,' said Rachel. 'He's not the type, plus have you seen his wife? She's an absolute stunner.'

'That doesn't mean anything,' said Jane.

Frankie sighed.

'Bloody men,' said Rachel. 'I know they can be a pain in the arse, but we can't keep Greg on the list just because he's a man.'

'Let's move on,' said Frankie, eager to stay on track. 'Sarah is next. We haven't really talked about her have we?'

'No,' the others agreed.

'She's slipped under the net... maybe she's been keeping a low profile on purpose.' Frankie tried to think back to the party. 'She was flirting with Greg, if I remember rightly.'

'No surprises there,' said Rachel.

'She does have a bit of a reputation,' agreed Jane.

'She was pissed on Prosecco,' said Rachel. 'Probably too pissed to murder anyone, if I'm honest.'

'Would be worth having a chat with her though,' said Frankie. 'See if she remembers anything.'

'Unlikely,' laughed Rachel.

Frankie smiled. 'I'll speak to her anyway. Just in case.' She paused, scanning the board. 'So, that just leaves Beatrice, the elusive sister. How are we going to track her down?'

'I could see if Grace will give me her address,' said Jane. 'Although, I'll need to get hold of Grace first.'

Rachel nodded. 'Go easy with Grace,' she said, and Frankie got a sudden knot in her stomach. *These were actual people, dealing with real grief.*

'Of course,' said Jane.

'Or maybe Ann would give you her address,' said Rachel. 'You said Victoria took in a letter every week. Maybe she can remember the address. I mean, I can't remember what I had for breakfast but you never know.'

'No harm in asking,' said Jane. 'She said the letters had little bees drawn on the envelope so they've obviously stuck in her mind.'

'Bees?' asked Frankie.

'Bee for Beatrice I presume.'

'Cute,' said Frankie, as she drew another square and in it doodled a picture of a bee. She wrote *Beatrice – sister* underneath. 'Just don't go getting Ann into trouble for giving out people's private informa...' She trailed off as a thought buzzed into her mind. 'Bee, bee, bee,' she muttered to herself.

'Are you okay, Frankie?' asked Rachel.

'Yeah, I'm just trying to remember something, I've seen something to do with a bee, I just can't... hang on.' She picked up the folder marked *evidence* and started flicking through the plastic wallets.

'Here,' she announced, showing them both a receipt.

'Key-cutting,' read Rachel. 'And...'

'A bee keyring!' Frankie's eyes lit up. 'Maybe she got a spare key cut and put it on a bee keyring.'

'For Bee,' said Jane.

'Exactly,' said Frankie.

31

JANE

Jane had bees on the brain, so when Flik, her nail technician, asked her if she'd like any nail art, she said, 'Could I have a bumble bee please?'

Flik let out a little gasp and then said in an exaggerated whisper. 'I did some bees a while back for a lady, and I just found out yesterday that now she's dead. Murdered they reckon!'

'Gosh!' said Jane. 'How awful!'

'Little daisies and a bee on a couple of nails...' said Flik snapping back into her happy nail tech voice. 'How does that sound?'

'It sounds perfect,' said Jane, realising that this random connection may prove to be very helpful. *Beauticians and hairdressers always know all the gossip.* 'Do you remember anything about her, the lady with the bees?'

'Urm, oh yes, I do actually.' She tapped the nail file on her chin. 'Her name was a cake I think... Battenberg? Bakewell... no, hang on, was it Sandwich?'

'Victoria Sandwich?' Jane smiled.

'Yes, that's it! How could I forget? What a great name.'

'I thought it might have been.'

'Oh, do you know her?'

Jane nodded. 'I knew her, yes.'

'What a small world,' said Flik.

She is literally from the next village, thought Jane, but she nodded.

Flik added, 'I am so sorry for your loss.'

Jane smiled and feigned a little tear.

Flik stopped and held Jane's hand between both of hers. 'I see why you asked for bees now,' she said. 'What a special way to remember her.'

Jane sniffed away the tears that weren't really coming, not sure why she was faking such distress. She wondered if she would get a more honest answer to her next question if Flik thought she was grieving. She smiled to herself. She was getting good at this detective lark.

'Any idea why she chose bees?' Jane asked. 'I knew she liked them but...'

'Hmm, not sure, something to do with her fella I think. It usually is,' Flik laughed.

'She didn't have a fella,' said Jane.

'That you know of,' said Flik, with a wink.

'Good point.' Jane made a mental note to add that to the whiteboard as a possibility.

'You still want to go with bees?' asked Flik, as she located some yellow and black bottles of polish from the shelf. 'It won't upset you too much?'

'Yes please,' said Jane. 'My fella and I love bees.' This wasn't even a lie. 'We met in Manchester.'

'Oh.' Flik smiled, looking confused.

'The bee is the symbol of Manchester.'

'Is it really? Well, who knew? Every day's a school day.'

Jane smiled and wondered if Flik knew that she shared her

name with another six-legged bug. A Disney Pixar bug no less. She decided not to mention it.

'Her sister is called Bee too,' said Jane.

'Whose sister?'

'Victoria's.'

'Oh right, is she?' said Flik. 'Ahh, maybe it was that then, I can't remember to be honest.' She paused, looking pensive. 'Well, I know who got the raw end of the name deal, don't you? I would much rather have a Victoria Sandwich than a Bee Sandwich!'

Jane laughed, and nodded. She really needed to speak to Bee. Bee could be the key to this whole thing. Maybe there was a secret fortune that she was set to inherit, or a family feud that meant she wanted her sister dead. Sibling rivalry is very common, it definitely needed delving into.

'They look beautiful,' said Jane, when Flik had finished fancifying her nails.

'I'm glad you like them. Now buzz off,' said Flik, and Jane's face dropped. 'Y'know, because of the bees.'

'Oh yes, of course.' Jane blushed.

'Sorry,' said Flik, who blushed too. 'Not the time for making jokes.'

'I disagree,' said Jane. 'We have to laugh, otherwise...' She didn't finish her sentence, but she didn't have to.

When Jane got home she made herself a cuppa and then got Facebook up on her phone.

She went to Victoria's page and scrolled through her *friends* until she found Grace. *Poor girl,* she thought. *What a lot to deal with at such a young age.* She clicked on her profile and hit the blue *message* button.

She started typing.

Grace, I don't know if you remember me. I'm one of your mum's friends from the village. I am so sorry for your loss. If there is anything that I can do, please let me know. Jane x

She ummed and ahhed about the kiss for ages before sending the message. Once she finally pressed send, she went to put her phone down but noticed the three little dots that meant that Grace was already typing a reply.

Thank you, Jane
    I appreciate you reaching out. You are the only person from back home that has.
    I know Mum sometimes rubbed people up the wrong way, but she didn't deserve this.
    ...

She was still typing. Should Jane reply or wait for her to finish? She waited patiently.

I'm coming home tomorrow. I couldn't face it straight away.

Jane typed in reply:

Well, just message me if I can help in any way. I could pop you some dinner round.

Grace responded:

Thank you, That would be nice. Auntie Bee is coming too, but I will be in touch if we need any other help.

Auntie Bee!

So, they definitely do call her Bee, thought Jane. *Perfect.* She replied with just an *x*. She didn't have to think for quite as long about that one. It just felt right. She would pop round with a meal – a casserole – and maybe some flowers. Then she could hopefully have a chat with them both. Rachel will be pleased. This could be the breakthrough that they need.

Jane opened up The Jam Sandwich Detectives chat and sent the other ladies two emojis: a bee and a magnifying glass.

> Rachel (Megan's mum): What's with the cryptic message?

> Jane (Lottie's mum): You will find out soon enough. 🕵️

> Frankie (Billy's mum): Oooh, I love all the mystery.

> Rachel (Megan's mum): Wish I could say the same... hope it's something useful.

Jane knew that Rachel was getting stressed about the whole thing, and she only wanted her to be happy, she did *not* want to give her more to worry about. That being said, she also wanted to make sure she had something useful – something that would help clear Rachel's name – before she got her hopes up, so she kept her cards close to her chest.

> Jane (Lottie's mum): I think you will be pleased.

Jane hoped she was right, and replied with a photo of her nails.

> Jane (Lottie's mum): Getting into the spirit of things!

> Frankie (Billy's mum): Wow, Jane. They look
> great!

Jane smiled and wondered if she should add the image to her Instagram.

She waited, but Rachel didn't respond.

She's got a lot on her mind, Jane told herself. Once she updated her about Bee, she would be really pleased and Jane would be well and truly in the good books. She really hoped that Bee would prove to be the key to all of this, but she needed to tread carefully. Bee would be grieving, and grief was a difficult thing, even if you were grieving for someone as bloody awful as Victoria Sandwich.

32

RACHEL

Rachel couldn't stop thinking about the bee keyring. She had seen one somewhere recently, but she couldn't for the life of her think where.

Did Natasha have one? They always called her the Queen Bee of the playground. But a bee was a bit quaint for Natasha, wasn't it? She probably had a flippin' Gucci keyring adorning the keys to her house and Mercedes. Surely the one that Victoria bought must have been for Beatrice, the sister. It made complete sense. She just hoped that Jane could get hold of her. Her recent coded emoji message indicated that maybe she was onto something, and had that area covered.

Fingers crossed.

Bee-adorned fingers, no less. What was Jane like? Fancy getting their main clue painted on her nails!

In the meantime though, Natasha was Rachel's project. She needed to find out whether she had any sort of motive and it occurred to her that the best way to ascertain this might be to make a beeline for one of her minions. Pun intended. She needed to bypass the Queen Bee and head for the worker bees.

As if on cue Amy and Beth chattered their way onto the playground.

After a prolonged goodbye between each of the designer-Lycra-clad mums and their children – like they were sending them off to war or on a year-long trip around the world rather than to a normal day at school – their kids went in and the two mums relaxed. They were no longer in 'heightened mum' mode, but still very much in 'on show in front of the other mums, must look busy and important but also on top of things' mode.

Rachel was certainly not on top of things, but the investigation was important so she breezed on over to Amy and Beth, hoping that the conversation would not be too awkward.

'Morning, ladies,' said Rachel, as they gave her a confused look. 'I wondered if I could have a quick chat.'

'We're off on a run,' said Amy. 'Things to do after that, so we haven't really got time, I'm afraid.'

'It's kind of important,' said Rachel.

'You can come with us if you like,' said Beth, and Amy scowled at her.

'Erm, I'm not really dressed for a run.' Rachel looked down at her old leggings, battered Converse and baggy T-shirt and realised that this was about as sporty as her wardrobe got.

'You'll be fine in that,' said Beth. 'You've got to start somewhere and we always start off slow.'

'Okay,' said Rachel. 'If you're sure.'

'We're sure.' Beth and Rachel both looked at Amy, who didn't look very sure at all.

'Fine,' she said eventually. 'Let's go. We walk for a bit anyway to warm up.'

The three women walked out of the playground together and Rachel caught Jane's eye as she went. Jane's eyebrows were well and truly raised and Rachel shot her a sly wink. She then passed Frankie who was trotting along, perfecting the definitely not late, just perfectly timed walk that Rachel had never mastered. She waved at Rachel but was apparently too focused on getting Billy to school to even notice anything weird about who Rachel was with.

'So, what do you want to talk about?' asked Beth.

'Does Natasha have a bee keyring on her keys?'

'What?'

'I thought you said it was important,' said Amy.

'It is,' said Rachel. 'Does she?'

'I don't know,' said Beth. 'I've never really studied her keys.'

'Amy?'

'I don't remember seeing a bee. What has this got to do with, well, anything?'

Rachel ignored the question. 'Did Natasha have any beef with Victoria at all?'

Amy stopped. 'Are you kidding, Rachel? Why are you asking about Victoria?'

'C'mon, Amy,' said Beth. 'Keep moving.'

Amy started walking again and Rachel said, 'I'm trying to clear my name.'

'I suggest you leave the investigating to the police,' said Amy.

'I will, I mean I am, I'm just trying to help.'

Beth looked at her with pity, then her watch beeped. 'Warm up over,' she said. 'Time to start a gentle jog.'

The first thing Rachel realised as she started running was that a sports bra would have been a welcome addition to her outfit. She had one tucked at the back of a drawer somewhere, but it was too late for that.

'You can't just accuse Natasha, to shift the blame from you,' said Amy.

'I'm not,' said Rachel, already struggling to talk. 'I'm just trying to cover all bases.'

There was a brief pause in the conversation as Amy and Beth got into a rhythm with their strides and Rachel just tried her hardest to keep up.

'They were friends,' said Amy, after an outward puff of air.

'Yeah,' agreed Beth. 'Apart from the photo incident they've always got on.' Then she squealed, 'Ow!' Amy removed the elbow she had dug into Beth's side.

'Photo incident?'

'Oh,' said Beth. 'I thought everyone knew.'

'You can talk to me openly,' panted Rachel. 'I'm not the police. I'm just a mum... a very unfit mum.'

Beth glanced at Amy for reassurance as to whether she should say any more and Amy shrugged. She took a long puff out and Rachel wasn't sure whether it was to help with the running or prepare herself for a big announcement. Maybe a bit of both.

'There was this night out a while back,' said Beth eventually. 'Natasha was drunk.'

'That's an understatement,' Amy chimed in.

'Hammered,' said Beth. 'And Victoria was taking photos. Everyone was just posing, y'know, messing about.'

Rachel nodded and tried to breathe as quietly as she could, when in actual fact she wanted to puff and gasp for air. She had no idea how Beth could just chat away and run at the same time. Presumably that's what happened if you ran regularly and like, got fit.

'And then the next day, Victoria sends this one group photo to our chat.'

'The Yummy Mummies?' asked Rachel.

'Yes,' said Beth. 'How did you...?'

'Jane.' Rachel virtually panted the word out. Jane might think she is a woman of mystery but Rachel had seen her phone screen light up with the words *Yummy Mummies* on more than one occasion. She glanced round to check that there was no one around to witness her attempt at running. Why was it that the other two still looked pristine, whereas Rachel looked like she had just run a marathon, not jogged a few hundred metres?

'Oh right, well, yes,' Beth continued. 'So, she sends this photo and Natasha replies straight away saying, "delete that now", but Victoria didn't delete it... she posted it on Instagram!'

Rachel faked a gasp.

'That's why she's not on the Yummy Mummies chat anymore,' Amy chimed in.

'I see,' panted Rachel.

'Well, that and now, y'know, the whole being dead thing.'

Beth shook her head at Amy. 'Anyway, not only did she post it on Instagram, but she also tagged everyone in it, including Natasha, and, well... Natasha has fifty-thousand followers!'

'So I hear,' said Rachel.

'So, everyone saw it, and...'

'I didn't see it,' said Rachel.

'Well, fifty-thousand people saw it and well, Natasha was not happy.'

'That's putting it lightly,' said Amy.

'She was severely pissed off?' suggested Rachel.

'She was livid,' said Amy.

'What was so bad about the photo?'

'Well,' began Beth, but Amy finished for her. 'Natasha just looked really drunk. Y'know, mascara down her cheeks, wine down her dress.'

'Not the best image for a fashionista on Instagram,' puffed Rachel, not sure how much longer she could keep running.

'Exactly,' said Amy.

'Yes,' said Beth, although Rachel got the feeling that there was something she wasn't telling her.

She opened her mouth to ask what it was but the words

weren't coming. She was well and truly out of breath. She stopped and put her hands on her knees.

'That's me done,' she said, wiping sweat from her forehead. 'You ladies carry on. Thank you, you have been very helpful.'

They both turned and jogged backwards as they finished the conversation with a crumpled and knackered Rachel.

'Any time,' said Amy.

'Same time next week?' said Beth, and Rachel laughed.

Who knew becoming a detective would involve so much bloody running?!

33

———

FRANKIE

Frankie wasn't sure how she was going to strike up a conversation with Sarah. She barely knew her.

Earlier she'd seen Rachel tagging along with Amy and Beth to quiz them but Frankie didn't have the confidence to just start talking to someone out of the blue. She had bottled it on the playground because Sarah had been with a group of mums, whispering and looking over their shoulders. Not the easiest place to intercept her.

The playdate with Gina had been daunting and she didn't want to put herself through that anxiety again. She thought about sending Sarah a private message, she was on the mum-chat after all, but would that seem a bit creepy? Or invasive? Or was she overthinking this? Probably.

Her overthinking led Frankie to loiter outside the school gates, then follow Sarah to the village shop. She had to dart behind a wheelie bin at one point when Sarah looked back over her shoulder because Frankie had trodden on a twig. Obviously this was far less creepy.

She went back and forth, both in her mind and along the shelves of the shop, hoping that she looked like she was actually shopping and not just following someone. She needed to buy something. She scanned the shelves for something more appetising than what she had at home for lunch. Her brain was far too full of suspects, and theories, and how to approach Sarah to think up an interesting meal, so she grabbed the first vaguely appealing thing that she saw.

As she turned the corner of the aisle she walked straight into Sarah. Honestly, what were the chances? Conscious that all she was holding was a tin of spaghetti hoops, she felt the sudden need to explain, which in this case was another word for *lie*.

'For Billy,' she said, waggling the tin. 'He loves these.'

Sarah smiled a knowing smile. 'Oh yes,' she winked. 'Mia loves them too.'

Frankie felt herself blush. 'She's just started Reception too, hasn't she?' she asked, knowing full well that Sarah's daughter had, but trying to sound as natural and blasé as possible.

'She has. How is Billy getting on?'

'Good, I think, I mean he doesn't tell me much but...'

'They never do!'

Frankie smiled and wondered what her next move should be. Sarah looked at her watch. She needed to think of something, quick, but then Sarah said, 'Hey, I'm free for the next hour or so if you fancy grabbing a coffee?'

'Sure,' said Frankie. Well, that was easy! The spaghetti hoops would have to wait.

'How did you feel after the Bake Off party?' They only had an hour and Frankie knew that she couldn't skirt around the topic forever.

Sarah took a sip of her coffee and glanced around the coffee shop to check no one was listening. The coffee shop was owned by Trace, one of the school mums, and she was a gossip!

'Bloody hell,' said Sarah. 'What a drama! Still can't really believe that it actually happened.'

'Yeah, I know what you mean,' said Frankie, although she believed it all right. Her, Rachel and Jane had been living the ins and outs of it ever since.

'I mean, who the bloody hell would kill Victoria? Don't get me wrong, I know she's a pain in the arse but, killing her is a bit O-T-T, isn't it?' Sarah said it how it was, or at least how it seemed from the outside. But The Jam Sandwich Detectives had started looking more closely, and were beginning to realise that things weren't always as they seemed.

Frankie was learning to be less trustful, and that meant digging a little deeper with Sarah, despite her seemingly obvious innocence.

'You were getting pretty friendly with Greg at the party, weren't you?'

'Don't you bloody start,' said Sarah. 'We don't all have youth on our side like you, Frankie. Some of us have to take our flirting where we can get it... and a PTA Bake Off party is the closest thing I've got to a social life, I'm afraid!'

Frankie raised one eyebrow.

'I was only having a laugh,' added Sarah.

Frankie held her hands up. 'Hey, I'm not disputing that, and I'm definitely not judging. I was only wondering because, well, do you think there's anything iffy about him?'

'Greg?'

'Yes!'

'Don't be so bloody ridiculous, he's as strait-laced as they come. Kind, considerate, he's always doing odd jobs for people...' Sarah paused briefly. 'Yeah, he's definitely a helper, not a murderer.'

'It's the odd jobs I'm thinking about,' said Frankie with a raised eyebrow.

'Give over.' Sarah laughed. 'You are barking up completely the wrong tree there.'

'So, you don't think there was something going on between him and Victoria?'

Sarah laughed so loudly that Frankie scanned the coffee shop to check everyone wasn't staring at them, and it turned out they were getting a few funny looks so Frankie lowered her voice. 'I'll take that as a no.'

'Listen,' said Sarah. 'Greg likes a bit of fun, just like me. We both mess around a bit and sometimes get a bit flirty after one too many grape juices, but that's as far as it goes. Now, unfortunately, the same can't be said for all the school parents. There are definitely a few people dipping their toes in other people's fountains if you catch my drift.'

'So, you think Victoria was, y'know, at it with someone else's husband?'

Sarah held her hands up. 'Hey, I am not about to start any rumours about a dead woman, but yes... absolutely!'

Frankie flopped onto the sofa as soon as she got home, not really sure what to do with this new information. She wasn't sure whether it helped or just added to the confusion. *Maybe that was Sarah's intention? Who even knew anymore?*

Her head was spinning, and all the new information going around and around made her feel dizzy. She picked up her notebook and as soon as she started to doodle, her jaw, her shoulders, and her whole body relaxed. She thought about what Sarah had said: *He's a helper not a murderer,* and she doodled a stick man, trimming hedges, baking cakes, making packed lunches, washing uniform, scheduling playdates... and then she decided that a woman must have murdered Victoria.

It had to have been someone who could multi-task.

The doorbell rang, snapping Frankie out of her dreamy doodle-daze and she thought about not answering it. She looked at the clock. There was only an hour until school pick-up and she hadn't even had any lunch yet. She looked longingly at the can of spaghetti hoops on the coffee table in front of her. She puffed some hair out of her face and reluctantly heaved herself up. She should really answer the door. It might be something important.

'Oh, it's only you,' she said, relieved, as she opened the door to see Rachel standing on the doorstep.

'Charming,' said Rachel. 'Can I come in?' She was already halfway through the door.

'Sure. I mean I'm very busy doing lots of very busy and important things, but I can probably spare a few minutes.'

Rachel laughed. 'Got anything to eat? I'm starving!'

'So, what's the goss?' asked Rachel, with a mouthful of spaghetti hoops.

'Not much really, apart from the fact that Victoria was most likely a bit of a floozy.'

'Interesting.' Rachel nodded as she chewed.

'Yeah, Sarah reckons she was having it off with someone's husband...'

'Very interesting!'

'But, I'm pretty sure that Sarah doesn't have anything to hide.'

'Well, that's helpful at least,' said Rachel. 'I didn't get much out of Natasha's tribe, except that there's a photo that caused some hoo-hah a while back. Apparently it was sent on that Yummy Mummy chat before all hell broke loose when it arrived on social media... I'll ask Jane if she remembers it.'

'Good idea,' said Frankie, mopping up the last of her hoop-juice with a slice of toast.

'Didn't get any further with the spare key or the bee keyring though,' said Rachel. 'I know I've seen one somewhere, I just can't for the life of me think where.'

'It'll come to you when you least expect it,' said Frankie. 'Now, talking of keys, I need to find mine. It's nearly that time. Goodbye peace and quiet, hello after-school chaos.'

'Gosh, yeah it is. Time flies when you're eating spaghetti hoops. Shall I stick the plates in the dishwasher?'

'Please,' called Frankie, as she threw cushions out of the way, lifted bags and books, and crawled around the floor looking under the furniture.

'They can't be far away,' said Rachel, scanning the room before wandering out to the hallway with their dirty plates. 'Where do you normally keep them, in this bowl?'

'Yeah,' called Frankie. 'Are they in there?'

'No!'

Where could they be? What did she do with them when she got back earlier? Frankie was starting to panic. 'What the hell have I done with them? We're gonna be late for the kids.'

'They will be here somewhere,' said Rachel, as she reappeared. 'You got in, didn't you? You must have used your key.'

'I guess so...'

'You need some key hooks on the wall like–'

Frankie rolled her eyes. Now was not the time to be lecturing her on how to not lose keys; they were already lost and she needed to find them, quickly.

'Oh my God, I know where I've seen them,' said Rachel.

'Where?' said Frankie, looking at her watch. 'C'mon, Rach, it's already twenty past.'

'Oh, sorry no, not your keys... the spare key and the bee keyring. I know exactly where I've seen them.' Rachel let herself fall back onto the couch, seemingly deep in thought, as Frankie sighed in frustration.

'Ow!' Something had dug into Rachel's bottom as she let herself sink into the cushions. 'What's that?' She produced the offending item from the depths of the sofa.

'My keys,' said Frankie. 'You found them, thank you, Rachel. Now come on, get up, no time for sitting around. We're going to be late!'

The two women scrambled out of the front door and dashed to school before they both got put on the naughty parent list.

***

Once they'd fought their way through the rabble of tired and grumpy kids and in-need-of-a-drink parents, and collected their darlings, Rachel asked, 'Are you free later? Friday drinks?'

'Um, it's Thursday!' said Frankie.

'Oh, shit, is it?'

Frankie laughed. 'Sounds like you need one. Amanda's away and it's a bit short notice for a sitter, so it'd have to be at mine...'

'I'll bring wine,' Rachel interjected before Frankie could think up any more reasons to say no. She was shattered and had been looking forward to an early night, which would never happen with Rachel and a bottle of wine involved, but it seemed like Rachel was keen to tell her what she'd remembered and Frankie didn't want to be the reason she forgot it again.

'Fine.' Frankie laughed. 'Ooh there's Jane.'

'I wouldn't...' Rachel started to say, but it was too late.

'Jane,' Frankie called. 'Drinks tonight?' Then she mouthed sorry at Rachel, who shrugged and wafted a hand.

'Can't tonight I'm afraid, ladies,' said Jane, winking and tapping her nose. Frankie thought she had a fly on her face at first. 'Busy, busy, hush, hush!'

'Right you are,' said Frankie. 'Looking forward to a catch-up soon.' Then in a lower tone just to Rachel, 'Very cloak and dagger.'

'She's a woman of mystery,' laughed Rachel.

'Sorry if you hadn't wanted me to invite her.' Frankie dug her teeth into her bottom lip.

'Oh, it's fine,' said Rachel. 'It's just... well, what I want to tell you, we can't risk everyone finding out, not until we've looked into it properly and well, I do think Jane is trustworthy, but...'

'You don't want all the Yummy Mummies finding out?'

'Ha!' said Rachel. 'Yeah, something like that.'

'Well, in that case it's a good thing she's busy. Do you want to pop over once the kids are in bed? Any time after seven-ish?'

'I'll be there at seven O-five. There's no way my two will be in bed, but Phil can deal with bedtime at the zoo tonight!'

34

———

JANE

Jane had made a casserole.

And some millionaire shortbread.

She rang the doorbell of Victoria's house and clung on tightly to the dish with her other hand, her arm wrapped around the front of it for both protection and warmth as she carefully balanced the Tupperware of sweet treats on top.

'Grace,' she said, as a tired face appeared at the open door. 'How are you? I've brought you a casserole.'

'Thank you, Jane,' said Grace, with a sad smile that made her eyes twinkle. 'That is kind of you.'

Jane smiled kindly at Grace and was momentarily lost for words. She was beautiful. She had her mother's piercing blue eyes but her beauty was more effortless than Victoria's. She looked fragile, and Jane tried to hold back the tears as she thought about what she must be going through.

Another face appeared behind Grace. It took Jane aback for a moment, because other than the longer, more wayward hair, she looked exactly like Victoria. Those same blue eyes were tinged with sadness. 'You must be Jane. Grace said you were coming. Hi, I'm Beatrice, Victoria's sister. Ooh, is that a casserole? How thoughtful. Much appreciated, thank you.' Beatrice took the dish. 'Come in, come in. Sorry, Grace is still in shock, understandably of course.'

'Of course,' said Jane, hoping that it would stop Beatrice's unnecessary rambling.

'Would you like a drink? Tea? Coffee? Something stronger?'

'Tea would be lovely, Beatrice, if you don't mind. Thank you,' said Jane.

'I'll make it,' said Grace, who seemed relieved to have a reason to escape.

'This must have been an unimaginably difficult week for you,' said Jane as Beatrice led her through to Victoria's living room. 'Please accept my condolences.'

'Thank you,' said Beatrice. 'Yes, it's not been easy. We're both still in shock. It didn't help that I was away at the time. I told Grace to stay at uni until I got back. I'm not sure she'd have coped well with coming back here alone.'

'I think you made the right call there,' said Jane, with her kindest smile. 'Had you seen your sister recently?'

'Yes, I had, which is something I suppose. I popped in just before I went away. She was getting ready for this Bake Off party. She seemed so excited about it. Little did she know it would be the death of her.' A single tear fell onto Beatrice's cheek and Jane quickly located a tissue in her handbag – she never left home without a pack of tissues – and handed it to her. 'If only I'd known what was going to happen at that party,' sniffed Beatrice. 'If I'd have stayed another day...'

'You can't blame yourself,' said Jane. 'There's no way you could have known.' She placed a hand on Beatrice's shoulder. 'And there's no way you could have done anything to stop it.'

Beatrice looked her straight in the eyes and Jane was hit again by the striking colour of them. 'How can you be so sure?'

Jane swallowed. She was unsure how much to say, but she

decided that it would be good to tell Beatrice that they'd been trying to help.

'We've been looking into it,' said Jane. 'To sort of, help out the police. We want to find out who did this and get justice for Victoria.'

Beatrice kept looking at her but didn't say a word.

'It looks like someone poisoned her glass, the one with her name on it. No one could have known,' said Jane. 'But it looks like someone did this deliberately. Have the police explained that to you?'

Beatrice took a deep breath. 'Yes, they have, but I... well, I couldn't quite believe it.'

'None of us could.'

'Thank you,' said Beatrice, after the briefest of silences. 'For trying. We appreciate your support, even more than we appreciate your casserole.' Jane smiled and Beatrice tried to. 'If there is anything I can do to help you, please just say.'

Jane thought for a moment. 'Do you know anyone who would have wanted to kill your sister?'

'Of course not,' said Beatrice.

Jane was about to ask about the letters, but Grace returned with a tray of tea.

'Sorry about that,' said Grace. 'Mum always made the tea so I had to remind myself where things were.' She set down the tray on the coffee table in the centre of the room and sat on one of the lounge chairs.

'Were you good friends with Mum?' asked Grace.

'Yes,' said Jane, with a pang of guilt about the little white lie. 'We got on well.' The truth was that they did get on well once upon a time, but as is often the case with village life, things can change quickly. 'I was absolutely devastated when I heard.'

'Oh, so you weren't there?' asked Beatrice. 'At the party?'

'No, it was for the new mums. Victoria was trying to get

them involved, drum up a bit of help. It always tends to be the same people who end up helping with the PTA events so it's good to get some new blood.'

The room fell silent. Jane wondered if perhaps that wasn't the best turn of phrase.

'Jane,' said Beatrice. 'I'm going to ask you what you asked me. Do you know anyone who would want to kill my sister?'

'No!' Another white lie. 'Absolutely not... But I intend to find out who did.'

'Thank you,' said Beatrice.

Grace smiled a timid smile, making her look even younger than her blossoming years. Jane felt the sudden urge to hug her but thought that might be overstepping the mark, so instead she simply smiled back.

'Well, I don't want to keep you,' said Jane. 'I'm sure you have lots to talk about. Thank you for the tea.'

She stood up and Beatrice showed her to the door.

Once they were out in the hallway Beatrice leaned in close to her and said in almost a whisper, 'I've got letters.'

'Oh?'

'Victoria used to write to me nearly every week.'

'How lovely,' said Jane, as she feigned surprise at this news.

'If her letters are anything to go by then I would say that she definitely upset a few people.'

'Really?' said Jane. She was heading into Oscar-winning territory now.

'I can send you them if you think it would help? The letters I mean. They might help you understand my sister and what was going on in her life.' Beatrice paused. 'I know I should send them to the police, but I think I'd feel better if someone who, you know...'

Her voice caught, so Jane helped her out. 'Knew her?'

'Yes, I think someone who knew her should read them first.'

'That would be extremely helpful,' said Jane. 'Thank you so much.'

Jane scrawled her address on a notepad that Beatrice found in a drawer of the console table. This was a result far better than she had been expecting from this little visit. This was the kind of information worthy of the detective title that she, Rachel and Frankie had given themselves. The question was whether to tell the others, or hold out until she knew a little more. After all, a little mystery never hurt anyone.

35

———————

RACHEL

Rachel looked at her watch as she stood on the doorstep.

She had promised that she wouldn't arrive before 7.05pm. Why was it that she ran around like a headless chicken every morning trying to be on time, but suddenly with a bottle of wine in hand she was early?

She waited.

At 7.05 on the dot she rang the doorbell.

'In bed?' she asked, holding up her crossed fingers as soon as the door opened the tiniest of cracks.

'Just,' said Frankie, rolling her eyes in jest and opening the door wide to let Rachel in.

Rachel held up the bottle in her hand. 'I hope you've got some large glasses!'

Frankie smiled. 'They are already out,' she said as she took the bottle.

'You know me too well.'

Frankie poured the wine.

'Keep going,' said Rachel, when Frankie went to stop.

'You do know that you're not supposed to fill the glass all the way to the top? You are supposed to let it breathe.'

'Bugger that,' said Rachel. 'I won't be able to breathe if I don't get some of that down my neck soon... I've been holding this thing in all afternoon!'

'What thing?'

'The thing I need to tell you,' said Rachel, swallowing a very large gulp of wine.

'Well, come on... spit it out then,' said Frankie. 'The thing, not the wine.'

Rachel took a deep breath and got ready for her Poirot moment. The moment where she announces that she has spotted something crucial that will absolutely, definitely lead to them solving the case, but not before creating a few more questions first, no doubt.

'I know where I have seen the bee keyring!'

Rachel waited for a gasp of amazement from Frankie, but she just said, 'Oh! I thought we'd decided it was Bee's?'

'Well, we thought it might be, but it's been bugging me because I knew I'd seen a bee keyring somewhere recently and I just couldn't think where, but–'

'Do we need some sort of drum roll?'

'Don't take the piss!' Rachel raised one eyebrow.

'Would I do such a thing? Anyway, c'mon... I'm on the edge of my seat here.'

'So, I went round to Jane's the day after...' Rachel paused. 'Well, the day after it happened and I was sitting in her kitchen. Have you been in Jane's kitchen?'

'Yes,' said Frankie. 'The night you got arrested!'

'Oh yes, of course... hang on, I did not get arrested, I–'

'It was a joke,' laughed Frankie. 'But I have seen her kitchen. Why?'

'It is the cleanest, tidiest, pristinest – is that a word?' Frankie opened her mouth to respond but before she could, Rachel continued, '– most spotless kitchen I have ever seen. It is like something out of a magazine. Anyway, I somehow ended up in the pantry – don't ask me why – and as I walked around, past the backdoor, I saw this little row of hooks on the wall. Named hooks, I mean, as if anyone is actually that organised. And there, under the beautifully inscribed name Ben was a bee keyring, with a key attached, hanging right there on the hook. I had totally forgotten, but you losing your keys earlier, made me think that you should get some – little hooks I mean – and then it just came to me...'

'So... it's Ben's keyring?'

'I think so, yes.' Rachel looked straight at Frankie and tried to read her expression. Was it shock or disbelief or something else?

'Ben? Surely it can't be, I mean he's our friend's husband, he's a police officer... none of this makes sense.'

'I can't make sense of it either. All I know is that Ben has a bee keyring and we know that Victoria bought a bee keyring when she got a spare key cut.'

Frankie nodded. 'Why the hell would Ben have a spare key to Victoria's house, and why a bee?'

'A very good question,' said Rachel.

'And why hasn't Jane told us that?'

'Another good question,' said Rachel. 'Maybe she doesn't know.'

'Or maybe she's covering for him?'

A silence fell between the two friends as they thought about what that could mean. Rachel started coming up with various scenarios, but before her head got too crowded she decided that knowing the answer would be much better than guessing it.

'I'm going to text her.'

Rachel (Charlie's mum): Any luck with the bee keyring @Jane? Trying to think where I have seen one…

Frankie looked at the chat on her own phone, and then at Rachel. 'You're testing her?'

'This is an investigation, Frankie. We can leave no stone unturned.'

She didn't reply straight away. Jane always replied straight away. *What is going on?*

'Where did she say she was going tonight?' asked Rachel, refreshing her phone screen.

'She didn't… she was being all secretive and mysterious.'

'Well, I wish she'd stop being so bloody mysterious and start being the prompt replying, non-secretive Jane we all know and love.'

'I've just thought,' said Frankie as she opened the screw-top bottle and poured them both more wine. 'If it is Ben's key, you don't think he's been doing *odd jobs* for Victoria, do you? You remember what Sarah told me… that it wasn't Greg or her we should be worried about when it came to other people's husbands or wives!'

'I mean, I can't see it.' Rachel thought about how gorgeous Jane always looked. 'Why would Ben be sniffing around Victoria when he's got Miss Perfect at home?'

'I have homemade premium beef burgers from Waitrose in the freezer,' said Frankie. 'But that doesn't stop me from nipping to McDonald's every once in a while.'

'True,' said Rachel. 'But Ben and Victoria? Surely not!'

Both of their phones pinged and they grabbed them.

'Don't spill the wine,' said Frankie, placing her glass carefully on a coaster. 'That's good stuff… it wasn't even on offer!'

Jane (Lottie's mum): Funnily enough I was just going to buzz you…

See what I did there?

Buzz…

Because of the bee keyring

Rachel (Charlie's mum): Very good!

They both looked up from their screens and Rachel rolled her eyes at Frankie, who sniggered.

Frankie (Billy's mum): 🐝

Rachel looked back down at her phone. 'Don't encourage her,' she said, as Frankie giggled.

Rachel (Charlie's mum): Anyway, the keyring?

Jane (Lottie's mum): Yes, well, I've just been with Bee and Grace. Had a lovely chat with them both. Grace seems distraught. Beatrice less so. Anyway, Bee had the key with the bee keyring. Victoria had left it under a plant pot for her.

Rachel (Charlie's mum): Really? That was very forward thinking of her… I guess she knew she'd be dead the next time Bee visited.

Frankie gulped down her mouthful of wine. 'Why have you written that? People leave their keys under plant pots all the time. I don't think we can read too much into that, can we?'

Rachel sighed. 'You're right.' She was just annoyed that the bee keyring on Ben's hook may have been a red herring after all and that bee keyrings were perhaps more common than she realised. *That or Jane is still covering for her husband.* Either way it was too soon to tell Jane her suspicions. There was no point in breaking her heart over something that may well turn out to be nothing. She typed some more...

> Rachel (Charlie's mum): Sorry ladies, ignore me. That was a stupid thing to say.

> Jane (Lottie's mum): 

Rachel hoped that she might *just* have got away with that stupid comment. She really must start thinking before she spoke, or typed.

> Rachel (Charlie's mum): So, did Bee seem genuine, or like she might have wanted her sister dead?

> Jane (Lottie's mum): Well, it's funny you should say that because I got the feeling there was something going on between the sisters. Some tension or something. They used to write letters to each other frequently, but she said they had been trailing off.

> Rachel (Charlie's mum): Interesting.

> Jane (Lottie's mum): And Grace didn't seem herself.

'I mean, her mum has just died!' said Frankie, as she read the message. 'Of course she's not her-bloody-self.'

> Frankie (Billy's mum): Well, that is to be expected.

> Jane (Lottie's mum): Of course.

> Rachel (Charlie's mum): Any idea what might have been going on between the sisters?

> Jane (Lottie's mum): No.

> Although Bee said she'd let us read some of their letters. She's going to post them to us. She is really pleased that we are trying to get to the bottom of what happened to her sister.

Oh God! thought Rachel. *That's one way to scare her off.*

> Rachel (Charlie's mum): You didn't tell her why we are investigating, did you?

> Jane (Lottie's mum): I just told her that we were friends of Victoria, looking for justice for her.

> Rachel (Charlie's mum): Okay, good.

'And justice for me too... the wrongly accused,' said Rachel to Frankie.

'Yeah, but she doesn't need to know that. It might put her on edge.'

'Very true, and we don't want another on-edge Sandwich Sister!'

'Christ no!' said Frankie. 'The main question is, if Ben did have a bee keyring on a hook in his kitchen then *surely* Jane knew about that... so why is she *still* not telling us?'

'A very good question indeed,' agreed Rachel. 'And one we definitely need answering, but the next question is, how do we go about asking it?'

Their phones pinged again and both pairs of eyes instinctively looked down, before their faces scrunched in confusion.

Jane (Lottie's mum): Oh and Grace is studying photography at uni…

'Okay!' Rachel shrugged.

Jane (Lottie's mum): …and we all know what photographers use to develop their photos, don't we?

'Do we?' Rachel looked puzzled.
'I'll google it,' said Frankie, and then, 'Oh…' She grimaced.
'What? What do they use?'
'Cyanide!' Frankie swallowed, audibly as the word also lit up both of their phone screens.
'Well, who knew?'

36

FRANKIE

'Perhaps I should ask her,' suggests Frankie. 'I'll just play stupid. Ask her straight out. Invite myself in, have a nosey and see if it's on the hook.'

Despite the fact they had just found someone with direct access to the poison, Frankie and Rachel were still fixated on why Jane hadn't mentioned the bee keyring.

'I mean, you could give it a go,' said Rachel.

'Okay, right. I'll nip over tomorrow after the school drop-off and I'll let you know what she says.'

'Are you sure you don't want me to go? Or at least come with you?'

'No, it's fine,' Frankie insisted. She didn't admit that she had an ulterior motive. She'd seen Jane's Instagram post earlier and knew that her house contained freshly baked millionaire shortbread. Her absolute favourite. 'I don't want her to think we're ganging up on her.'

'You're right,' said Rachel. 'Well, make sure you message me as soon as you've spoken to her. Oh, and while you're there, ask her about this photo... the one that upset Natasha.'

'I will.' Frankie yawned. She didn't even do it on purpose but Rachel got the hint.

'Oh, is that the time? I'd better get going.'

'You don't have to,' said Frankie.

'It's fine,' said Rachel. 'I am bloody knackered too. Who knew proving your innocence would be so flippin' tiring?'

'Who knew indeed?'

As Frankie stood on Jane's doorstep the following morning her first thought was, *I hope Jane doesn't think I'm rude just turning up like this* and her second thought was, *I hope she's got some shortbread left.*

She tried not to show her disappointment when Ben answered the door. *Is he authorised to dish out the millionaire shortbread?*

'Oh! Hi, Ben, I was after Jane. Is she...?'

'She's out,' he said. 'Just dropping Lottie at school. Did you not see her?'

'Um no, I didn't actually,' said Frankie, telling a white lie. She had totally spotted her on the playground, but knew that if she spoke to her there, she'd have no hope of getting her hands on any shortbread.

Frankie had quickly mastered the art of the *blinkered playground walk*; reserved for times when you are in a rush, or need to speak to someone specific and can't get distracted by idle chat, or when you simply don't have the headspace for any mum-chat that day. Which was most days for Frankie. This, however, was the first time she had used said blinkered walk in the pursuit of chocolatey goodies.

'Do you want to come in and wait for her?' asked Ben.

'Oh, um, okay. I could do. If it's not inconvenient.'

Ben stepped aside and ushered her in.

As Frankie stepped through the front door, a thought hit her: Ben had just been added to their list of suspects. She tried to shake it off as it dawned on her that she was now alone in the house with him.

'She must have nipped to the shop or something.'

'Yes, probably.' She tried to stay calm.

As the front door slammed shut behind her, the vibrations shuddered through her.

She took a deep breath.

He was her friend's husband. He couldn't have been responsible for the murder, he was just a dad after all. And even if he did have something to do with it, what possible reason could he have for wanting to kill Frankie? Other than her poking her nose into the investigation. *Oh crap! That is actually a fairly rock-solid reason.*

'Tea?' asked Ben.

'Oh, err, go on then. Yes please.'

Oh crap, no! What was she thinking? Did she really want to risk drinking tea from someone who *possibly, maybe,* had form for poisoning?

'Actually no.' Although it would distract him while she had a poke around. 'Oh, go on then!'

'So, yes?' Ben looked confused.

Frankie nodded. She followed him into the kitchen and immediately scanned the room to locate the key hooks. There they were, by the back door, just as Rachel had described.

'Is everything okay?' he asked, his eyes trying to follow her gaze. 'Are you looking for something?'

Frankie flicked her eyes straight back to look at him and realised that her nosing was perhaps not as subtle as she had intended. She rapidly searched the depths of her brain to think up an excuse for her nosiness, but then realised that she should just tell the truth. A new plan began to form… She shouldn't ask Jane – it might upset her and rock The Jam Sandwich Detectives boat after all. She should ask Ben.

'I thought I'd remembered seeing a bee keyring on those hooks when I was here last time. No?'

Ben looked at the hooks and then back at her. He seemed lost for words. 'I'm sorry what?' he finally managed to say.

'A keyring, with a bee on it. Do you have one?'

'Oh yes, I do have a bee keyring now you come to mention it. Jane bought it for me in Manchester. Why do you ask?'

'Manchester?' Frankie raised her voice into a question, which she hoped meant that she could avoid his.

'That's where we met. She's always buying bee knick-knacks.' He nodded towards a bee vase on the windowsill that was home to some rather sorry-looking chrysanthemums.

'Oh, really?' mused Frankie. 'Strange she never mentioned it.'

'Is it?' Ben raised an eyebrow. 'I mean, it's quite a specific anecdote.'

'I suppose,' nodded Frankie, remembering Jane's bee nails; it did all add up. 'Where is it now?'

'Where is what?'

'The bee keyring.'

'Oh, right. I have no idea.'

'So, you've lost your keys?'

'No, well I mean, yes, I technically don't know where *that one* is right now, but it's just a spare. My main keys are right here.' He produced a set from his pocket and jangled them in front of Frankie's face.

'A spare.' Frankie nodded and scratched her chin.

'What exactly is going on here, Frankie? I thought I was supposed to be the cop, but why do I feel like *I'm* being questioned?'

'Just conducting general enquiries.'

'Not related to...?'

'People think that Rachel killed Victoria, and Jane and I are trying to help her prove that she didn't.'

'Jane? I knew she was up to something,' said Ben, shaking his head.

'We are just helping out our friend.' Frankie gave him the sweetest smile she could manage.

'Well, be careful,' said Ben. 'The police don't always appreciate amateur sleuthing.'

'I mean, if they pulled their finger out, we wouldn't have to!'

Ben laughed. 'I'll pass that on to DI Harding.'

'Please do,' smiled Frankie. 'Anyway, thank you for your time. You have been *very* helpful.'

She stood up. *There was no sign of the millionaire shortbread anywhere.*

'You're going? I thought you were here to see Jane? I've no idea where she's got to!'

'I was, but I must be getting on. I'll catch up with her later,' said Frankie. 'I'll see myself out shall I?'

Suddenly she felt flustered, like she shouldn't be here snooping on her own, like she was going against their friend Jane by secretly talking to her husband about all this. She went to step over the post that was lying on the doormat, but then picked it up and handed it to Ben who had followed her down the hallway. Her eyes lingered on the top envelope.

'Sorry.' Why was she apologising? 'Looks like a bill. Oh, and your chrysanths could do with some water!'

Frankie typed.

> Frankie (Billy's mum): Ben has a bee keyring
> and guess what?

She didn't wait for a reply.

> Frankie (Billy's mum): He's lost it!

> Rachel (Charlie's mum): Convenient!

> Frankie (Billy's mum): Exactly! AND more to the
> point...

She sent the first part of her message and paused for dramatic effect, but then...

> Rachel (Charlie's mum) is typing...

Frankie typed out the rest of her message, but didn't hit send as she was eagerly awaiting whatever Rachel had to say. Before long she grew impatient and pressed send, just as her phone pinged with Rachel's message.

> Rachel (Charlie's mum): Why did Jane never
> mention this?

> Frankie (Billy's mum): Why did Jane never
> mention this?

Great minds think alike.

She heard a knock at her front door, then the doorbell rang too. *Why do delivery drivers always do both and then disappear and just leave the package on the doorstep anyway?* As she walked up to the front door she automatically peeped through the spy-hole.

Shit! she typed frantically. *The police are here.*

Rachel (Charlie's mum): 😨 Don't panic!

Frankie (Billy's mum): Easy for you to say.

Rachel (Charlie's mum): They will be questioning everyone who was there. I'm surprised it's taken them this long to talk to you.

Frankie (Billy's mum): What do I say?

Rachel (Charlie's mum): Just answer their questions truthfully… you've got nothing to hide!

Frankie (Billy's mum): Except that we've been doing our own private investigation.

Rachel (Charlie's mum): Yeah, maybe don't mention that.

Frankie started to type a reply but then the doorbell rang again.

37

JANE

Jane found herself walking the long way home after school drop-off.

Her route took her past Victoria's house and she lingered, unsure of her intent.

She heard, then saw, the front door start to open and had the sudden urge to hide, which she resisted. Being spotted hiding would make her look like she was up to something. Perhaps she *was* up to something, but she herself was not sure what that was.

'Oh, Jane,' called Beatrice, from the doorway. 'I'm glad I've seen you. Hold on...'

She disappeared back inside before Jane could say anything, and reappeared a minute later with a clean and sparkling casserole dish.

Jane who had wandered up the front path, took it from her. 'I was in no rush for it back.'

'It's fine,' said Beatrice. 'I decanted the leftovers into some Tupperware and popped it in the freezer, so we're all set.'

'Well, thank you.'

'No, thank *you*. It was absolutely delicious. Best casserole I've had since... well, since Vee last made one.'

Jane smiled. 'You call her Vee?'

Beatrice nodded.

'And she called you Bee?'

'I suppose she did, yes.'

'Hence the bee keyring?'

'Bee keyring?' Beatrice scrunched up her forehead.

'On the door key.'

'Oh yes, how did you...?'

'Oh, I saw it on the side table,' said Jane, hoping that it wasn't obvious she had been snooping. 'What a lovely gesture; your sister getting you a special keyring for the spare key.'

Beatrice smiled. 'To be honest, I hadn't even realised the significance. It was under the plant pot by the back door. The bee did make me smile though, when I saw it, so perhaps my subconscious knew.'

A single tear fell down Beatrice's cheek as she took the key out of her pocket. Jane looked away, down towards the dish she was cradling in her arms. She was intruding on a special moment between a woman and her late sister.

'Are you okay, Auntie Bee?' said Grace, joining them at the doorway.

'Oh,' said Beatrice, wiping the tear away. 'You *are* up. We need to get going. I don't want to get stuck in traffic and miss our flight.'

'Okay,' said Grace. 'Give me a sec.' And she darted back inside.

'Are you leaving already?' asked Jane, as Beatrice heaved her case out of the front door and walked down the path towards Victoria's red sports car.

'Yes,' said Beatrice, then lowering her voice. 'Grace is finding it difficult being in her mum's house, y'know, with all the reminders. She's going to come up and spend a few days with me... until we can start planning the funeral.'

'Oh, you haven't started that yet?' Jane hoped she wasn't coming across too nosey.

'We need to wait for the okay from the police,' said Beatrice.

'I see,' said Jane. 'Well, anything I can do, please just shout.'

'Oh, Jane, you are doing more than enough by helping to find out who did this. And that reminds me, I will get those letters sent down to you as soon as we're back.' She looked at her watch. 'If our flight is not delayed I might even be able to post them today. I live right by the Post Office.'

'That would be really helpful,' said Jane. 'Anyway, I'll leave you to it. Safe travels.'

'Thank you so much,' said Beatrice. 'For all of your kindness. Victoria was lucky to have such a wonderful friend.'

Jane smiled what she hoped looked like a genuine smile and not one racked with guilt at the fact that she was playing the role of friend to a dead woman to help her actual friend prove her innocence.

***

The second Jane opened her front door, Ben appeared in the hallway.

'Where have you been?' he asked.

'I just popped to pick up my casserole dish from Victoria's sister.'

'Your casserole dish?' He scrunched up his forehead in that way that always irritated Jane. 'Why did Victoria's sister have your casserole dish?'

'I made them a casserole.'

'Them?'

'Beatrice and Grace, Victoria's daughter.'

'Why did you make them a casserole?'

Jane sighed. 'They are grieving, Ben. That's what you do when people are grieving... you make them a casserole.'

Ben shook his head. He brushed his hand through his hair and it fell back into place in that perfect way that it always did. 'Well,' he said. 'While you were off picking up our kitchen items from a murder scene, I've had your nosey mate round here, asking me questions about a bloody keyring.'

'Which one?'

'The bee one, the one on that spare key.'

'I meant which friend? Rachel?'

'No, the other one...'

'Frankie?' Jane's eyes widened.

'Yes.'

'Fine. Well, don't worry,' said Jane, wondering why Frankie was asking Ben questions and why she hadn't mentioned any of this to her. They had become a bit obsessed with this bee keyring as if it was the only one in existence and Victoria was the only person ever to have bought one. 'The one in question is Bee's, Victoria's sister, and she has it; a bee keyring for Bee. So, don't worry about yours, it's got nothing to do with anything.'

'Oh, right! So, that's definitely the one Rachel's looking for?' Ben asked.

'Yes.' Jane smiled.

'Right, okay, well I told her that you bought me mine anyway,' said Ben.

'Why did you do that?'

'Because you did!'

'Of course I did.' Jane let her frown relax. 'Silly me.'

'Well, can you tell your mate before I have her Miss Marple-ing around here again please?'

'Of course, darling.' Jane smiled. 'Shall I put the kettle on?'

'Yes,' replied Ben. 'Fine.'

Jane sensed a tone to his reply. A sarcastic: *sure, just make a cup of tea and everything will be fine* kind of tone, but she didn't let his shortness or tense shoulders faze her.

'Shall we have a day out tomorrow?' She had to do something to ease the tension. 'The weather is supposed to be nice... it might be the last nice day before autumn fully hits. We could drive to the seaside.'

Ben smiled and put his hand on hers. 'That sounds nice.'

She waited for the *but...* but to her surprise it never came. 'Great,' she said. 'That's settled then.'

She needed the solidarity of her husband. Female friends were so fickle. Even Rachel and Frankie, who she had been really enjoying bonding with over the investigation, now seemed to be liaising behind her back. She had put her absolute all into sticking up for Rachel, but now Jane was wondering whether she could be trusted after all.

A day not thinking about The Jam Sandwich Detectives, not thinking about the investigation, not thinking about murder, would do her good. The sea air would be good for her soul and good for her marriage, which had been more than a little strained lately. She always kept smiling and carried on, but maybe she needed to reset a little. Hopefully an ice cream covered in sand and a stick of rock hard enough to break your teeth would be the perfect way to do that.

38

RACHEL

'Mum, what's a murderer?'

'What?' said Rachel, rubbing her eyes. 'Good morning to you too, Charlie!'

Rachel shimmied out from under the Charlie-shaped bundle of duvet and propped her pillows and cushions into a pile so that she could sit up. What had she done to deserve this question before her first coffee on a Saturday morning?

'Charlie! I told you not to ask her.' Megan appeared and sat down carefully on the edge of the bed.

'It's okay, darling. What has brought this question on?' Rachel asked, buying time to come up with an appropriate answer.

'Well, someone at school said that you are one, so I asked Miss Williams like you normally tell me to do when I don't know something, and she said "ask your mum" so that's what I'm doing.'

Rachel's face dropped.

'Are you one, Mum? And is it something bad?'

'Miss Williams said "ask your mum"?' Her eyes filled with

tears and she held her breath in an attempt to stop them from spilling out, but it didn't work.

'Charlie! You've upset her now,' said Megan, putting her arm around Rachel's shoulder.

'I didn't mean to. I just wanted to know... Sorry, Mummy.'

'It's okay, love, you've got nothing to apologise for. You're entitled to ask.'

'So, what is it?'

Rachel took a deep breath. 'It's when you hurt someone on purpose so badly that they... well, they die.'

'Oh,' said Charlie, the ends of his mouth turning down. 'Like when you tread on a spider?'

'Yes, kind of.'

'Oh, okay.' His eyes lit up. 'Well, I'll just tell Freddie that it's fine then. His mum must be a murderer too, anyway. He says she treads on spiders all the time!'

'Hang on. It was Freddie that said I was a murderer?'

Charlie nodded. 'His mum told him you were.'

'Did she now?'

The tears turned to anger. Rachel could feel her face turning red. It was one thing for Natasha to tell all the other mums that she thought Rachel was a murderer, but telling the kids was a low blow.

'C'mon, Charlie,' said Megan. 'Let's give Mum a minute.'

The kids disappeared and Rachel picked up her phone. She refused to have anyone telling her kids' friends that she was a murderer. *How dare Natasha!* Rachel decided to confront her, and she decided to do it in a public forum.

She opened the *Reception Mums #inittogether* chat, ready to type and instead read:

You can't send messages to this group because you're no longer a member.

'What the fuck?!' she said out loud. 'They've bloody removed me!'

She buried herself back under the duvet. She had the whole bed to herself. Phil must already be up; she hoped he had the coffee machine on.

———

A while later Megan reappeared holding a steaming cup of coffee.

'Oh, Megan. You are a good girl.'

Megan put the coffee on her bedside table, sat down next to her mum and gave her a squeeze.

'I'm sorry I've been a bit stressed recently, darling,' said Rachel. 'It's just...'

'You're sad about that lady that died,' said Megan. 'The one at the cake party.'

Rachel smiled. 'Yes. It is very sad, isn't it?'

Megan nodded. 'I made you this,' she said, handing Rachel a small string of colourful beads.

'And I drew this!' Charlie burst into the bedroom. He thrust a bit of paper at her and she un-crumpled it to reveal a picture entitled *My Mum* in scratchy crayon letters.

Rachel beamed. She put the beads around her wrist and found some Blu Tack in her drawer to fix Charlie's picture to her dresser. She took a sip of freshly brewed coffee and wondered why she'd ever fretted about being *just a mum*. Being Charlie and Megan's mum was everything.

'Thank you,' she said, kissing each of her children. 'I love you both and I want you to know that I'm not a murderer... I'm just a mum.'

———

> Rachel (Charlie's mum): They've removed me from the fucking mum-chat.

> Frankie (Billy's mum): Good morning to you too, Rachel.

> Rachel (Charlie's mum): Sorry, yes, good morning.

> How did it go with the police?

Rachel really must remember not to make everything about her.

> Frankie (Billy's mum): It was fine. It kind of made me think that…

> Frankie (Billy's mum) is typing…

> Rachel (Charlie's mum): What?

> Frankie (Billy's mum): That maybe we should just leave it to them… that they will get to the truth.

Fucking hell, thought Rachel. *Is she turning against me? What the hell did the police say to her?* Disappointment washed over Rachel. Like she had been let down by a teammate, but maybe Frankie was right, maybe they should take a step back. They had become friends, but all they talked about was the murder. Maybe they should get to know each other a bit more outside of a criminal investigation.

> Rachel (Charlie's mum): It's a nice day. How about an afternoon out? No murder talk. We could go to the country park down the road. Kids can play. We can chat.

> Frankie (Billy's mum): That sounds great.

> No murder talk?

Rachel (Charlie's mum): Promise!

Frankie (Billy's mum): It's a deal.

This was just what Rachel needed. Some quality time with the kids. Some quality time with Frankie. She did have a slight pang of guilt that she and Frankie had arranged a day out without Jane. She didn't want her to think they had been snooping around behind her back.

It was also playing on Rachel's mind that Jane had never mentioned Ben's bee keyring but she had promised Frankie she wouldn't talk about the murder all day. Perhaps she should pop round and have a quick word with Jane beforehand? She could invite her along and then subtly quiz her about the keyring without Frankie ever knowing she'd broken her promise. She needed to grab some bits for a picnic anyway and with any luck, Jane would have been baking!

'I'm just popping out,' she called to Phil. 'Need some picnic-y bits from the shop.'

'Fine,' called Phil, who of course, had no actual say in the matter. 'I'll have the kids dressed and ready for when you get back.'

'Thank you, love.' He was a good egg. She had really hit the jackpot with Phil.

She knew that some dads just let the mums get on with it without any involvement whatsoever, and to some extent looking after the kids was her department – he was the main bread winner after all, and she wasn't someone who was bitter about this or had a chip on her shoulder about it.

When they had first had children they had discussed it. They had decided between them that this was the way that worked for them. She gave up her twenty-four seven on-call job as a PA for a new twenty-four seven job called motherhood, and she had never had any regrets – well not many – although lately she had started to feel like she was losing her identity. Like she was just a mum and nothing else anymore.

She loved her kids more than anything, but the more she thought about it the more she knew that she needed to be more than just a mum, *and the murderer label was not exactly what she had in mind.*

She typed out an email and pressed send without overthinking it. She still hadn't heard back from her interview and surely a polite nudge wouldn't hurt. Then she put it out of her mind.

She planned to enjoy a day in the fresh air with Frankie, and hopefully Jane too. The kids playing, while the mums ate jam sandwiches and drank Prosecco; that was what being a mum was all about... wasn't it?

As Rachel walked up to Jane's front door, she fumbled about in her handbag looking for tissues. Her nose was tingling and she didn't want to greet Jane by sneezing in her face.

Her handbag-rummaging obviously looked like key-hunting, as the postman – or post boy; he looked really young but that could have just been her getting old – handed her a stack of envelopes and said, 'Cheers, love.'

Love? she thought. *I'm old enough to be his mother.*

She took the stack, found a tissue, and once she was satisfied that, in fact, no sneeze was imminent, she rang the doorbell. While she waited, she glanced down at the stack of post in her hand. The top letter was something for Ben.

She pressed the doorbell again. *Surely they aren't all up and out this early on a Saturday morning?* She looked back down at the post and started casually flicking through it. She didn't mean to be nosey, it was like a reflex. Perhaps she was turning into a proper detective. *Everything could be a clue.* Underneath the top letter was some bumpf for the occupier, but right at the bottom of the pile was a Jiffy bag. It was quite heavy, as if it had a book or a stack of papers in it. She tried the bell one last time. If they didn't answer this time, she'd come back later.

Nothing.

She tried to put all the post through the letter box but the Jiffy bag wouldn't fit. She moved the Jiffy bag to the top of the pile and tapped it in her hands, wondering what to do with it. That is when she looked at it more closely. It was addressed to Jane and Co. – which was a bit odd – and when she turned it over it said: Sender: B Sandwich.

'Shit!' she said out loud, before glancing over her shoulder to check the postman was out of earshot. 'These are Victoria's letters.'

She stared at them for a moment. Jane clearly wasn't in. *Was it bad to take them and have a quick look at them while she was out?* She would bring them straight back around later... they were a team after all. And it did say *and Co.* on the front of the Jiffy. She wasn't really sure why she was trying so hard to convince herself because she had already decided. She had the letters in her hand, they could contain the key to proving her innocence, there was no way she *wasn't* going to read them.

She stuffed the package under her arm and went to post the other envelopes through the letter box. Something about the letter to Ben caught her eye and made her look twice. At first she wasn't sure what it was but then it hit her, like being slapped in the face with a Jiffy bag full of letters. It was obvious. Why had she never thought of it before?

Should she take the letter too? No, she didn't need it. What was she thinking? She took a deep breath. 'Calm down, Rach,' she said to herself. She posted the letters through the door and practically sprinted home with the Jiffy bag under her arm. She was late to meet Frankie and she had no food for the picnic, but she had something much better. A nugget of information that had given her a flash of inspiration, along with a packet full of actual evidence.

As she turned the corner into her road, she saw Phil loading children into Frankie's car, which was by the kerb outside their house.

'There you are,' said Phil, looking up as his wife ran down the road. 'Where's all the picnic food?'

'Change of plan, gonna raid the fridge,' panted Rachel. 'Be with you in a jiffy, Frankie.'

After Rachel had cobbled together a picnic from what was left in her fridge, she ran out to the car.

'I'm afraid the *no murder talk* plan is out the window, Frankie.'

'Rach!' said Frankie, through gritted teeth. 'Not in front of the kids.'

'It's fine, they can help.' She leaned round and looked over her shoulder. 'Do you want to help solve a murder kids?'

'Yeah!' they chorused from the back seat and Rachel shrugged at Frankie, who shook her head and rolled her eyes.

'Are there jam sandwiches in your picnic, Frankie?'

'Of course!'

'Then we're all set... the kids can join the club!'

39

———

JANE

'Let's take a family selfie,' said Jane, the moment they set foot on the beach.

'We've just got here!' groaned Ben.

'But the sun's out. We don't know how long that will last.'

Ben sighed as they stood together and posed for a photo.

'That's a nice one,' said Jane, peering down at her phone.

'Can we paddle?' asked Lottie.

'Of course,' said Ben, kicking off his flip-flops. 'We're British; we're at the beach; we paddle at the slightest hint of the sun.'

Ben and Lottie ran down to the water's edge and Jane looked up, following them with her eyes, before her gaze fell back down to the screen in front of her. She had parked herself in the camping chair that probably wasn't really meant for the beach, and already felt a bit unstable. It was fine, she decided, as she didn't plan on moving any time soon.

She fiddled with the settings until the photo looked like they were in the Caribbean, as opposed to Costa del Norfolk. Then *ping!* It was uploaded to Instagram with the caption: *Getting away from it all! #autumnsun*

She looked up briefly and smiled at the sight of her rapidly growing daughter, playing around in the shallow waves, kicking seawater at her dad and splashing his rolled up jeans. Her mind briefly wandered back to days at the beach when Lottie was little, and shells were treasures that amazed and dazzled, and ice creams were exciting treats of which every mouthful was savoured.

This was nice though. Relaxing. Getting away from the monotony of the school run and the keeping up of appearances. Even here though, Jane felt the urge to portray the perfect life. She tried not to think about the fact that her new friends – the ones who she had thought she was in a team with – were having secret discussions that she wasn't party to; then cornering her husband to answer questions that she didn't know about. They were probably having secret meet-ups without her too.

It gave her that feeling in her stomach that she remembered from her own school days. The feeling of being left out, of not being part of the gang. She shook it off and swiped down on the screen of her phone, to refresh it, and see if she had any likes or comments.

One like.

From her mum.

Then another appeared. From Frankie.

Her phone pinged with a notification from The Jam Sandwich Detectives chat.

Rachel (Megan's mum): @Jane where are you?

Jane didn't reply straight away. She didn't want to seem too eager.

Frankie (Billy's mum): Looks lovely, wherever you are xx

> Rachel (Megan's mum): Let us know when you're back… loads to discuss.

Perhaps Jane's plan was working. The girls were missing her. Realising that they needed her.

> Jane (Lottie's mum): Just needed some sea air.

> Back tomorrow.

> Frankie (Billy's mum): Enjoy!

> Rachel (Megan's mum): Okay, yes, have a nice time.

Jane could picture Frankie, nudging Rachel, saying, 'Say something nice,' before Rachel typed: *have a nice time*. It was obvious they were together – without her – although she only had herself to blame today. She had chosen to escape.

She closed her eyes and leaned back in the chair trying to let her worries float off into the breeze, but then Ben plonked himself down in the chair next to her and her peace was shattered.

'When did she get so big?' he asked, smiling at Lottie who was still picking up shells on the shoreline.

'I have absolutely no idea,' said Jane.

They both sat in what was either a contented or awkward silence. Jane could no longer tell.

'This is nice,' she said finally, to break the uncomfortable silence more than anything else.

'Yes,' agreed Ben. 'Good suggestion. Nice way to spend a Saturday.'

The silence crept back.

'Fish and chips later?' he asked eventually.

'Of course,' said Jane. 'What else?' And they both laughed

and started to relax a little. 'I suppose it's my turn to help with the shell hunting.' She got up and wandered down towards the sea and towards Lottie, enjoying the sand between her toes.

'Look, Mum, a yellow periwinkle!'

Jane smiled as she thought about how Lottie had always loved shells, ever since her first trip to the seaside, and she had always liked learning the names of the different varieties. The little yellow periwinkles had always been her favourite, and during one holiday to Cornwall, when she was tiny, she had collected a whole jam jar full, which is still sat on a shelf in her bedroom to this day.

'Aww, I love the little yellow ones,' said Jane. 'You could add it to your jar.'

'I think I will... can we get an ice cream?'

'Of course.'

Jane's heart burst with joy as she watched her daughter and her husband run off up the beach, towards the little wooden café, giggling as they went, and for a moment she felt happy. She felt alive. She forgot that she was caught up in the middle of a murder investigation. One she had only really become embroiled in because she hoped to make new friendships, which already seemed to be strained.

She sat back in her camping chair and watched the waves come and go. Just like the mums on the playground. Just like the friendships in her life. Just like the love and then the anger that she felt towards her husband. All that washed away with the tide and for a few moments her mind was empty of worry and full of ice-cream expectation, the smell of the seaside and the seagulls circling, children playing and kites flapping in the breeze.

She took a deep breath in.

She wanted to preserve this moment and keep it in a jam jar.

40

RACHEL

'So,' said Rachel as she spread out the picnic blanket. 'I may have done something slightly sneaky.'

'Ooh, do tell,' said Frankie.

Megan, Charlie and Billy were running amok in the play area just next to where Rachel and Frankie were setting up their picnic feast. Rachel had given Megan a fiver earlier and asked her to keep the boys occupied, so that she and Frankie could have an uninterrupted chat.

'I might have just intercepted the postman at Jane's house.'

'Well, it's funny you should say that, Rach, because I saw something interesting amongst Jane's post yesterday too.'

'Go on...'

'No, you go first.'

'Does yours have anything to do with Ben's middle name?' Rachel asked.

'Yes!' nodded Frankie, her eyes lighting up. 'Edward? Ernie? Ethan? I don't know what it is, but according to the mail I saw, it starts with an *E*.'

'Exactly!'

'Um, *Exactly* would be a strange middle name.'

The ladies laughed at the lame joke, but Rachel stopped suddenly when it sunk in that they had clearly both reached the same conclusion.

'Benjamin E. Evans,' said Rachel.

'Bee!' said both women at once.

'BEE!' yelled the kids as they ran towards their mothers.

'Charlie's been stung by a bee,' announced Megan.

Charlie was wailing.

'Oh, Charlie my darling,' said Rachel as she threw her arms around her sobbing son. 'You were supposed to be watching him, Megan.'

'I was watching... I saw it happen.'

Rachel shook her head and rubbed Charlie's throbbing finger. 'Let me see if I can find an ice pack or...' It was too late, Charlie had already popped his finger in her plastic glass of Prosecco. 'Thanks for that, Charlie!'

Megan giggled and Charlie managed a little smile.

'Are you sure it was a bee?' asked Rachel. 'They don't usually sting unless they have to.'

'Yes,' said Charlie. 'It was mean and... there it is again.' He jumped up and started hopping about.

Rachel followed the buzzing sound and started swiping the air with a Tupperware lid that she had grabbed.

'Get it, Mum! I don't like it,' wailed Charlie.

As Rachel swiped she realised that it was a wasp. 'Come here, you little bugger,' she yelled as she whacked it with a napkin. 'Yes! Got it.' The wasp fell to the floor and Rachel stomped a victorious foot down onto it. 'Take that, you horrible little thing.'

Megan turned white. 'You killed it, Mum. You killed a bee.'

'It was a wasp, love, and it hurt your brother, so it deserved it.'

'But...' Megan seemed lost for words for a moment. 'You can't just kill something because it hurt you.'

'If you hurt someone and they die you are a murderer,' said Charlie, looking up at Rachel. 'You said so.'

She felt her cheeks flush. 'It was just a wasp,' she just about managed to say.

<hr>

Once Charlie had calmed down and his finger wasn't throbbing as much, and Megan had stopped crying about the dead wasp, the children ran off to play again.

Rachel sighed. 'Bloody wasps!'

'Forget wasps,' said Frankie. 'Do you think Ben *is* the BEE on Victoria's calendar?'

'I don't know what to think anymore.' Rachel scratched her suddenly tight forehead. 'Why would Ben be on Victoria's calendar? Unless, he was doing *odd jobs* for her after all!'

'Maybe we should ask Jane!' suggested Frankie.

'Maybe Jane doesn't know,' said Rachel. 'If he's off having hanky-panky he's not exactly going to tell his wife, is he?'

'You really think it could be a secret liaison?'

'Victoria seems to have form.' Rachel rummaged in her bag. 'Anyway, back to the post. I have something interesting to show you. Now, I know I probably shouldn't technically have this but it's kind of addressed to us all and Jane has swanned off to the seaside, so...'

'Jane and Co.' Frankie read from the package that Rachel thrust under her nose. 'Who is this from? Who knows that we...?'

'It's from Beatrice,' said Rachel, showing Frankie the sender information on the back of the pack. 'Jane said she'd told her we've been looking into things and Beatrice said she would send over her letters.'

'Well, she doesn't hang about.'

'I guess she's keen to find out who killed her sister.'

There was a pause while both women stared at the package.

'So, we can open it then, right? Without Jane I mean?' Rachel spoke to Frankie like a child asking permission to eat another lollipop.

'Well, it does say Jane and Co. and I guess that we are Co. So, I don't see why not. We can catch her up tomorrow.'

Permission granted, Rachel ripped open the package like a kid on Christmas morning, and as she did so a cascade of letters spilled out and landed on the picnic blanket.

'Are they in any kind of order?' asked Frankie.

'I don't think so,' said Rachel, pulling one of the letters out of its envelope.

A silence fell on the picnic blanket as the two women absorbed themselves in reading. The chatter and rumblings of their children playing sounded distant, as if it was outside a window, and the avid readers were inside a quiet library, studiously reading the gripping texts. What they were reading was as engaging as a classic novel, only this story was true, if the words on the pages were to be trusted, that is. And why would they lie? They were two sisters writing to each other. Presumably neither ever intended these letters to be seen by anyone else. And presumably neither sister ever expected them to be evidence in a murder enquiry.

'Listen to this,' began Rachel, but she was interrupted by the sound of approaching feet and whines of, 'When can we eat?' so the reading had to pause while they fed and nurtured their children, and listened with faux interest to the details of the intricate game they'd been playing.

'Okay, who wants a jam sandwich?' asked Frankie.

After lunch Rachel and Frankie settled down for another spot of light reading while the stuffed children went off to finish playing their game, about which, despite the lengthy explanation, their mums were still none the wiser.

As Rachel read, something most unexpected began to happen, she started to feel sorry for Victoria. Even her death hadn't filled Rachel with a great deal of pity, but now, reading about her life, finally pulled on Rachel's tough heartstrings.

The letters made her seem lonely, as if her sister – who was 300 miles away – was the only person she had to talk to. She really opened up to her in these letters. They were very personal and Rachel shifted uncomfortably on the blanket as she read. She felt like she was intruding on a secret exchange between two sisters. She *was* intruding. She did have permission from one sister – well, via Jane – but the other sister was in no position to grant such permissions, and guilt crept over Rachel as she read.

But she couldn't stop. She was engrossed.

Frankie was also reading in silence next to her. Apparently just as gripped. Who would comment first? Who would announce something intriguing from within the pages? Who would give away Victoria's secrets? Did they have any right to? *Yes*, Rachel decided… if it proved her innocence then she had every right.

Rachel finally broke the silence. 'So, it seems like they were close, Victoria and Beatrice, but I don't get the feeling they saw each other very often. It's almost as if that bit of distance gives Victoria the confidence to open up. She talks about being lonely, about missing Grace and feeling like she has no purpose any more. It is really quite sad.'

Frankie was silent.

'Frankie, do you agree? That she seemed to have lost all sense of purpose…'

'Oh, I think she had a purpose all right,' said Frankie, finally.

'You do?'

'It's here in black and white… like the stripes of a bumblebee.'

'Bumblebees are black and yellow.'

'Oh, yeah! That's a shame, would have tied in nicely.'

'With what?' asked Rachel.

'With Victoria's purpose… Benjamin *Engelbert* Evans. It says so right here. Those BEEs on the calendar were definitely visits from Ben. And I think he was doing a lot more than pruning her bushes.'

41

FRANKIE

'We need to talk to Ben,' said Frankie. 'We need to talk to him before we talk to Jane.'

'You're probably right,' said Rachel.

'I am definitely right,' said Frankie. 'She will be heartbroken. We can't do that to her if there's a simple and reasonable explanation.'

'Is there likely to be?'

'Not from what I've read, but we have to give him a chance to explain.'

'You seem very certain about this,' said Rachel.

'I am certain,' said Frankie. She had been involved in crossed wires before and it was not nice for anyone involved. 'A good detective always get their facts in order before making any wild accusations.'

'That is very true,' agreed Rachel. 'How are we going to talk to Ben? He's at the beach with Jane and Lottie.'

'I guess we have to wait,' said Frankie. 'It's going to be hard though, knowing what we know.'

'What we *think* we know,' said Rachel. 'There is still a chance that Victoria has fantasised the whole thing.'

'I suppose,' said Frankie. 'So, what do we do until then?'

'Back to the pinboard,' said Rachel. 'Let's check we haven't missed anything. Plus, there's still a stack of letters we haven't read here. Should we not read them all before we talk to Ben?'

'I can't read anymore,' said Frankie. 'It's like reading someone's diary. It feels intrusive. I think we need to be open and honest about what we know and hope that Ben is open and honest back.'

Rachel nodded and put the letters back in the package and slid it into her bag. Frankie knew full well that Rachel would read them; that she wouldn't be able to help herself, and maybe they should be read. After all Rachel had something to prove: her innocence. That was definitely worth invading someone's privacy for. But Frankie didn't like the secrecy. She needed to face this thing head-on.

The clouds started to gather, so Frankie and Rachel gathered their children too and packed away the picnic things. They took a gentle stroll back to the car park not saying much. Anything they might have said would have been drowned out by the chitter-chatter of the children anyway.

Then over the murmurings they heard an ear-splintering, 'Cooey!'

Rachel's face dropped as she saw who was calling them.

'Oh! Hello, Natasha,' said Frankie in her friendliest voice.

'Hello, ladies. Out escaping the village gossip, are we?'

'Could ask you the same question,' said Rachel.

'Oh, I just ignore all that,' said Natasha. 'I don't believe for one minute that you're capable of murder, Rachel.'

Rachel's face flushed and Frankie wondered if Natasha knew she was making such a back-handed compliment.

Then out of nowhere, Rachel pushed back her shoulders and spoke with confidence. 'Well, it certainly is convenient for whoever *did* kill Victoria that all eyes are on me, so anyone pointing people in my direction is suspicious in my book.'

Well said, thought Frankie, and she shot Rachel a congratulatory smile. She wanted to fist pump the air or high five her, but just about managed to stay composed.

Natasha seemed slightly flummoxed by Rachel's new-found confidence. 'Anyway, I need to be off,' she said as she fumbled around in her bag, before dropping her keys.

The last few rays of sunlight that were still peeking through the cloud hit the keys and Frankie spotted the criss-crossed pattern of the wing of an insect glinting in amongst the gravel.

'Let me get them for you,' said Frankie, pretending to be helpful but actually wanting a closer look. 'Here you go.' She held out the bundle of keys in front of Natasha's face. 'Is that a bumblebee?' she asked.

Rachel's ears pricked up.

'It is not,' said Natasha, snatching the keys from Frankie's fingers. 'It's a dragonfly.'

And sure enough the long slender body of a dragonfly glistened in the light.

'So it is,' said Frankie.

'So it is,' sighed Rachel.

'What's going on?' Natasha scrunched up her forehead. 'Why do you two care what insect is on my keyring?'

'Um...'

'We think that a bumblebee keyring might hold the answer to who Victoria's killer is.' Rachel's elbow dug into her ribs as she spoke.

'Oh, guys! You are not still playing detective, are you? Why don't you leave it to the actual police?'

'Because the actual police haven't arrested anyone yet,' said Rachel. 'And last time I checked they still seemed to think that I had something to do with it.'

'Well, that's ridiculous,' said Natasha. 'You wouldn't have the balls to kill anyone.'

Frankie raised one eyebrow. *The back-handed compliment was much less subtle this time.* She waited to see how Rachel would take it. The answer being: *not well!*

'Why don't you try me, *Natasha?*'

'Is that a threat, *Rachel?*'

'Ladies, c'mon, calm down.' Frankie did her best to defuse the situation. 'It's been a stressful couple of weeks, let's not take it out on each other.'

'Fine,' said Rachel, smoothing her hair and clothes down.

'Fine,' said Natasha. 'See you later, ladies.' She walked off towards her car, but stopped suddenly and turned back around, luckily just missing Rachel's eye roll.

'You *do* know who has a bumblebee keyring don't you?'

'Pardon?' Frankie wasn't sure if she was supposed to guess the answer or wait with bated breath.

'Gina, that new mum,' said Natasha. 'She was standing next to me on the playground the other day, and she was like *"Ooh look, we've got similar keyrings,"* which is perhaps the dullest thing anyone has ever said to me on the playground, and I have talked to my four year old about *exactly* what he had for lunch.'

'Why would she bring something like that to your attention?' asked Rachel, taking the words right out of Frankie's mouth. 'I mean it's a clue in a murder case.'

'But she wouldn't know that...'

'...unless she was the murderer!'

'Then why mention it?'

'Hmm,' Rachel thought out loud. 'On the one hand it indicates her innocence, as she wouldn't have mentioned something that would incriminate her, so it must just have been an innocent passing comment. On the other hand...'

'She may not realise the significance of what she has said,

and she may just have dropped herself right in the middle of this mess.'

As Frankie and Rachel turned to ask Natasha what she thought, they saw the dust kick up from underneath her wheels as she drove out of the gravelly car park.

'Thanks for all your help,' said Rachel, rolling her eyes at the back of the car. 'Do you get the feeling we are going round in circles?'

Frankie didn't say anything as she let the cogs in her head slowly turn.

'Did you hear me, Frankie? I said, *do you feel like we're...*'

'Going round in circles, yes I heard you.' Frankie was lost in her thoughts, there was something niggling at her, banging at the door to get into her mind, she just needed to let it in. If only she had a key to give to the niggle... she could leave it under a plant pot. 'But Gina and her bee keyring may be more helpful than we realise,' she said, eventually.

42

RACHEL

Rachel sat in her favourite chair, wrapped in a blanket and cradling a mug of hot chocolate. It wasn't a particularly cold evening, she just liked being snuggled up and cosy... by herself... while Phil put the kids to bed.

Bedtime wasn't going well. She could hear her bedsprings being sprung above her head and knew full well that Charlie was using their bed as a trampoline again.

'Charlie!' she heard Phil yell through the ceiling. 'You are going to ruin the mattress.'

She smiled as she wondered in what world Phil thought that an almost-five-year-old cared about whether or not he ruined a mattress. Gone were the days of her and Phil having much chance to wear it out. Now they were just constantly worn out themselves instead.

She took a sip of hot chocolate, then winced as it was too hot on her lip. She put her mug down on the side table and picked up her evening reading; not a spicy novel or a trashy magazine, but a stack of letters, written by the woman she was accused of murdering.

The more she read the more she became engrossed in this

unlikely love affair between her friend's husband and the bossy ex-chair of the PTA. And the more she read, the more she realised that is exactly what it was, a love affair. Rachel had been assuming that this misdemeanour was some sort of fling, but the way Victoria was describing it to her sister there were actual feelings involved. Most definitely from her and, if her written words reflected the truth, from Ben too.

Poor Jane.

He's going to leave his wife, she read. *He's going to tell her everything very soon.* These pitiful, desperate words didn't seem in keeping with the brash, bolshie woman who had written them. *Would he have left Jane? Would he have told her everything?* Rachel couldn't see it somehow. And that is when she found it, the sentence she had been dreading. The sentence that confirmed the fear that had been bubbling up for the past couple of days: *And I've told him that if he doesn't tell her soon... I will.*

Ben had a motive.

Rachel picked up her hot chocolate, took a sip and winced as she swallowed it. It had gone cold. She slammed the mug back down. She hadn't meant to be so aggressive but a sense of urgency had come over her. She scrolled through Instagram and found Jane's most recent post.

Home for the night. #cosy

She had tagged the hotel that they were staying in, so Rachel googled it. It looked pretty fancy, which was presumably why Jane had tagged it. That is how Instagram works. Put on your best show. Keep up those appearances.

Rachel grabbed her car keys and ran upstairs. She popped her head around Megan's bedroom door where the rest of her little family were sat huddled together watching *Bluey* on Phil's phone.

'Books at bedtime, Daddy, not screens.'

'He's not *your* daddy,' said Charlie.

'No, but I'm your mummy and I say: books at bedtime, not screens!'

All three of them stuck their tongues out at her and giggled.

She rolled her eyes. She didn't have the time or energy to argue. 'I've got to go out,' she said, in a loud whisper.

'Now?' Phil glanced at the clock on the wall.

'I'll be back as soon as I can, but it will be after midnight.'

'What's going on? Is everything okay?'

'It's fine,' Rachel reassured him. 'But it's important, so I need to go. Okay?'

Phil paused. 'Okay.' He raised his eyebrows, sighed and went back to watching *Bluey*.

It *was* important. It was also madness, but it was important.

She kept telling herself this as she got in the car and drove. The satnav said two hours and seven minutes. She was aiming for under two. She put her foot down and hoped that she didn't get stopped by the police or snapped by any speed cameras. *But this is worth sitting through a speed awareness course for.* The roads were pretty clear, so she tried to relax a bit and eased into the steady, monotonous pace of the A-roads.

It was about an hour and forty minutes into the journey that she realised she was still wearing her pyjamas.

As Rachel pulled into the hotel car park her phone started ringing.

'Hello?' she said, pulling over by the entrance, as she couldn't see any space in the car park. She was not sure why she was whispering.

'Where are you?' asked Frankie. 'I've just been to yours, and Phil said you're out.'

'Can't a woman have any secrets?'

Rachel was trying to sound mysterious, but Frankie snapped straight back, 'Not when we're investigating a murder, no!'

She had a point.

'I've come to talk to Ben,' Rachel admitted, eventually.

'I thought they were in Norfolk?' Frankie sounded confused.

'They are.'

'Wait, you haven't driven to bloody Norfolk, have you? It's the middle of the bloody night!'

'I needed to speak to him!'

'They're coming back tomorrow,' said Frankie. 'Couldn't it have waited one day?' Rachel could feel her eyes rolling through the phone.

'No! I needed to speak to him *now*.' She looked at her watch, it was just past ten. *Hardly the middle of the night.* 'Why are you calling so late anyway?'

'I messaged Gina,' said Frankie, before leaving a dramatic pause. 'You won't believe it, but... Victoria bought her that bee keyring.'

'What! Really?'

'Yep, so she says. So, maybe we've been barking up the wrong tree?'

'No way,' said Rachel. 'Not from what I've just read...'

'Oh,' Frankie started to whisper. 'Have you read the rest of the letters?'

'I have indeed. And let's just say they make for *extremely* interesting reading.'

Someone, who was probably a receptionist, had come out of the front door of the hotel and was eyeing her car.

'I've got to go,' she said, before hanging up and manoeuvring the car into a space she had spotted at the far end of the car park.

She quickly walked back over to the hotel entrance, smoothing down her top and desperately hoping that the receptionist thought she was wearing stylish loungewear, not fifteen quid Asda pyjamas.

'Can I help you?' asked the receptionist.

'Oh hi,' said Rachel, politely. 'So sorry to arrive at such a late hour, but I was hoping to speak with one of your guests... it is quite urgent.'

'Fine.' The receptionist smiled in the way that only receptionists can. 'Do come in and take a seat in the lobby. Which guest were you after?'

The lobby, thought Rachel. *Are we suddenly in an American gangster movie?* but she just said, 'Ben Evans, please.' Then added, 'It's a work matter,' so that it didn't seem too clandestine.

'And who shall I say is wanting to see him?'

Before Rachel had time to think, the words, 'Detective Inspector Harding,' had escaped from her lips.

'Of course,' said the receptionist, with a sudden sense of urgency. She scurried back behind her counter and tapped furiously at her keyboard. 'I will call his room right away, detective.'

43

JANE

Jane had just turned off her bedside light when the phone rang. It took her by surprise; it was the first time she had heard the chirp of a landline in quite some time.

'Hello,' she said in a sleepy slur. She listened for a moment before sitting up straighter in bed and saying, 'Oh, okay, I will send him down.'

Jane put the receiver down and turned to Ben. 'DI Harding is in reception to see you.'

'What?' said Ben. 'She can't be.'

'Well, she is! That was the hotel reception on the phone.'

Ben looked at the radio alarm clock by the side of the bed. Another thing that Jane hadn't seen in quite a while. *Were all coastal hotels stuck in the nineties or was it just in Norfolk?*

'It's past ten,' said Ben, as he hopped out of bed and pulled on some trousers. He looked in the mirror and flattened down his crumpled T-shirt, then did the same to his untamed hair. 'What the hell could she want at this hour?' He paused. 'In Norfolk?'

'I was about to ask the same thing.' Jane folded her arms and leaned back against the tower of pillows she had propped up.

'Don't look at me like that, love. It'll be some work thing.'

'What work thing is important enough to drive all the way to Norfolk for? At this time of night?'

He shrugged. 'I honestly don't know.'

Jane sighed.

'I'd better go,' he said. 'I don't want to keep her waiting.'

'No,' said Jane. 'Just keep me waiting instead.'

'Sorry, love,' he said before slipping out of the bedroom door.

Jane looked over at Lottie, flat out on the sofa bed. All that sea air had wiped her out. She wished she was in her place, dreaming of crashing waves, sea breezes and kaleidoscopic shells. Instead she was wide awake, wondering why her husband was being called upon, late at night, by the detective inspector in charge of a murder case. The same murder case that she and her friends had been looking into. The murder case that her husband was definitely *not* assigned to. Something was up. There was no chance she was getting to sleep now, she would be wide awake until she found out what the hell was going on.

She tapped out a message and sent it to The Jam Sandwich Detectives chat.

> Jane (Lottie's mum): What the bloody hell is going on? DI Harding has just turned up at our hotel.

> Frankie (Billy's mum): What?! 😮

> Jane (Lottie's mum): She's talking to Ben. Has something happened?

> Frankie (Billy's mum): Not that I know of. It is probably just routine. They've been talking to everyone.

> Jane (Lottie's mum): Have they followed anyone else to Norfolk?

> Frankie (Billy's mum): Try not to panic, Jane. I'm sure everything will be fine. Does your hotel room have a mini bar? Maybe have a drink to calm the nerves.

Jane threw her phone onto the bed. *Have a drink?* That was Frankie's advice. A fat lot of help she was, and it took every fibre in Jane's being to stop herself from typing this. She took a deep breath and tried to stop the anger rising in her chest. If she was honest with herself, that anger had been bubbling away long before today. Probably ever since Frankie had started muscling in between her and Rachel.

Jane had been getting on really well with Rachel. She had started to feel like she had an actual friend, more than just a polite *Hello*, on the playground and someone she could actually talk to. Then, just as they started to really click, Frankie had turned up. Jane *knew* that she could have helped Rachel prove her innocence, and that they didn't need Frankie's help, but Rachel had insisted and now Jane felt like Frankie was gradually stealing Rachel away from her. She wouldn't let that happen. She hadn't wanted Frankie to get involved in the first place, and now here she was telling her to calm down and have a drink, when her husband was being questioned by the detective in charge of the case.

She would not calm down. She needed to know what was going on.

It was hard to tell from a text message but Jane had this niggling feeling that despite the shocked emoji, Frankie wasn't actually very shocked at all about DI Harding's unexpected visit. She was starting to wonder whether she could trust

Frankie at all, and why hadn't Rachel replied? Something wasn't right but she couldn't quite put her finger on what it was.

> Jane (Lottie's mum): Where is Rachel?

> Frankie (Billy's mum): …is typing…

Jane waited for a reply, but one didn't appear.

That's it, she thought. *I refuse to be ignored.*

She stormed towards the door. Then hesitated. *Lottie will be all right for a minute,* she thought. After all, she would only be downstairs. But then she saw herself in the mirror. Could she go down like this? She had no make-up on, her hair was scraped back in a ponytail and she was in her pyjamas. She didn't want DI Harding to see her like this; who she really was... no filter.

She went into the bathroom and grabbed her make-up bag. She would feel better about sticking up for her husband with a bit of lippy on, and coming face to face with DI Harding would be easier with a squirt of perfume and brushed hair.

Her eyes filled with tears as she let her mind wander and come up with its own reasons about why DI Harding might be there. She wondered what Ben might have done. She hadn't wanted to believe that Ben would do anything so stupid, but DI Harding had come all this way to speak to him. It must be serious.

She dabbed the mascara from under her eyelashes, took a deep breath and walked towards the hotel room door.

44

———

RACHEL

Rachel sat up straight, on a velour armchair in the corner of the hotel reception. Ben was taking a while to appear and occasionally the receptionist glanced up at her, over her glasses, so Rachel tried to look, well, detective-like.

She took in the decor and noted that it didn't look quite as luxurious as Jane's Instagram photos had made it seem. The wallpaper was peeling at the corners and some of the picture frames looked like they hadn't seen a duster in a fair few years.

She scrunched up her face as she tried to make out what one of the pictures that hung in an over-elaborate frame was supposed to be, but the sound of her own name snapped her out of her thoughts.

'Rachel?' Ben's expression dropped to the floor as he walked into the otherwise deserted reception area. 'Are you here with DI Harding?'

'Not exactly,' said Rachel, standing up and smoothing down her creased pyjama top.

He raised an eyebrow.

'I am DI Harding.' Rachel smiled.

Ben looked confused.

'I knew you wouldn't come down to speak to me if I said who I really was.'

'So, you lied?'

The receptionist lowered the glasses that were balanced on the end of her nose. 'Is everything okay?'

'Fine,' said Ben, and Rachel was relieved that he wasn't about to cause a scene. He turned back to her. 'Shall we sit down?'

He gestured to the seating area that Rachel had just been sitting in. She nodded and sat back down, slowly and carefully, remembering that she had fallen ungainly into the soft cushion last time she had done so.

'So, what's going on, Ben?' she asked, trying her best to sit still in the slightly wobbly chair.

'I could ask you the same question... following us all the way to Norfolk in the middle of the night?'

'You know exactly why I'm here.' She raised her eyebrows and stared him straight in the face.

'I'm not sure I do,' said Ben, and Rachel let out a puff of air, frustrated by his stubbornness. 'All I do know is that you've been snooping around in things that don't concern you and getting my wife caught up in things that don't concern her either.'

'But they do concern her, don't they, Ben?' said Rachel. 'And they concern me too. They concern me very much!'

Ben didn't seem to have anything to say to that, so Rachel continued. 'How long had you been sleeping with Victoria?' She decided that getting straight to the point was the best way.

'I beg your pardon!'

'Are you denying it?'

He opened his mouth to speak, then hesitated and sighed.

'Is there any point? You seem to have made up your mind already.'

'So, that's a no?'

Ben was silent again.

'I didn't kill her,' he said eventually. 'If that's where this is going. I didn't. I wouldn't.'

'Listen,' said Rachel, more softly this time. 'Just tell me what happened and I might be able to help you... if you really didn't do it then you've got nothing to hide.' *Well, apart from an affair.*

She hoped that this different approach might be more effective. She was getting into detective mode after all. And Ben had the look of a man with a lot to confess.

He took a deep breath. 'I used to go round and do odd jobs, y'know, water her garden, mow the lawn. She was on her own and I think she missed having a man around the house.'

'Sounds like she's had a few men around the house lately.'

Ben blushed, and it made Rachel feel uncomfortable; seeing a strong man look so vulnerable.

'Anyway, one day a while back, Jane realised that the spare key Victoria had given me was on the bee keyring that she had bought me, and she flipped.'

'Oh,' said Rachel, surprised at this revelation. 'So, Jane really did buy you that bee keyring? I had a niggling feeling you had made that up.'

'Why would I make it up?' asked Ben.

For a lot of reasons, thought Rachel, but she didn't say that. Instead she asked, 'So, what happened when Jane flipped about the key?'

'She told me that I couldn't go round there anymore.'

'And did you?'

'Did I...?'

'Did you go round there, Ben?'

He paused and Rachel already knew the answer.

'Is that when it started?' she asked.

He lowered his head.

'Is that when it turned into something more?' she probed. 'Were you proving a point? That she couldn't tell you what to do. Is that how it all began? What started as a few innocent odd jobs grew into a whole host of other jobs? Just so that you could prove a point.'

'It wasn't like that,' said Ben, almost inaudibly.

'So, what was it like?'

The silence was suddenly unbearable, but Rachel knew that she had to let it hang in the air so that he would answer the question.

'I liked her,' he said finally. And there it was, the truth. He liked Victoria, and she liked him too, and Rachel could guess the rest.

'You fell for each other,' said Rachel, and Ben's head was now in his hands. 'Did she threaten to tell Jane?' He didn't respond. 'Is that why you killed her?'

She thought he was going to shout, scream at her that he didn't kill Victoria, but he looked her straight in the eyes and said, 'I don't have to answer your questions, Rachel. You are not the police. I'm going to bed.'

She watched him get up to leave.

'No,' she said. 'But I am your wife's friend.'

He walked back towards the staircase and she wondered if she should call her friend now and tell her that her husband – the murderer – was on his way back to her. Tell her to run. Tell her to hide. But somehow she knew that he wouldn't hurt Jane, not physically. After all, he loved her so much that maybe he would kill to protect their marriage.

But he didn't love her enough to not sleep with another

woman. And he didn't love her enough to take that woman's key off their special bee keyring. Rachel's mind was working overtime as she wondered whether that crime was actually worse. Maybe the sex could be forgiven, but the disregard for the significance of a special keepsake... that was heinous.

45

JANE

As Jane finally made it to the bottom of the stairs a flushed Ben was walking towards her, and the main hotel entrance door swung shut as the shape of a woman disappeared out of it.

DI Harding.

'What the hell is going on, Ben?'

'Just give me a minute to process it all, will you, love?' said Ben, as he walked straight past her and headed off up the stairs.

She followed him up, staying silent for as long as she could manage, but inside her were a million questions. She was bursting to speak, but knew she had to time it right to get anything even close to an honest answer.

Once they were back in the relative safety of their hotel room, Ben sat down on the side of the bed and put his head in his hands.

Jane took a deep breath. 'Tell me the truth, Ben,' she said in a quieter and more controlled tone. 'You owe me that.'

Ben sighed. He looked over at their daughter, her breath slow and steady as she slept. Jane knew that he wished, like she did, that he could be that relaxed. Jane wished that their life could always be as simple as looking at Lottie made it feel. But then her actual life swamped those thoughts and she was back to feeling at a complete loss.

'I think you know the truth,' he said eventually, looking down at the stiff carpet, the kind you have in hotels to disguise the stains.

Jane didn't say anything... until she did. 'I want to hear it from you.'

Ben just shook his head and his silence annoyed her more than anything he had already done to hurt her. Maybe it was time for Jane to be honest with her friends. Maybe she should tell them what her husband had been up to. Or maybe they had already worked it out for themselves.

Lottie stirred. 'What's going on?' she asked in a sleepy voice. 'Is it morning already?'

'No, darling,' said Jane, tucking her daughter back under the duvet. 'Everything is fine. You go back to sleep. We've got a long drive in the morning.'

A long drive back to face the music, Jane thought as she looked at Ben.

A single tear ran down his cheek. Some were welling up in her own eyes, but she refused to let him see her cry.

They sat in silence in the car.

Lottie had her earphones in, so they could have talked in confidence, but there was nothing to say.

Jane's phone pinged and she ignored it at first, but after three more chirps, Ben snapped, 'Just look at your phone, will you? I'm trying to drive.'

She took her phone out of her handbag and wondered why couples always did that, get cross at each other about mundane annoyances, rather than the things that actually mattered. Was it because they were easier to confront? Less heartache involved? Easier to resolve? She presumed it was for all of those reasons, and so she said, 'Sorry, I'll put it on silent.' And they were the first words she had spoken since they got onto the main road towards home.

She scrolled through the messages in The Jam Sandwich Detectives chat.

> Frankie (Billy's mum): Sorry about last night @Jane, I fell asleep so I didn't see your last message.

Jane knew this was a lie as her phone had told her Frankie was typing, but then she had stopped.

> Rachel (Megan's mum): @Jane We need to talk.
>
> It's important.
>
> What time are you home today?

Jane started typing a reply but then stopped. She was doing exactly what Frankie had done to her the night before, but she didn't have the words right now to explain what had been going on.

> Rachel (Megan's mum): It's important @Jane We are worried about you and we want to protect you.

It was too late for that. Jane's heart was already broken in two. Broken by Ben. Broken by Frankie. What did Rachel even want to protect her from?

Eventually she typed out a reply.

> Jane (Lottie's mum): We'll be home in an hour.

Rachel (Megan's mum): Great, come to mine.
Phil is taking the kids swimming. You too
@Frankie if you're free.

Frankie (Billy's mum): As a bird!

Then Frankie sent a GIF of three little birds, sitting on a branch together and Jane wondered if they would ever get back to that. The closeness of The Jam Sandwich Detectives had begun to dissolve more and more the longer that the investigation had gone on. At the start they had been three birds solving a mystery, but now they seemed to be weighed down by secrets and lies and Jane wondered if sometimes mysteries were best left as just that.

'I'm popping out when we get back,' said Jane, making sure it was a statement rather than a question.

'I thought we could stop for lunch,' said Ben.

'I haven't got time,' Jane insisted. 'I said I'd be back in an hour.'

'Of course you did,' said Ben. 'Off to see your crazy stalker friends I guess?'

She looked at him but his eyes were on the road.

'What do you mean, *stalker*?'

'Oh nothing, just can't get rid of them that's all.'

'I don't want to get rid of them,' said Jane.

And then the silence returned, and lingered for the rest of the journey home.

As Jane sat and soaked it in, she thought about her words. She absolutely *did not* want to get rid of her friends, especially Rachel, the first person to really be kind to her. In fact she wanted to cling onto her for dear life.

46

RACHEL

'Thanks for coming, Jane,' said Rachel, as she opened the front door. The first thing she noticed was how tired Jane looked, like she had the weight of the world on her shoulders.

'Of course,' Jane responded. 'You asked me to, so of course I would come.'

'Come in and sit down.' Rachel ushered her through to the kitchen, where Frankie was already sitting.

'Oh,' said Jane. 'Frankie, you're already here.'

'Yes.' Frankie smiled, and Rachel wondered whether she had correctly detected the irritated tone in Jane's voice. 'We wanted a quick chat.'

'There's something we need to tell you,' said Rachel, and she patted the table indicating for Jane to sit down opposite where she was now sitting.

Jane obliged and the friends all sat politely, and with uncomfortable formality, for a moment.

'Jane,' said Rachel, taking a moment to compose herself. 'There's no easy way to…'

'We think that Ben has been having an affair,' Frankie

blurted out and Rachel frowned at her, annoyed that she had jumped in.

Rachel's and Frankie's eyes met. Rachel gave her a look of *I was supposed to say that,* and received back a *So what? Someone had to say it* look, from Frankie.

Rachel had been taking it slowly, thinking about how to put it into words; thinking about the gentlest way to tell Jane. She also thought it should have come from her, but then, after seeing Jane's reaction, she realised that it didn't matter, that the words had the same meaning however they were spoken and whoever they were spoken by.

As she looked away from Frankie and back at Jane, she saw the heartache. She had been so wrapped up in how this revelation affected the investigation, she had barely thought about how upsetting it would be for Jane. Even now, she was so distracted by her thoughts, that at first it didn't fully register when Jane responded.

'I know.'

Jane looked down.

Rachel shrank into herself and when she eventually spoke, it was almost in a whisper. 'You know?'

'Of course I bloody know,' said Jane. 'How many odd jobs can one woman need? He was always popping round there to prune a hedge or water her plants. *Why can't she do it herself? I* thought one time, so I followed him and there was Greg, mowing the sodding lawn while Victoria was inside shagging my husband!'

The room fell silent.

The cogs turned in Rachel's mind. *Why would Ben kill Victoria if Jane already knew?*

'Does Ben know that you know?'

'No,' said Jane. 'I didn't tell anyone. I was so ashamed.'

Frankie's eyebrows shot up her forehead at this.

'Oh, Jane.' Rachel placed a hand on her shoulder. 'You have nothing to be ashamed about. It is Ben that should be ashamed.'

'How?' asked Frankie. 'How did you keep all that inside, Jane? The heartache, the betrayal, the anger?'

Suddenly, Jane burst into the most tears Rachel could remember seeing for quite some time, and she had a four year old. She sat and sobbed, her perfect make-up streaming down her face. All traces of confidence and strength had vanished and Rachel sat looking at a fragile shell of a woman. Rachel and Frankie did their best to console her. It was like she had held it in all this time and she was finally letting it out.

Rachel was about to ask her why she didn't tell them, her and Frankie, but then it dawned on her that she had no idea how long this had been going on. Presumably long before they really became close friends, long before the murder of her husband's lover.

Hang on. Those cogs were whirring again.

If Jane knew, then she must have had the same suspicions that Rachel and Frankie had got from those letters. Jane must have thought the murderer could have been Ben. All this time, had she been playing along? She had supposedly been helping them to prove Rachel's innocence, but had she just been doing so to protect her husband? Did she still love him enough to protect him after everything he had done?

'And do you know what the worst thing is?' said Jane, wiping the snot from her nose and the tears from her eyes with one swoop of her arm. 'Her spare key. He had her spare key on the keyring that I fucking bought him!'

And there it was, all that anger. It had built up and built up and been toppled over by a final act of betrayal: the bee keyring. More central and important to this whole case than Rachel could ever have realised. But Victoria *had* bought one; it was on that receipt. Had it really been for Gina? Or was that some sort of cover-up?

Rachel needed to escape for a moment, to think this through. 'I'll put the kettle on,' she said. Standard procedure when somebody cries.

She went to the sink and filled the kettle but the thought of another cup of tea gave her the sudden urge to pee.

She sat on the toilet and the five cups of tea she had already drunk that morning trickled out of her, and as they did so, a swirl of thoughts trickled into her mind. This was so often the case as she sat on her throne of thought, the perfect spot for reflection and revelations. Her thoughts started stacking up like Jenga blocks and slotting together to make sense, but then one critical piece slid out, and the whole tower came crashing down.

Jane knew.

Did Jane know that Ben was going to leave her? Was he planning to start a new life with Victoria, take Lottie with him to live in her beautiful cottage? Jane wouldn't have let Victoria take away her family; take away her life...

And now, was it happening again? Frankie and Rachel were becoming close. Did Jane feel like she was getting pushed out? Was Jane worried that Frankie was going to take away her friend? Just like Victoria took away her husband.

Rachel pushed the button on the top of the toilet and everything that she thought she knew flushed out of her mind and left a new truth floating there.

Did Jane love her family enough to kill for them?

And that's when it hit her... did Jane love their friendship enough to kill again?

She plunged the door handle down and her hand, still wet from washing, slipped off and it sprang back up. She pushed it down again, gripping tighter this time, but the door wouldn't move. Something, or someone, was blocking it.

'Jane!' she called. 'Let me out... Frankie! Are you okay?'

Nothing.

'JANE! FRANKIE! SOMEBODY? HELP!'

She rammed down the door handle and shoved at the door. Tugging it. Banging it. Pushing it. Pulling it.

'HELP!' she cried again, but there was no one there to help her. She could no longer hear anyone through the door. No sound at all. No sign of life. Where had they gone? Where had Jane taken Frankie? What was she going to do to her?

She kicked the door and a bolt of excruciating pain shot up her ankle.

'Shit!'

She leant against the door to regain her balance, and then it opened and she fell. She anticipated the hard smack of the ground but it didn't come. She fell into softness. Into the arms of her husband.

'Phil,' she gasped.

'What's going on?' he asked. 'Why was the dresser in front of the door?'

And with that she knew. She knew it was deliberate. She knew Jane had taken Frankie.

47

FRANKIE

Jane ran a trembling hand through her usually pristine hair and left it dishevelled.

The other hand gripped Frankie's arm tightly, the bee-adorned nails almost piercing her skin. Beneath the smudges of tear-streaked mascara, there was panic in Jane's eyes. Their sparkle had gone and they looked wild and angry.

'Where are we going?' asked Frankie. 'Rachel is making us tea.'

'Tea,' said Jane, her voice harsh and gravelly. 'Of course she's making fucking tea. That will sort everything out, won't it? Her answer to bloody everything is tea.'

Frankie swallowed the lump in her throat. 'I think she's just trying to help. To offer support. It has been a difficult time for her too.'

'Oh and don't we bloody know it,' sneered Jane. 'All I have heard lately is what an awful time Rachel is having. So caught up in her pathetic little murder mystery that she doesn't even stop to see that other people have their own stuff going on. That other people's lives are falling apart.'

'Jane, where is this coming from?'

'You're just as bad, Frankie. You have no idea what I've been through.'

'Then tell me.'

Jane didn't listen. 'Swanning around with your red string and your mug shots. Each pin you stuck in that stupid board, was like a stab in my heart.'

'Jane, I... I thought we were a team.' Frankie's heart raced. She had never seen Jane like this. The Insta-smile had vanished, replaced by a hardened frown. A mist had descended over her eyes and they were now dark and serious. Frankie started to feel something that she had never felt towards a friend before.

Fear.

'Jane.' Frankie took a deep breath. 'Let's talk about this. Rachel will be wondering where we are, and–'

'Let her wonder,' said Jane.

'And you're hurting my arm.'

Jane loosened her grip slightly. Her eyes filled with tears. 'You hurt me too you know, Frankie.'

'Well, that was never my intention.'

Jane's bottom lip quivered, but she held on firmly to Frankie's arm and kept walking.

They walked all the way to Jane's house, but this wasn't a friendly stroll. Frankie was being forced there.

As they entered Jane's kitchen, Frankie wondered why they were there and then she saw Jane's phone on the countertop.

Jane swiped it up and started tapping frantically on the screen.

'What now?' asked Frankie.

'Sit,' Jane ordered, and Frankie sat on one of the kitchen stools. They were quite high and she would normally have asked Jane for a hand getting up and they would have giggled as she struggled onto the seat, but not today. She wriggled her way on as quickly as she could manage, with minimum fuss.

Sweat was dripping down Frankie's forehead and she dabbed it with her sleeve. Jane's eyes were wide and frantic, but as Frankie took a deep breath, Jane seemed to make a conscious effort to calm the situation. 'Would you like a glass of water?' she asked.

'Erm, yes,' said Frankie, worrying more about what her answer *should* be than whether she actually wanted one or not.

Jane took a jug from the fridge and poured out a glass of water. 'Ice? Lemon?'

Ice and lemon? This was the most ridiculous hostage situation in the history of hostage situations. If that was what this even was... Frankie had no idea. 'No thanks, just water will be fine.'

She couldn't understand what was going on. She understood that Jane was upset about Ben's carrying-on, and about Frankie and Rachel knowing about it, but grabbing her and forcing her halfway across the village just to give her a glass of water seemed a bit extreme.

'What do you want from me, Jane?' she asked eventually.

'I want to show you something.'

Oh God! thought Frankie. They had been so keen to find out everything about this case, but now she was not sure if this was something that she wanted to see.

'Are you sure?' she asked.

'I'm sure,' said Jane.

RACHEL

'Where's Frankie?' Rachel gasped.

'I don't know,' said Phil. 'I haven't seen her. Is something wrong?'

'Yes! I mean, I don't know. I mean, I think so.'

'Take a deep breath and tell me what is going on,' said Phil, placing his hands on his wife's shoulders.

Rachel breathed slowly, in through her nose and then puffed out a steady stream of air. Phil did the same as he faced her.

Then Rachel spoke as clearly and calmly as she could manage. 'I think that Jane killed Victoria, and I think she's about to try and kill Frankie too.'

'Okay,' said Phil. Rachel could see the shock in his face, she could see the million questions behind his eyes, she could see the disbelief, but he remained the calm presence that she needed and he simply said, 'Do you have any idea where they might be?'

And that was why she loved him. He was always so calm in a crisis. Act now, think later. Get things sorted.

She thought about his question. Where might they be? 'Maybe Jane's house.'

'Really? Is she likely to murder her friend in her own house?'

'Good point.' Rachel thought for a second. 'Then, maybe Frankie's house, the café, the woods, the graveyard... I have no idea where you murder someone, I mean, I'm not a murderer after all.'

'I think it might be best to call the police,' said Phil. 'Your amateur sleuthing has got you this far, but it might be time to leave it to the professionals.'

From anyone else this sentence might have sounded sarcastic and almost certainly would have been as patronising as hell, but somehow from Phil it seemed kind. He had stuck behind her the whole way. Left her to her investigation, never belittled it or laughed at it. He had been reassuringly faithful and told her on many occasions that he knew she was innocent. She was lucky. She guessed that was all that Jane had wanted. For Ben to stick by her. To love her and not to betray her.

'I'll call DI Harding,' she said, as she fumbled through her handbag. 'I'm sure she gave me her card.'

'Do you think we should call Ben too?' asked Phil, and it made Rachel stop in her tracks.

She had spent the past couple of days assuming Ben's guilt and now realised she had been way off the mark. He was guilty of something, but it wasn't murder. She should call him. She should apologise. She had followed him half way across the country and hounded him with questions in the middle of the night.

'Yes,' she said. 'I probably should. He might know where Jane is. But I'll call DI Harding first.' She held the crumpled card aloft and Phil nodded.

'I'll put the kettle on,' he said. He really was a good egg.

'Actually...' Rachel was thinking out loud. 'I'll text Ben, then I can wait for a reply while I speak to DI Harding.'

Phil had disappeared to make the tea.

> Rachel (Megan's mum): Ben! Is Jane with you? She's got Frankie and I'm worried that she's going to do something stupid.

But she didn't have to wait any time at all. She didn't even have time to tap DI Harding's number into her phone.

> Ben (Lottie's dad): I think you might be too late!

Rachel nearly dropped her phone, but the need to know what he meant gave her the strength to cling onto it.

> Rachel (Megan's mum): What do you mean?

> Ben!

> You're freaking me out!!!

> Ben (Lottie's dad): Message forwarded: Ben, I've done something stupid. I don't know what to do. I don't know how to make things right. I think it's over. J x

Shit!

49

FRANKIE

'Jane!' said Ben, letting the front door slam behind him and bursting into the kitchen. 'What the hell is going on? What was with the cryptic message?'

Despite her suspicions about Ben, Frankie felt a wave of relief at his arrival. She was glad to not be alone with Jane anymore, and although he probably wasn't her first choice of backup, at least he was something. He was someone.

'It's over, Ben,' said Jane.

His face fell.

'What are you talking about?'

'We can both stop pretending that we don't know what the other has done. You have torn this family apart and I, well, I have thrown the pieces into the fire.'

Frankie averted her eyes and looked down at the floor, feeling that she was intruding on this private moment, despite the fact that she had been dragged here unwillingly.

'Here!' said Jane, thrusting her phone in Frankie's face.

She took the phone from Jane and studied the photo that filled the screen. Pressing her lips together she looked over at Ben and then back down at the phone. She was trying to take in exactly what she was looking at, and as she stared down at it, everything began to make sense.

'Oh, not that photo again,' said Ben, rolling his eyes. 'I told you, it was nothing.'

'You're a liar,' said Jane. 'I know it was more than just this photo. It was humiliating, and you let it happen.'

'Love,' said Ben. 'Can we talk about this?'

'What's going on?' said Lottie, wandering into the room.

'Nothing,' snapped Jane. 'Go back to your room.'

Lottie looked taken aback and turned to leave, her eyes filling with tears.

Ben put his hand on her shoulder. 'It's okay,' he whispered, and Jane scowled at him.

A tear fell down Jane's cheek as Lottie left, quickly and quietly.

'I never meant to hurt Lottie,' she sniffed. 'I wanted to hold on to her so tightly. I couldn't bear that Victoria was going to take her away.'

'What?' asked Frankie.

'She had already taken my husband, I couldn't bear it if she took my whole family.'

'But Lottie loves you,' said Frankie. 'She would love you no matter what.'

'We'll see,' said Jane. 'Will she be able to love me after what I have done?'

Frankie frowned, trying to understand what Jane was telling her.

'I was at my lowest... and then... and then you took Rachel.'

'What are you talking about?'

'You have been trying to take her away from me from the moment you started poking your nose in.'

'Hang on,' said Frankie. 'You came to me.'

'To question you, and then suddenly you wheedled your way into the team.'

'I never meant to–'

'It's the story of my life.' Jane's anger seemed to have dispersed and been replaced by sadness.

'I thought we were friends,' said Frankie.

'*Were!*' Jane laughed. 'Like I said: story of my life.'

Frankie studied her face. She couldn't believe the change in the woman standing in front of her. Something had happened and Frankie was still not entirely sure what. She had been worried about what Ben might do but now it seemed as if Jane was the person to fear.

As Ben paced up and down the kitchen, Jane leaned on the counter shaking her head and muttering to herself, words that sounded like, *What now?*

'Guys,' said Frankie, eventually. 'Can I go?'

'No,' snapped Jane, staring at her like thunder as Ben kept pacing.

'Okay!' Frankie held both hands up. 'In that case... why don't we have a cup of tea?' Jane scowled at her but she persevered. 'We could sit and have a nice, calm chat. You could tell me exactly what has happened and I can see if there is any way I can help. And if I can't help,' Frankie was determined to get this all out, 'then I can listen, and that might be good for you too.'

Ben stopped pacing and looked from his wife to Frankie, and then back to Jane.

'You don't realise what you're asking me to do, Frankie,' said Jane. 'I could tell you, but then I'd have to...'

And in that moment Frankie realised what was going on here.

'Don't say it,' said Frankie, as she swallowed hard. 'I don't want to hear you say it.'

50

RACHEL

Rachel waited for the ringing to stop and as soon as the call clicked in she spoke.

'Something awful's happened!'

'Hello? Who is this?' DI Harding's voice sounded concerned but kind. Not harsh, like someone being called by a stranger on a Sunday could have been. Except of course, Rachel wasn't a stranger. DI Harding had questioned her about a murder just days ago, and now here she was phoning the detective about what she hoped and prayed wasn't about to become another one.

'It's Rachel Walker. I'm sorry to call on a Sunday, but I think that my friend Frankie is in trouble.'

'Okay, tell me everything.' DI Harding paused. 'Tell me the quick version.' She could obviously sense the panic in Rachel's voice.

So, Rachel did. She told her everything. She told her about the bee keyring, and the letters. She told her what Ben had said and what Jane had said and she told her how Jane had been *helping* them with their investigation; throwing in what Rachel now knew were red herrings all over the place, accusing other people when it was her all along. And as she said all this, the tears came.

'I trusted her,' said Rachel, realising why the lies stung so much.

DI Harding sighed on the other end of the phone. 'Why didn't you come to me earlier? Why didn't you tell me you were investigating all this yourselves?'

Rachel wasn't sure. 'Because I was your prime suspect,' she said, although this wasn't the truth. The truth was that she wanted to do something for herself. A project. She wanted to be the leader of her little mum crew. She wanted to be in control. Proving her innocence was an added bonus. Just the cherry on top of the jam sandwich cake.

'Well, you should have,' said DI Harding. 'We could have worked together. Everyone is innocent until proven guilty. I would have listened.'

'Sorry,' said Rachel. 'I will next time.'

DI Harding laughed. 'I'll hold you to that.' She let their conversation hang in the air for a moment and then said. 'Right, let's find Frankie. I'm on my way.'

He picked up straight away when Rachel called him.

'Ben, the police are on their way. We need to find her. I really hope the stupid thing she has done isn't what I'm thinking. I would never forgive myself. But I'm worried that it is. She knows about you and Victoria, Ben. She knew all along and I think that Frankie is in danger.'

'Slow down,' said Ben. 'Take a breath, Rachel. They are here. Jane is here and Frankie is fine.'

'She is? They are? Why didn't you... Oh, thank God! I'm on my way.'

She ran all the way to Ben and Jane's house. The adrenaline must have kicked in somewhere along the way as she arrived calm and composed, and not the slightest bit out of breath. *Screw you Couch to 5k. Who needs an app when you think one of your friends is about to get murdered?*

As she walked into Jane's lounge and saw Frankie sitting there, the relief overwhelmed her. Ben had told her on the phone that she was fine, but she didn't know what to believe any more and the panic had bubbled away inside her until she saw Frankie with her own eyes.

Frankie stood up and Rachel threw her arms around her.

She saw the frown appear on Jane's face, and the daggers that shot towards her from Jane's eyes. It was a look of jealousy, and Rachel couldn't quite believe that even now, after everything, Jane could still be jealous of a hug between friends.

'Jane,' said Rachel, turning to the woman who used to be her friend. Who, she supposed, still was her friend. Everyone makes mistakes after all and isn't friendship all about forgiveness?

'Rachel,' said Jane. 'Let me explain.'

Jane's phone was lit up on the coffee table between them all. A picture filled the screen. The picture was of a group of glamorous women. Natasha was at the centre looking rather drunk, mascara smeared down her face and red wine spilt down her pale dress. Victoria was at the edge, an arm draped around her. The arm belonged to a man who was kissing her on the cheek. The man was Ben. The man was Jane's husband.

'There is no need,' said Rachel, with a timid smile. 'I already understand.'

And she did.

———

After a uniformed officer had taken Jane away in handcuffs and DI Harding had taken statements from everyone, Rachel and Frankie left Ben and Lottie to come to terms with everything, and they walked home.

'She was just trying to protect her family,' said Rachel. 'She didn't want to lose *everything* just because her husband couldn't keep it in his pants.'

'The irony being of course, that she has now lost it all anyway,' said Frankie.

'I know, but I'm sure DI Harding joined the police force to get dangerous and evil people off the streets, not mums who have been let down by their partners and acted in a moment of desperation.'

Frankie nodded. 'Victoria was just a lonely mum too. She didn't deserve to lose her life for it.'

Rachel sighed. 'Us women should be sticking together, not killing each other over a man. And mums shouldn't be competing with each other. It is not a competition; it's survival. We're all on the same ship. We should be supporting each other, not showing off and trying to out-mum one another.'

'Hear hear,' said Frankie. 'Rachel for PM or actually, I hear they are looking for a new chair of the PTA!'

'Frankie!' Rachel rolled her eyes and dropped her head into her hand.

'Too soon?' asked Frankie.

'Definitely too soon,' said Rachel, stifling a smile.

51

JANE

The door opened and joy bubbled up in Jane.

'Rachel,' she said, as her friend sat down in front of her holding a brown paper bag.

Rachel smiled. 'How are you, Jane?'

Jane paused, and swallowed. 'I'm okay,' she said, eventually. 'All things considered. Thank you so much for coming. I didn't think...'

'Well,' said Rachel. 'I wanted to see you.'

Jane smiled and pushed some wispy strands of hair behind her ears. 'I just can't believe you actually came.'

'Try and stop me,' said Rachel. 'I've always wanted to look inside a real lock-up. Exciting, isn't it? Like a proper detective now I am...' Jane didn't say anything so Rachel continued. 'Sorry, I don't mean *exciting*, I didn't think... well no, I didn't think, Jane. Sorry.'

Jane smiled. Rachel was exuding nervous energy.

'I'll start again,' said Rachel. 'You look...' Jane could tell that she didn't really know what to say about her grey marl sweatshirt and joggers, her scraped back hair and the much-less-glamorous-than-usual metal bands adorning her wrists.

'Bloody awful,' said Jane. 'I am fully aware of how I look… but don't worry, I won't be posting this *look* on Instagram any time soon.'

Rachel laughed and Jane couldn't help but let out a little giggle.

'Whyever not? Grey is the new black, so I've heard.'

Jane smiled and her mind wandered. She started wondering whether starting a *fashion behind bars* or a *prison cell decor* Instagram page might be fun, although she wasn't sure she was even allowed social media in prison. *Oh God!* She hadn't thought about that. How would she cope?

'Are you going to be okay, Jane?' Rachel asked, snapping back to serious.

'I think so,' said Jane. She wasn't sure that she would be, but rather than say that, she made a stupid joke. 'Prison will be like a rest… no laundry, no cooking, no cleaning, no school runs. What will I do with myself?'

Rachel didn't laugh. 'Oh, Jane.'

Jane sighed.

'Have you spoken to Ben?' Rachel asked.

'He's been in once, which is more than I expected to be honest, and more than I deserve, but he has at least acknowledged his part in all this and he has apologised, so that is something.'

She looked down at the handcuffs around her wrists, which to her were ridiculous. She knew that she wasn't a danger to anyone else, but no one else knew that, she supposed.

'Will you keep an eye on him for me?' she said eventually. 'I don't expect him to wait around for me, I don't mean keep an eye on him in that regard, I just mean… y'know, check he's okay.'

'Of course,' said Rachel.

'And Lottie…' a tear fell down her cheek. 'She's got two

parents to be angry at, but I want her to know that we both love her.'

Rachel smiled. 'She will know.'

Jane lifted both hands so that she could wipe her tear away, and then rested her forehead on her palms for a moment.

'They are going to be fine, Jane, and so are you.' Rachel paused. 'And, Jane...'

'Yes?'

'I'm sorry.'

Jane looked confused. 'Why are *you* sorry?'

'I was too busy making it all about me,' said Rachel. 'Even before the investigation and proving my innocence, I was always focused on myself. How *I* could make the best cake for the Bake Off party... I didn't stop to think about you.'

Jane shook her head. 'Don't be silly.'

'But maybe if I'd asked how you were instead of instructing you to bake me a cake–'

'It is not your fault, Rachel. You are, and have *always* been completely innocent.'

Rachel smiled and looked at her watch.

Please don't leave yet, thought Jane, but she didn't say it. She didn't want to seem too needy.

She looked around the room. She got it. Why would anyone want to stay here a moment longer than they needed to? Why did Rachel even come in the first place? She didn't have to. Jane suddenly felt overwhelming gratitude towards her friend.

'Why did you go along with the investigation?' asked Rachel. 'Was it just to throw us curveballs? You could have just thrown me under the bus. If you'd let me take the blame, you would be a free woman now.' Rachel's voice was starting to rise and Jane was worried that it was dawning on her that she should be more angry than she had been so far.

'You want the truth?' asked Jane.

Rachel nodded. 'It is probably about time for it.'

'I was enjoying it,' said Jane, and it was the absolute full and honest truth.

And Rachel who had looked ready to shout and scream, just nodded. 'Yeah, me too.'

'It's me that should be saying sorry to you,' said Jane, after a reflective pause. 'At first, I was trying to throw you off the scent, but before long I got caught up in the camaraderie. It was exhilarating, and I was trying to prove your innocence as much as you and Frankie were.'

'Just ideally without dropping yourself in it?'

'Well, yes. Why do you think I chose to do it on the day of the Bake Off party? Plenty of other suspects,' said Jane. 'Bit late for that now though!'

Rachel let out a very soft laugh.

'I'm not expecting us to go back to what we had before,' said Jane. 'But I want you to know that I value your friendship. You have no idea how much it means to me that you have come to visit me today. I mean that.'

'I know.'

When Rachel got up to leave, Jane said, 'Rach, never take what you have for granted. I would give anything for a week in the sun right now.'

Rachel smiled and nodded. She had been clutching a brown paper bag ever since she arrived, but Jane had not asked what was in it. Her place in the pecking order had dropped considerably and she had no right to be nosey or inquisitive any more, but she couldn't help wondering. *Was it something for her?* She had been wanting to know the whole time Rachel had been there, but she knew that she had to wait.

Patience was something she was going to need in this place, plus, it was not polite to ask someone if the package they were holding was a gift for you, even if you were the only other non-uniformed person in the room, and especially if that room was in a prison.

Before Rachel left, she placed the brown paper bag in front of Jane, who looked at it and said, 'Thank you,' despite not knowing what was inside.

'Bye, Jane,' said Rachel.

'Goodbye, Rachel,' said Jane, and as her friend turned to leave, she opened the brown paper bag.

52

———

RACHEL

Rachel laid the table with their best cutlery.

She put out her crystal champagne flutes, then decided that fizz was inappropriate so swapped them for ordinary wine glasses, the nice ones though, from John Lewis. The television chattered away in the background, but she wasn't paying any attention to it. Not until she heard Jane's name.

'Local mother-of-one Jane Evans, who has been on remand for almost a month after being charged with the murder of another local woman, Victoria Sandwich, attended her plea hearing earlier today. Ms Sandwich was thought to have died from anaphylactic shock caused by traces of nut, but it later emerged that she had been poisoned. Ms Evans, who is awaiting trial, pleaded guilty to murder at today's hearing.'

Rachel dropped the glass she was holding and it shattered into tiny shards.

'Shit!'

At least it wasn't a crystal flute! She cleaned up the broken glass as quickly as she could and glanced at the clock. Frankie and Amanda would be here soon. It would be the first time she had met Amanda, who was finally back from her army tour.

Rachel had no idea how Frankie did it. She always seemed to have motherhood so under control, despite doing a hell of a lot of solo-parenting. Rachel had Phil, who was great, and she still spent most of her time running around like a headless chicken.

'I'm excited to meet her,' Rachel had said when Frankie had told her she would be back soon. 'You must come round for dinner. Maybe the kids could have a sleepover and we could have a few drinks.'

'That sounds lovely,' Frankie had said and Rachel was relieved because she just wanted, more than anything, to do something normal. To have friends over for dinner and talk about something other than suspects and motives and alibis.

And so, here they were. And they were talking about holidays and cars and how expensive swimming lessons were, and work and pensions and how it was important though, to learn how to swim. And Rachel was glad, and she was relaxed, but after a while she started to feel uncomfortable that no one was talking about the big, fat elephant in the room. So, she said, 'I went to see her a few weeks ago – Jane – when she was first on remand.'

And the room fell silent.

Amanda looked at Phil, who gave her a reassuring nod that it was fine, don't panic, it was good to talk about these things. At least that's how Rachel read the nod – but she had been married to him for over a decade. Amanda took a sip of her wine and carried on eating, so she must have got the same nod-vibe too.

'What did you say to her?' asked Frankie in a whisper. Lottie was upstairs, at the sleepover too. Rachel had explained to Frankie that it was to keep Megan company and help Ben out a bit. Frankie had said that she understood and that she had nothing against poor Lottie.

Frankie put her glass down and leant forwards, as if there was about to be some big revelation.

'Not much,' said Rachel, pushing the food around her plate with a fork. 'I got her some Jammie Dodgers. It was the best I could do from the prison shop.'

Amanda's eyebrows raised, but she remained silent. Phil half smiled.

And Frankie nodded. 'The right decision,' she said, and then she added, 'Prisons have a shop?'

They all laughed and then there was a brief silence. Just before it turned into an awkward one, Phil asked, 'So, what now, ladies? Now you've got no Miss Marple-ing to do?'

'Why do people keep comparing us to Miss Marple?' asked Rachel. 'I see myself more like that woman from *Line of Duty*...'

'Or her off *The Fall*?' Frankie chipped in.

'Ooh yes,' said Rachel. 'I wouldn't mind hunting down serial killers if they looked like that guy off *The Fall*.'

'Rachel!' Frankie tutted, shaking her head. 'But yeah, comparing us to someone under retirement age would be a good start!'

'Well, that's the thing, you ladies are way off retiring, so what's the plan?'

Rachel raised one eyebrow at her husband and waited for him to dare to say that it would give her more time to do the housework. 'No crimes to solve and kids all in school...'

'I might speak to Jess, see if I can fast-track to detective like she did...' Rachel's fist clenched and shot to her mouth; she hadn't really meant to say that out loud. It was half a joke and half a test of her husband's and friend's reaction.

Both their eyes widened.

'Sorry, who's Jess?' asked Amanda.

'DI Harding,' said her wife. 'The one who led Victoria's case.'

'How do you know she fast-tracked?'

'Oh, we got chatting,' said Rachel. 'She's actually really nice and I feel kind of bad for referring to her as *Die-Hard* early on!'

Frankie laughed, then said, 'All this job chat reminds me, what happened with that job interview, Rach?'

'Oh, they offered it to me – must have been desperate – but I turned it down.'

'What? I thought you were keen?'

'I was, but this whole drama has made me reassess things. I kept feeling like I had something missing, like I wasn't doing anything for me, but then I realised that this *is* me. Being a mum. I think that sometimes we get pressured into thinking we need to be something more, like there is some sort of shame in being *just a mum*, but when I thought they were going to lock me up and throw away the key, all I could think about was Megan and Charlie. I didn't care about the job, I didn't care about anything, but I did care about being their mum.'

Frankie nodded, Phil smiled and Amanda did too.

'Well, they're lucky to have you as their mum,' said Phil, putting an arm around his wife.

'I bet Lottie would give anything for Jane to be just a mum right now,' added Frankie.

Rachel smiled. 'Plus, of course,' she continued, thinking that the wine was making her sentimental, 'there is no such thing as being *just* a mum. We just have to enjoy the good bits, deal with the difficult bits and not get weighed down by the nonsense.'

'Well, here's to that,' said Frankie, raising her glass.

Rachel clinked it with hers, and the two spouses raised theirs and nodded too.

'What about you, Frankie? Have you done anything with your doodles?'

Frankie flushed a deep shade of pink. 'Well... I did think about starting an Instagram page. Mummy Doodles or Sketchy

Mutha; something like that. Drawing those silly little doodles helps me to relax, so I thought they might help other people too.'

'I *know* they would,' said Rachel, and the two ladies clinked their glasses together again.

Sunday morning came around far too quickly and Rachel's much needed lie-in was interrupted by two very excitable four year olds. Charlie and Billy came bounding into her room at 6:04am.

'What's for breakfast?' asked Charlie.

'Are my mummies still here?' asked Billy.

'Cornflakes and no, they went home, but they are coming back to get you at ten, which is...' She focused her eyes on the clock by her bed. 'Nearly *FOUR* hours away!' *Wow!* she thought as she stumbled downstairs in search of the coffee machine. *What am I going to do with a whole extra child for nearly four hours?*

Make that two extra children.

Rachel had almost forgotten that Lottie was there, she was so understandably quiet.

'Megan's still asleep,' said Lottie, as she wandered into the kitchen and perched on a bar stool.

Rachel poured cornflakes into bowls for the boys in her own still-half-asleep state.

'Can I get you a cup of tea, Lottie? Milk? Juice?' Despite having an eight year old herself, Rachel had temporarily forgotten what they drank.

'Juice is fine,' said Lottie.

'Anything to eat?'

Lottie shook her head.

They sat in silence until Rachel couldn't bear it any longer. 'How's your dad?'

'Fine,' said Lottie, and for a moment Rachel thought that was all she was going to get. 'He knows he messed up, so he's trying to make up for it.'

Rachel smiled. 'Is it working?'

Lottie shrugged. 'I suppose so. Luckily for him, Mum messed up worse!'

'Very true.' Rachel nodded. She put her hand on Lottie's. 'Now, promise me that you won't let their mess-ups mess you up! You are not them. You are you, Lottie Evans. The world is your oyster.'

'Eww, I hate oysters!'

Rachel was pleased to detect a little smile.

'Okay, well the world is your... what do you like?'

Lottie thought for a second. 'Biscoff spread on pancakes.'

'Then the world is your Biscoff pancake,' said Rachel, producing a jar from the cupboard and waving it excitedly. 'Shall we?'

Lottie's smile widened. 'Yes, please!'

53

———————

RACHEL

Despite Rachel's initial panic, the rest of the morning went smoothly.

Her morning coffee re-humanised her and once all four children were full of pancakes, she relaxed and enjoyed the contentment that came with knowing that the kids were happy. The Biscoff spread was their hair-of-the-dog after a sugar-filled sleepover.

Last night the adults had all gone to bed happy too, after an evening filled with fizz and fun, that had lifted the stress of parenting for a moment and helped Rachel put the whole thing into perspective.

At bedtime she had hugged her kids a little tighter, knowing that they were the most important thing in her world, and that them wearing the wrong T-shirt to school or her forgetting to give them a cardboard box and a yoghurt pot to take in, didn't mean that she loved them any less. Hearing Jane's name on the news and the announcement that she had pleaded guilty, and thinking of her in that grey tracksuit, with her unwashed hair and grubby fingernails, made the stress of PE kits and uniform and World Book Day and reading records, flutter away.

None of it mattered.

Being there for her kids was what was important. Loving them unconditionally was what was important. But now Rachel knew that looking after herself was what was important too. She was sure of all this, and the only thing she wasn't sure of was why it had taken a murder to make her realise it.

'What are you going to do this morning, love?' asked Phil, breezing into the kitchen. 'With no murder to solve?'

Rachel sighed.

He had made this joke before and she had laughed, but it was losing its funniness, and she was genuinely missing the sleuthing.

'Scroll through my phone until I lose the will to scroll any longer and then give in and get dressed, I guess.' She hadn't meant for it to sound quite as sarcastic.

She looked Phil up and down; he was in his full football kit.

'I was gonna go for my Sunday morning kick-about with the lads,' said Phil, clearly clocking the raised eyebrows from his wife as she noticed his attire. 'But I could take the kids to the park instead, if you like? And run you a bath? I'll get changed... I didn't think.'

'It's fine,' said Rachel. 'I've got this.'

She got up to take her cold cup of coffee to the microwave and unexpectedly Phil wrapped his arms around her. In the warmth of his embrace she softened a little and let her vulnerable side escape for a moment.

'What do I do now?' she asked her husband.

'Anything you want,' he replied. 'The world is your...'

'Biscoff pancake!' She smiled.

He raised one eyebrow. 'If you like!' Then, after a pause, he asked, 'Are you really thinking of joining the police?'

'No.' She laughed. 'When would I have time to do that?' She paused and thought. 'I might join the PTA!'

Phil's face dropped. 'You're kidding?'

'I am.' Rachel smiled.

'Thank God,' said Phil.

'They don't need me anyway. I hear the FoCUPS cobbled together a brilliant coffee morning. It even made some money for a change!'

Rachel sighed a contented sigh. 'But I will find my something. Something that's right. I know now that I don't have to be just a mum, but also that being one is just fine.'

When the doorbell finally rang, Rachel was calm and relaxed for the first time in ages.

'Billy, your mum's here,' she called up the stairs, and the giggles and pounding feet told her that the boys had either not heard her or chosen not to hear her. 'Frankie!' she beamed as she opened the front door.

'How are you so chipper?' croaked Frankie.

'Sore head?' Rachel laughed.

'Just a bit,' said Frankie, rubbing her forehead. 'Not sure I'm ready to parent today.'

'Of course you are,' said Rachel. 'But come and have a cuppa in the garden first. The boys are happily playing upstairs.'

Rachel put the kettle on and a few minutes later the two women wandered out to the garden with their steaming mugs. It was a beautifully autumnal day and Rachel breathed in the crisp air as she walked across the cool patio in her bare feet.

They sat down on the rattan-effect sofa and made the most of a mild autumn morning. Summer seemed like a distant memory but the October sunshine felt warm on their faces.

'So,' said Rachel. 'Not to dwell on things, but I can't get my head around all the bee keyrings. Victoria only brought one, right?'

'For Gina,' said Frankie. 'Victoria had a soft spot for her. She empathised with her and wanted to look out for her.'

'By buying her cute little gifts?'

Frankie nodded.

'And Jane bought Ben's,' said Rachel.

'Hence why she was so pissed off that he used it for his bit on the side's key.'

'Hmm,' said Rachel. 'So, where did Bee's come from? The one that Victoria left under the flower pot for her.'

'Same key!' said Frankie.

'Ahh...' Rachel suddenly remembered bumping into Jane as she loitered outside Victoria's house. 'Jane must have put it there, as a decoy.'

'Disposing of the evidence,' said Frankie. 'After all, she'd used it to sneak in and poison Victoria's glass earlier in the day.'

'As well as get her hands on the cyanide in the first place? Grace must have had some for a photography project.'

Frankie shook her head. 'Anything Grace might have had from uni wouldn't have been strong enough to kill Victoria, but Jane has police training; she knows her way around the dark web. You can get all sorts on there!'

Rachel's eyes widened. 'How do you know all this?'

'Oh, it's amazing what you have time to chat about when you are being kidnapped.' Frankie smiled.

Rachel bit her lip. 'About that, I haven't asked you how you...'

'It's in the past,' said Frankie. 'She was emotional; she wasn't thinking straight. I am fine.'

Rachel nodded. 'She showed you the photo, the one that Natasha had her knickers in a twist about.'

'Everyone was too busy worrying about what Natasha

looked like,' said Frankie. 'Except Jane, she hadn't even noticed that. All she saw was her husband kissing another woman, and luckily for her, Natasha eventually ordered Victoria to take the photo down. So, Jane just kept quiet. She didn't tell anyone that she was heartbroken. She was so afraid of anyone seeing that her perfect life wasn't as perfect as it seemed, that she hid her problems and it ended up costing her everything.'

The ladies fell silent.

Rachel reflected on everything that had happened. She uncrossed her legs and put both her bare feet firmly on the ground.

'Shit! Ow! Fucking hell!' Her mug of tea crashed to the floor. 'What was that?'

'Are you okay, Rach?' asked a concerned Frankie. 'What happened?'

'Something stung me...' said Rachel, trying not to hop on any bits of broken mug.

'Shit, Rach.'

'Mummy,' Megan came running out of the back door followed by Lottie. 'We heard a crash. Are you okay?'

'I'm fine, darling. I just got stung,' she said, flapping her foot vigorously. 'Can't see the little bugger that did it though.'

Megan scanned the floor. 'Look there on the floor... it's a bee.'

'Sounds about right,' said Rachel, as she sat on the garden sofa and held up a glowing red toe to examine the stinger that was poking out of it.

'Oh no!' wailed Megan. 'That means it's going to die.'

'Aww, come here.' Rachel beckoned her over and Megan sat down next to her mum.

'But bees are nice,' sobbed Megan. 'They make honey.'

Rachel put her arm around her daughter and wiped a tear away from her eye, but as she kept her arm held firmly around

Megan's shoulder, Rachel's eyes were focused on Lottie. 'Bees are very protective creatures. They look after their hive and they only sting when they absolutely have to.'

Later on, when the throbbing in Rachel's toe had died down, she opened up the *Reception Mums #inittogether* chat for the first time in weeks. Natasha had added her back into the group – without even a hint of an apology – once Jane had been arrested. No one had said anything since her return. She assumed that an alternate group, without her in it, had been set up. Either that or everyone had been stunned into silence. Rachel had never asked Frankie whether there was a new chat, mainly because she didn't really want to hear the answer.

She wondered what would happen if she said something in this group now... would anyone respond? Would they be nasty? Would they ignore her? Would they act like nothing had happened?

Did she even want them to respond? Did she want them to ghost her? Did she want them to react? She wasn't sure herself, but one thing she was sure of was that life is short, too short to hold a grudge, and that you don't know what will happen unless you give things a go.

So she typed...

> Rachel (Charlie's mum): Is it PE kit tomorrow?

THE END

ACKNOWLEDGEMENTS

Readers, you are everything. Thank you so much for spending some time with my characters, I hope you love them as much as I do.

To everyone at Bloodhound Books, thank you for believing in my book. Particular thanks to Tara Lyons, for guiding me through the process and Clare Law, my wonderful editor, for helping *The Jam Sandwich Detectives* to shine.

Completing #TeamClare is my agent and cheerleader Clare Wallace and the team at Darley Anderson, thank you for all your guidance and support, I couldn't have done it without you.

Mark Jennings and Heidi Sweeney, thank you for your most excellent police advice, without which my research would have mainly been based on old episodes of *The Bill*, and Chris Herbert, your knowledge of poison was invaluable, thank you. (Chris is a chemist for anyone wondering!)

A big thanks to my writing pals Sarah Dollar and Nadine Holland for your unbelievable writing support, and everyone else I have met on my writing journey, especially my Monday night eggs. Katie Blagden, thank you for being the first person to read this manuscript and telling me to pursue it.

To my long suffering husband, Luke, thank you for putting up with me and my dream of becoming an author. Your patience and support has got me through. My two wonderful kids, Alba and Nico, thank you for making me a mum, without you I would never have been able to write this book.

Special thanks to my parents, Helen and Roger, and my

sister, Laura, for always checking in and for reading early drafts. Dad, I can finally answer, 'Yes' to your question: 'Is there any book news?' and Mum, sorry that I've used the word 'shit' so many times!

To all my other friends and family who have been through the ups and downs of becoming an author with me, thank you for your unwavering support. And to my beautiful friend Kelly, you were the most wonderful of mums. I miss you every day.

And finally, to the mum-friends I have made on the school run, especially those who have become more than just mum-friends, thank you for the inspiration... any similarities are purely coincidental and I promise there are none of you that I want to murder!

ABOUT THE AUTHOR

After studying Film at university, Clare worked as a production co-ordinator in the television industry for several years, where she organised crews and made cups of tea for presenters. She now co-ordinates two young children, organises school bags and occasionally gets to drink a hot cup of tea herself!

Clare is a Penguin WriteNow shortlistee, who lives in Northamptonshire with her husband, two children and far too much Lego. She writes for both adults and children, and tapping away at her keyboard helps to keep her anxiety in check so that she can deal with the chaos of mum life.

Find out more at:

https://x.com/claretbooks

https://instagram.com/clarethompsonbooks

https://www.facebook.com/clarethompsonbooks

A NOTE FROM THE PUBLISHER

Thank you for reading this book. If you enjoyed it please do consider leaving a review on Amazon to help others find it too.

We hate typos. All of our books have been rigorously edited and proofread, but sometimes mistakes do slip through. If you have spotted a typo, please do let us know and we can get it amended within hours.

info@bloodhoundbooks.com

www.ingramcontent.com/pod-product-compliance
Lightning Source LLC
Chambersburg PA
CBHW050547190726
48283CB00007B/2037